A Shimmering Thread

Laura Di Martino

This book is a work of fiction based on historical research. While the places and events described are based on actual places in Italy and South Australia, and actual events which occurred from 1914 to 1924, all the characters are the creation of the author's imagination and any resemblance to actual persons is purely coincidental.

First published 2026 by KLMN Publications
Email: lauradimartino.author@gmail.com
Socials: http://linktr.ee/lauradimartino

ISBN: (paperback) 978-0-09756214-4-8
ISBN: (ebook) 978-0-9756214-5-5

Cover illustration: Mariel Kempt (mariel.kempt@gmail.com)
Image: Vecteezy.com (Ahmad Umam)
Text typesetting: David Bradbury (www.dbtype.com.au)

Contents

Contents

CHAPTER ONE

Abruzzo, Italy – February 1920

Clementina slides out of bed and throws her heavy woollen skirt over her chemise. Her stiff fingers struggle to button up the short, padded velour jacket. With every exhaled breath, a puff of moisture lingers in her unheated narrow room under the eaves. Winding her long black plait around her head, she secures it with a pin and attaches a short scarf over her head, making sure to cover her ears. She needs to hurry if she wants to get to the fields at the edge of the forest before the other villagers. There's little left to forage at this time of the year, but she's determined to keep looking until she can bring something substantial home. The children went to bed crying last night, their bellies sore after several days of only thin soup.

In her stockinged feet, she quietly grips her way down the ladder into the kitchen. Her short boots were left by the fire to dry. She stokes the embers and adds a log, so that the room will be warm when the family awakes. Finally, covering herself in her thick shawl, she silently slips out the door, heading down the street to the fields. The full moon sitting just above the horizon lights her way. As she passes, she says a prayer for good luck to the Madonna of the little church built at the edge of the forest.

Filomena drags a rickety handmade wooden chair out to the front stoop with a sack of the last of the dried broad bean pods gathered in spring. Tightening the knot of her thick winter shawl under her chin and squeezing into fingerless gloves, she cracks her knuckles in readiness for her task. As she splits the pods, she drops the hardened beans into the copper saucepan at her right foot and the wrinkled discarded pods onto an old hessian cloth at her left. Nothing is wasted. These shrivelled cases will be useful for plumping up her grandson's mattress.

The ping of the beans hitting the pan is occasionally interrupted when one of the neighbouring women passes down via Giardino, expertly balancing on her head, a large copper conch filled with water. The young women of Rapino are renowned for their sturdy backs and muscular necks, developed in childhood. They ferry their family's supply of water several times a day, using only a slim towel rolled into a snake coil on their heads to keep the copper conch aloft. It will still be many decades before piped water will reach these slim, two-story stone cottages built above animal and produce barns in the shadow of the Maiella Mountain range.

'Ueh zi zi gna stia?' They invariably call out in greeting, politely addressing her as 'aunty' and asking her how she's doing, on their way to and from the village fountain in the little square at the top of the street.

Hunching her shoulders, Filomena nods and sighs. '*Insomm.*' How else could her old body be feeling at this early hour?

The stoop at the top of a dozen stone steps above the snowline is where Filomena spends a good part of her day. Her husband, Nino, died 3 years ago from an infection when his scythe tore through his upper leg as he was gathering the flax. He'd been startled by a snake slithering over his foot. Their usual herbal ministrations, poultices and prayers had been insufficient. When the limb had turned black, they'd called the doctor, but it was too late. Thankfully, her only son, Giovanni, more robust than his father, adeptly took over the fieldwork. With her grandson, Tonino, now

13, they continued the family enterprise of growing and harvesting flax. Her daughter-in-law, Sabia, spins and weaves the flax to make lengths of linen cloth to sell to the itinerant merchant from Chieti.

The door of the stone house next door scrapes open a little later than usual. Without losing her rhythm, Filomena glances over at her cousin Antonia, who has brought out her basket of mending and her own chair into the growing daylight. Also in her mid-50s, the woman has developed a permanent hunch from her years spent at the edge of the ancient village laundry trough built into the riverbank. She washes, irons and mends clothes for the better-off families who live in the cluster of towns surrounding her village, situated in one of the many valleys of the Maiella mountain range. Antonia lost her husband, Rocco when he was still in his early 30s, but with three young boys and her mother-in-law to feed, she'd simply resigned herself to the continuous slog without complaint, never letting her twinkling laugh fade or her delight in gossip and company diminish.

Catching Filomena's eye, Antonia juts her chin towards the figure approaching from the forest end of the street. The young woman is dressed entirely in black. Her head and most of her face are shielded by a thick black knitted shawl, which reaches past her knees. Long-fingered hands are the only signs of flesh, and these are clutching possessively at a hessian sack. As she nears the stone houses, she lifts her face from the cobbled path to reveal large, almond-shaped, deep brown eyes. Antonia nods as the figure reaches her, careful not to reveal her dismay at seeing the air of wretchedness enveloping this young woman.

Antonia had eagerly welcomed Clementina Vitale into her home upon her marriage to her second son, Nicola. Before this, Clementina had lived across the street with her siblings, parents and paternal grand-parents. She'd grown up in a flax family too, like most of the families of via Giardino on the western border of the rural village of Rapino, which flanks the fields bordering their tributary of the Foro River. With its source in the glacial reaches of the Apennine Mountains, the crystalline waters meander through the Abruzzo ranges and wooded valleys for almost 80 kilometres to empty into the Adriatic Sea.

The men of Rapino always worked as a cooperative to grow and harvest the flax, while the women took charge of spinning and weaving the fibres on their narrow looms. As a village, they had a reputation to uphold. Clementina's mother, Rosa, had the expert eye so she ensured that each house spun the thread to a consistent thickness and that the tension of each family's loom was also set to produce consistency in weft and warp. Over many generations, they had built a reputation as skilled and dependable weavers of raw linen cloth.

When she was 12, the whole street had been involved in the decision to send Clementina to the nuns in the nearby town of Guardiagrele so that she could finesse her already exceptional embroidery skills. After 4 years, she had returned with a completed *corredo*, her glory box the envy of the other mothers. But Clementina's generous and patient tutoring of other young girls in her street soon banished any petty jealousies.

Antonia's second son, Nicola Della Valle, had been sent away too, to be an apprentice ceramicist. Living in the attic of his master's house, he'd been well-treated and well-taught. Yet, a growing boy could never get enough food, and all he talked about when he returned home one Sunday a month, was his empty belly. But he'd done well for himself, and it was no surprise to anyone when Nicola asked Clementina's father for permission to court his daughter. The young ones had been firm friends most of their lives, with their experience of living away from home further cementing their bond.

Clementina was engaged at 17, married at 18 and widowed at 19.

In the spring of 1915, only a month after their April wedding, Italy had declared itself at war against the Central powers, and many young men had been compulsorily drafted to fight in the Italian Army. At least a third of the conscripts from Rapino had died on the battlefield. Nicola had perished in the Sixth Battle of the Isonzo, fought in the very north of Italy, in Gorizia, during August 1916. He was among the almost 200,000 casualties in Italy's first year of war.

A few months before the November 1918 armistice, Antonia lost her third son, Domenico. He had turned 18 in June and had rushed off to enlist without his mother's approval. In their grief, they hadn't imagined the terror that was to come. With the return of the surviving men came a decimating disease. The Spanish Influenza they called it. By the end of the summer of 1919, at least half of the village population had been lost to the outbreak. The infants and the infirm went first, but then seemingly healthy young adults also succumbed. House after house was struck down. Antonia also lost Lorenzo, her eldest and only remaining son. He left his wife, Rosaria, with two young children to bring up on her own.

Across the street, all perished. Clementina lost her grandparents, her parents and her two brothers. The only blood relative she had left in the world was her eldest brother Francesco, who'd left in1907 and had never returned. He'd sent only a single strange postcard from a place Father Ernesto said was at the opposite end of the world.

Labouring up the steps to her mother-in-law, careful not to slip on the icy crust, Clementina holds out her sack. Rising to peek inside, Antonia shrieks and stumbles back into her chair.

'Bbell' mì—ndò 'lē truvat stu cunigghiu?' Antonia gasps at the sight of a rabbit, stunned by the extraordinary find in the middle of winter.

Clementina doesn't reply but tips out the still-warm animal onto the stoop and uses her eyes to direct Antonia's gaze to the wealth of mushrooms and chestnuts tumbling after it. Tears spring unfettered from Antonia's eyes. They've had no meat in over a year, scraping by on their store of dried beans supplemented by the meagre greens they can grow or forage.

'Filomè, ven' qua, ven' qua! Uè mò facéme na fèsta.'

It's time for a feast. Antonia calls to her cousin Filomena to come help her prepare. Both households will celebrate this bounty. In famine or feast, they survive by sharing, as they have always done.

CHAPTER TWO

Rapino, Abruzzo – May 1920

'*Entrate. Accomodatevi, signore.*'

Father Ernesto welcomes Clementina and her sister-in-law, Rosaria, to the sacristy of the village church.

'*Padre*, we've come to ask for your help with a few matters,' begins Clementina. She opens the linen bundle she's carrying to show him the handful of freshly picked wild asparagus she's brought him.

Smiling and nodding his thanks for the fresh vegetables, he sets out two extra chairs and sits facing them, giving them his full attention. Clementina pulls out a wrinkled postcard. In the 13 years since he'd left for Naples to do his compulsory 3 years of military service, this was the only communication they'd received from her eldest brother, Francesco. It was a black and white postcard showing a wide, elegant boulevard in a modern metropolis with the words 'Adelaide, Australia,' stamped on the front. On the back was his name, signed with a hurried scribble, and nothing else.

'Can you tell me if there's any way I could contact my brother in this place?'

'Give me time to make enquiries. I'll do my best,' he promises.

A month later, Father Ernesto gets on his bicycle and makes his way down the hill to the bottom of the village in Via Giardino. Arriving at Antonia's, he's swarmed by a group of children. One girl tells him that Signora Antonia is at the communal wash troughs down by the river, but it's Clementina he's after. Sending the girl inside to fetch her, he waits on the stoop, leaning against the cold metal railing for support. He taps his chest pocket and reaches inside his soutane, his chubby fingers feeling for the bishop's letter, reassuring himself that all is in order.

Clementina emerges with her sleeves rolled up, her apron wet. At her temple, tendrils of hair have escaped from her tightly wound scarf, and the curls add a vulnerability that her narrowed eyes dispel. She's been working with her sister-in-law Rosaria to starch and iron yesterday's bundle of laundry for the schoolteacher's wife, who expects it delivered to her by the end of the day, otherwise she won't pay the full price.

'Father Ernesto. To what do we owe this unexpected visit?'

'I'm sorry to disturb your work, my child. I won't keep you long, but I believe we finally have an answer to our prayers.'

Clementina shields her eyes against the afternoon sun, but her face doesn't move a muscle, waiting for the small man with his black pom-pom topped cap to elaborate. He hands Clementina the letter, knowing she can read it on her own.

'Think about it carefully, my child. Talk it over with Antonia. The bishop will want a definitive answer as soon as possible.'

★ ★ ★

'Read it again, Titina,' whispers Rosaria, careful not to stop rocking her almost asleep 2-year-old son Rocco, tucked up against her torso with his head lolling over her shoulder.

Filomena from next door and her daughter-in-law Sabia and Sabia's two young daughters are also sitting around the fireplace, eyes trained on Clementina, eagerly awaiting the second reading of the letter.

'Well? What do you think, Filomé? Should she take this chance?'

'*Chi dorme no ppiglia lu pesce.*'

It would be madness to turn down this offer. What's left for her here but sad memories and slow starvation? Filomena thinks to herself.

'*Mannaggia la Maiella!*' Antonia utters the ancient curse as she pokes the fire and makes it spark, hoping to ward off any more evil spirits.

* * *

Three days later, Clementina stands at the door to the little room tucked into the attic that she shared with her husband Nicola, for only 63 days before she waved him off to war. Her love for him has not wavered, but she's recently found herself unable to recall him. Yes, she's known him all her life, so there are plenty of memories of their growing up together, but her time as a bride was so short, she struggles to recall how he was as a husband for those few months. And she dares not recall his caresses and the nights they lay together, as it will be her undoing.

She picks up the photo postcard he sent her from Vicenza before his unit's deployment to the front. She traces his outline. He's posing stiffly in his new woollen uniform and hastily grown moustache. Wrapping the palm-sized cardboard frame in one of her linen tea towels, she stows it in her mother's old brown leather handbag with the only photo of her parents, taken on their wedding day nearly 40 years ago. The rest of her belongings are stored in the hand-carved wooden trunk her father built for her as a child. She debated about whether to take her *corredo*—the linen bath towels her mother had woven for her, and which she'd finished with a macrame fringe and her initials embroidered on one edge in lucky red thread; three sets of sheets and pillowcases with lace edging and embroidered hearts; a woollen bedspread her grandmother had woven and finished with a crocheted lace border; and a couple of nighties and matching bed jackets—one set in fine linen and the other set in fine wool, adorned with little pink field flowers. She couldn't leave behind her famous tablecloth. It had taken her 2 years to complete this masterpiece of pulled thread work, tatted lace inserts and delicate crochet lace fringe. A noise alerts her to Giovanni and Tonino from next door, here to bring her *cascia* downstairs and load it onto the cart they hired to take her the 40 kilometres north to the main town of Chieti, where her mission is waiting for her.

Clementina has been offered the opportunity to accompany a 5-year-old orphaned girl called Margherita to the only remaining relative willing to take her in. Margherita's mother's cousin is paying handsomely for this service. The coincidence that this woman lives in Adelaide, Australia, from where her eldest brother, Francesco, sent his only postcard, still makes Clementina tremble. But she's taken it as a sign from heaven. She has no idea if he is still in this place, or even if he is still alive, but Father Ernesto has told her to keep believing that she's meant to be re-united with him.

Glancing one last time at her room and through the window to her parent's abandoned house opposite, she reminds herself that she has no other choice. Despite Father Ernesto's fervent search for new clients, Antonia's laundry business has dwindled almost to nonexistence, and Clementina has had no orders for her embroidery work in over a year.

Since the war, the fortunes of their village have plummeted. Most of the men who survived the war have already left to find work elsewhere, leaving only old people and mothers burdened with children. Those in the village who have a relative overseas or in the industrial cities of the north, and whose migrant fathers, sons or husbands remember to send home regular remittances, are the only comfortable ones. The rest are barely scraping by, their permanently drawn, unsmiling faces a testament to their misery.

Clementina reminds herself of both Antonia and Filomena's advice: 'You're too young to be a tired old woman wishing your life away.'

She's terrified of leaving everything she's held dear, but she knows they're relying on her to send money home, for the children's sake.

Coming down the stairs, she wipes the tears from Antonia and Filomena's faces. Rosaria and Sabia are being braver, with the merest hint of quivering lips giving away their sorrow at losing their lifelong friend.

'Don't forget to write. We want to hear about everything,' chokes out Sabia.

'And don't hide anything; tell us the good news … and the ugly,' reminds practical Rosaria, who'd remained stoic and determined to protect her two young children after her husband Lorenzo's sudden death from the influenza.

The remaining residents of the eight occupied houses on via Giardino come out to wave her off. As soon as the news that she accepted the bishop's offer was out, they had all come to farewell her, to reassure her she'd made the right choice, to encourage her to be strong and to honour the memory of her parents and grandparents by taking this chance to make something of herself. Many promised they would clean the family graves and make sure to lay some wildflowers on feast days. All hoped that she would remember to write, and secretly, that along the way, there might come some opportunity for their own sons and daughters.

* * *

By late afternoon, Clementina is standing outside the orphanage in Chieti where her charge, Margherita, has been transferred. She pulls the chain of the bell attached to the inside of the ornate cast iron double gates, over 2 metres high. She can see into a gravel-lined courtyard. A window on the second floor of the façade opens and a nun appears in a dark blue habit, her face completely engulfed by a stiffly starched white cornette, a veil with enormous side wings giving her the appearance of a stork. She calls out, '*Paziena, signora. Arriviamo.*'

Giovanni and 13-year-old Tonino, still waiting on the cart with her wooden chest, give her an encouraging smile. Within moments, a young woman comes scurrying to the gate and pulls a large brass key from the depths of her apron pocket.

'*Signora Vitale?*'

Clementina nods.

'*Dà, n'anz, vè n'dà.*' The smiling young woman gestures her forward, stepping aside to open the gate further. Noticing the wooden chest, she instructs Giovanni to deposit it in the alcove to the right of the gates.

Clementina watches the proceedings. Her realisation that this may be a last goodbye to anyone from her home makes her eyes water. She accepts kisses on both cheeks from Giovanni and Tonino without a word, her emotions too raw.

The young woman closes and locks the gate once more and, pointing to the wooden chest, reassures Clementina. 'I'll get old Fernando to sort that out in a few minutes.'

Tucking her arm through Clementina's, she nudges her gently forward.

'*Jamme.* We have a bed prepared for you. But first let's stop in the kitchen.'

Sipping on a tumbler of warmed milk and chewing her way through a generous slice of bread drizzled in olive oil and a sprinkle of salt, Clementina watches a couple of nuns directing the work of some older girls in the large refractory kitchen. With her full belly and the enticing smell of the soup reviving her jagged senses, she quizzes Angelina about the convent's daily routines.

'We have 80 children here, all female, ranging in age from babies through to 18-year-olds. There are 10 nuns, including Mother Superior. The older girls help in the nursery, taking care of the babies, or take turns in the schoolroom or kitchen. They also work in the laundry or garden. We grow all our own fruit and vegetables. We have a cow for milk, and chickens for eggs. The children all receive a basic education in reading and writing, and training in domestic skills so that when they leave here, they're able to find a job. Or, if they're lucky, they'll find a husband, like I did,' she giggles.

'What about you, can you cook?' Angelina asks.

Clementina clears her throat.

'Only basic country fare. I'm an embroiderer, trained by the nuns at the Franciscan Convent in Guardiagrele.'

'Well, if you've spent time in a convent, you'll soon get used to us. Mother Superior will be very interested to hear of your skills.'

Glancing up at the sound of a bell, Angelina stands. 'Come along now, she's ready to meet you.'

CHAPTER THREE

Chieti, Abruzzo — May 1920

Mother Maddalena reaches for Clementina's elbow and draws her to a well-worn, upholstered armchair. Sinking into its plump softness, Clementina is surprised by the welcome of this little luxury after a full day of bumping along on the backless, narrow seat of Giovanni's hired cart.

'I imagine you've had a long day?'

'Yes, Mother. We left early this morning.'

'I'm sure you have many questions, so we'll start with yours. How does that sound?'

Mother Maddalena retreats to her little desk tucked under the window.

'Thank you, Mother. I'm mainly concerned about the details of the travel and about my charge, Margherita. Will I get to meet her today?'

'Yes, yes, of course. You'll meet Margherita soon. But there are a few things I must explain about her circumstances.'

Clementina slides back further into the armchair. With the worn leather handle of her mother's handbag still clutched in one hand, she nods for Mother Maddalena to continue.

'Margherita and her mother and three older siblings were made refugees when their village in the Veneto became part of the battleground against the Austrians. She was just a baby when she arrived. Many of the women and children from their village were kept together and offered shelter at the Red Cross Tent City erected at Porta San Giovanni on the eastern outskirts of Chieti. They were happy enough and well looked after, but when the Spanish influenza arrived, many were afflicted, and Margherita was the only one of her family to survive.'

Clementina's hand tightens around the armrest, and her eyes glaze at this news. She straightens her back and stares resolutely at the window above Mother Maddalena's head, trying not to let her own terrifying memories swamp her. To still her racing heart, she takes short, shallow breaths, tilting her head back to get as much air as she can into lungs squeezed tight by overwhelming emotions.

'I understand, *cara*,' whispers Mother Maddalena, giving the young woman time to return to a normal breathing pace. It is only when Clementina looks at her again that the nun continues.

'She came to us 6 months ago and has never spoken a word. We believe she can hear, but we've been unable to find out whether she's always been mute, or whether the shock of losing her family has rendered her dumb.'

Clementina's eyes widen, and she nods her head vigorously, making it clear to Mother Maddalena that she understands.

'Our young Sister Agnese has been looking out for her, and we've noticed that she's started to participate in the children's games, but we haven't heard a peep from her yet. Since she's been with us, we've made extensive inquiries with the military authorities regarding the whereabouts of her father. As people have been returning to her village, we've also alerted them that Margherita is with us, but the only correspondence we've had is with a woman from Australia who claims to be her mother's cousin. We're yet to verify whether this is true, because the church records for the village were lost in a fire. I've written to a sister convent in Treviso, asking them to look into the State Archives held there, but these things take time. Meanwhile, this woman has generously forwarded a substantial sum of money for Margherita's upkeep and for her travel to Australia with a governess.'

'When would we leave?' asks Clementina.

'Oh, I don't think it will be for a while yet. You can understand, can't you, *cara*, that we must ensure that her father is officially declared dead before we can presume to make any decisions for her future. We must also be certain that this woman who claims to be her relative is truly related to her and can look after a child in a fit manner. In that regard, I've written to the Vatican representative for Australia to request that he make his own enquiries.'

'So, why have I been brought here now?' Clementina asks.

'We want you to get to know Margherita, and for her to know and trust you. After all, the voyage to Australia will take 3 to 4 months, I believe. And we must be confident that we can entrust Margherita to you.'

'I see,' mumbles Clementina, lowering her eyes, trying to come to terms with this development.

'I was informed that the bishop received a letter from your parish priest, looking for information about connections in Adelaide. The bishop, knowing of our dilemma with young Margherita, proposed that you come here. I believe we may be of mutual benefit to one another since I've also been told that you have a very fine hand for embroidery. In fact, while you're waiting for the situation with Margherita to be resolved, I'd like to offer you a position as an embroidery teacher.'

Startled, Clementina's back stiffens, and she finally dares to look directly into the nun's eyes. 'A teacher?'

'Yes, for however long you are with us, which I expect will be at least a year. Naturally, you may live here with us, but you will have the freedom to come and go as you please when you are not required. We can pay you one hundred lire a week. How does that sound?'

'A year!' is all Clementina can utter, but then a thought springs to her. 'What happens if Margherita's father is found alive?'

'Well, it would be up to him to decide whether he still wants Margherita to go to Australia or to remain with us, but you too will be free to decide. You will have the option to stay here, in whatever capacity you choose. Or you may wish to go elsewhere, and we would assist you as best we could to fulfill your wishes. Certainly, if Margherita did need to go to Australia, then we'd hope that you would still accompany her.'

'I'll need time to think about all of this,' Clementina stutters. 'You see, Father Ernesto led me to believe that the matter was urgent, and that I would need to board the ship within a matter of days.'

Mother Maddalena bestows a warm smile on the young woman. 'There may have been some miscommunication between your Father Ernesto and the bishop's office, but we are very excited to have you here. I made my own inquiries about you with the Mother Superior of the Franciscan Convent in Guardiagrele. I received her reply this morning. She remembers you fondly, and she wrote glowingly about your talent.'

On hearing this, Clementina's mind returns to the warm sandstone walls of the Guardiagrele convent and of her special time there, mastering embroidery, but also learning to read and write. On hearing Mother Maddalena's kind words, her heart softens, and she begins to feel some of the binds loosen and stretch a little.

'That's very kind of you to say, Mother Maddelena. These last few years in my village have been very difficult for many. All our usual work has dried up, so for my family, I'm just another mouth to feed. The money you are offering me will be of great help to them.'

'We sometimes get requests for embroidery work from local families, so if you are interested, I could let the parish know that you're available for that sort of commission.'

'Thank you, I'd be keen to take on whatever extra work you could find.'

Clementina asks to have the night to think and pray on her decision, but she knows that there is little alternative. After the tragedy that befell her family, she had lost her status in the village. When she dared to go to the village well to fetch their daily water, the other women gave her a wide berth. They weren't rude, but the easy camaraderie was gone. It was clear they feared she was cursed and would bring the attention of evil spirits down on them if they dared to linger in her presence. At least here, she doesn't have to hide, and she's relieved to learn that she can earn some money too and send help to Antonia and Rosaria almost immediately. One hundred lire a week will buy enough flour for a month in Rapino.

* * *

'Clementina, Mother Maddalena is looking for you.'

Clementina nods to Francesca, one of the older girls who occasionally helps her with her classes. She removes her apron with its accumulation of snipped white thread ends and heads to the chapel.

'Mother Maddalena?' she calls softly as she enters the dark space.

'Over here, *cara*.'

The nun is kneeling at a side altar, almost blending into the black and white chequered marble floor. The pink marbled alcove and altar above her harbours a statue of the Foundress of the Daughters of Charity, Mother Maddalena's order. Clementina gazes upon the representation of Saint Louise de Marillac. She's an older woman with kind eyes, wearing a simple blue tunic and veil. A long wooden rosary hangs from a leather belt cinching her waist. Saint Louise is not looking out as most statues do but looking lovingly upon a little peasant girl in a patched skirt, who is holding the hand of the saint while showing her the exercise book she is carrying in her other hand. Enclosed in the saint's free hand is a sturdy Bible. The message Clementina has drawn from this image is that of a kindly mother, an educated woman, one who reads the word of God for herself and is dedicated to the care and education of poor girls.

In Clementina's village, especially in the flax-growers enclave where she grew up, few children completed more than the compulsory two years of education provided by the local authorities, just enough to learn to add their meagre coins and to sign their names. She was the only girl of her generation who'd been lucky enough to receive an extended education while at the convent in Guardiagrele. A momentary sense of guilt assails her. She knows that without her, the flax families will need to rely on the schoolteacher and the priest or second-hand information, leaving them prey to gossip and half-truths.

Clementina slides onto a bench in the alcove and waits respectfully for the nun to finish her contemplations. She gazes up at the statue. In her last 8 months here at the convent, she's come to know this little hideaway well, making it her own refuge from the noise and hectic activity of a daily life surrounded by so many people.

She shares a room with three other young women her age, all employed by the convent in various capacities. Luigina teaches the piano-forte and accompanies the choir for special services and Sunday masses, supplementing her income with private music lessons for the children of local dignitaries. Carolina and Maria are seamstresses, sewing and repairing clothes for the whole convent and the monastery nearby. Like Clementina, their room and board are included, and they are also paid for their services. Luigina and Carolina have parents and siblings living nearby, so they spend Sunday afternoons visiting them, but Maria has been in the convent most of her life. In the early days, she often invited Clementina to take a stroll through the town on their free afternoons. At first curious, Clementina joined her, but once private embroidery commissions started coming in, she spent her free time working.

When not tutoring or working, Clementina likes to find herself a quiet corner of the convent for her thoughts. She also reads books available to her from the nuns' library and completes the English language exercises sent to her by a convent in London.

Not long after her arrival in Chieti, Mother Maddalena had made an appointment for her at the Provincial Archives, where she found information on her brother's military enrolment. This had given her the name and location of his unit. A letter to the unit headquarters in Naples revealed her brother had served in Libya, in one of the new Italian colonies. When he had been honourably discharged at the end of his 3-year term, he'd returned to Naples. Unfortunately, there was no clue as to why he hadn't come home or how he had travelled to Australia.

At Christmas and Easter, Giovanni came to fetch her, so she could return to Rapino for a few days. It was good to see the family, but returning to Rapino reminded her even more acutely of her losses, and she struggled in the weeks following the visit to lift herself from the lethargy that descended upon her once again. She found solace only in this small alcove, fingering her rosary and mechanically reciting her Ave Marias until the noise in her head subsided.

Chieti, Abruzzo – May 1920

'Our foundress, Saint Louise, was a very humble woman, able to make do with little and trusting in the Lord to provide whatever she would need to help her community. I always come here when I have an important decision to make, hoping she'll guide my thoughts,' says Mother Maddalena as she comes to sit with Clementina.

The nun pulls a wad of envelopes from inside the breast pocket of her habit.

'Letters from Linda Scarpa, Margherita's relative in Australia. She's written once a month without fail, sending donations for our work and asking for updates about Margherita and her father's status. I have been very open with her about Margherita's condition. I have briefly explained your circumstances too. But news has come about Margherita's father, so it's time to make a decision.'

Clementina's jaw drops, and she utters a breathless, 'Oh, has he been found?'

'In a manner. The military authorities have confirmed through a witness that he was left for dead on the battlefield, and he has been declared killed in action.'

Stilled by the memory of those shocking words, Clementina freezes. Her eyes clench shut and her hands tremble in her lap. Mother Maddalena pulls Clementina's hands into her own lap, sitting still with her until the shaking stops and the young woman's breath returns to its normal rhythm.

'What happens now?'

'The War Reparations Office has issued a certificate declaring that we may act *in loco parentis*, giving us full authority to make decisions on her behalf until her majority at 21. Or we may hand that authority over to her mother's cousin, as no other relative has come forward.'

'So … are we still going to Australia?'

'The Vatican Delegate has reassured me that this Linda Scarpa is a good Catholic, and genuine in her desire to have Margherita come to her. She is a woman in her early 50s, married, but not blessed with her own children. However, she has her own business and her own income.'

'What does she do?' Clementina's high-pitched voice reveals her surprise and eagerness to know more.

'Apparently, she's a very successful seamstress, well-known in her local area.'

'How did she end up in Australia?'

'All of the information you'd likely want is in these letters. Please take them, read them carefully and consider the information contained, as well as the nature of the writer revealed by the letters. When you think you've digested the information, come back to me and we will discuss how to proceed. Will you do that?'

'Yes, Mother, certainly.' Clementina clutches the bundle to her chest. 'Thank you for trusting me with these, Mother Maddalena.'

'You're a clever and sensible young woman, Clementina, with a generous heart. I value your opinion, and I'm very curious to see what you make of these.'

Returning to the courtyard, Clementina looks over at barrel-sized Sister Costanza energetically ringing the 4 o'clock bell to announce the change of activities. It's time to pack up so the little ones can have an hour to run around expending their energy before Vespers. That will be followed by their evening meal and nighttime routines. The girls quickly roll their linens and stash them in the basket near Francesca's feet. This leaves Clementina free to attend to her own needs, and she's eager to go to her room to read the letters in peace, but little 5-year-old Margherita slides up to her and tugs her sleeve, pointing to the orchard. Taking the little one's hand and smiling down at the dishevelled blonde braids,

Clementina sets off for a stroll. Soon, a group of Margherita's friends is following, knowing that there'll be an exciting game of hide-and-seek on offer when Clementina is in charge.

CHAPTER FOUR

Decisions – April 1921

'Come, Margherita. Mother Maddalena is waiting for us in her office. There is some important news for you.'

As the pair make their way up the stairs, Margherita's eyes are downcast and she bites at her lip, but Clementina holds her hand, giving it a quick squeeze to reassure her.

Clementina hoists Margherita onto her lap when she takes a seat in the armchair by Mother Maddalena's desk. Despite having marked her sixth birthday, Margherita is so diminutive, Clementina has no trouble lifting her, looping a comforting arm around her tiny waist.

'May I begin, Mother Maddalena?' Clementina asks.

With a smile from the older woman, who sits facing them, hands tucked into the voluminous sleeves of her blue habit, Clementina begins.

'Margherita, *cara*, you know that Mother Maddalena has been doing her best to find your relatives, and especially your father?' She stops to make sure Margherita is listening. 'Well, we have learned that your father was very brave, and that he fought hard to defend our country, but that he also lost his life in battle.'

Margherita's face plummets, and she swivels to look deep into Clementina's eyes, searching for a clue for how she is supposed to respond.

'I know you were a baby when your father went to fight in the war, so you don't remember him, but you've heard the other children talking, especially the older ones, and you've heard the names we've read out at mass for the departed souls, haven't you?'

Margherita nods slowly, still unsure, her fingers fidgeting with the edge of her smock.

'Well, at mass on Sunday, we'll give thanks for your father's sacrifice, and we'll pray for his departed soul in heaven. Will that be alright with you, do you think?'

The little one nods again. A flicker of relief scampers across her face before she resumes her more natural serious expression.

'There is more news though.' Clementina pulls Margherita further into her embrace. 'Mother Maddalena has found a relative who would like to adopt you. Do you understand what that means, Margherita?'

Margherita thinks for a minute, her eyelashes fluttering as she tries to recall whether she really knows the meaning of the word. But she soon shakes her head from side to side.

'To be adopted is to leave here and go to a new mother and father. The lady who wants to adopt you is your mother's cousin, your Zia Linda.'

Margherita's chin trembles and tears form in her eyes. She shakes her head vigorously, then launches her arms around Clementina's neck and buries her head in her chest.

'There, there, *bella mia*. There's no need to be afraid because I'm coming with you.'

Margherita lifts her head, and once again, she peers desperately into Clementina's eyes. She uses her hands to point at Clementina and then at herself and uses her fingers to motion walking together.

Clementina smiles and repeats the gesture.

'You and I are going on a big adventure! Your Zia Linda lives in a faraway country, a long way from war and sadness. We're going to catch a big ship and sail on the ocean to a country called Australia. We'll take lots of books and paper and colouring pencils, and you'll have new clothes. And I'll be with you every step of the way, so there's no need to be afraid. Do you understand, *cara*?'

Mother Maddalena pulls out the box tucked under her desk and sets it in front of the chairs.

'Look inside, Margherita.'

Clementina encourages her to hop off her lap, releasing the flaps of the cardboard box for her. An exquisite straw hat, trimmed with a white ribbon and a shiny silver buckle, sits on top. Next, Clementina pulls out a white cotton dress adorned with layers of flounces below a satin-banded low waist with Chantilly lace around the collar and cuffs. On the back, filigree metal buttons catch the light. Black leather short boots with black laces and black stockings finish the outfit. At the bottom of the box are ribbons for her hair, a set of picture books and blank books to fill with her own writing and drawings, and a wooden pencil case filled with pencils, plain and coloured.

Margherita's little face crumples. Her eyes are shut tight, and she keeps shaking her head. Pushing the box away, she leaps towards Clementina, who is standing beside her and latches furiously onto Clementina's waist, threatening to topple her over. Clementina reassures her with soothing words and shuffles awkwardly back to her seat, pulling Margherita onto her lap. She strokes the girl's head, rocking backwards and forwards for several minutes until the girl's shaking subsides.

Mother Maddalena approaches with a flyer for the steamship they'll be travelling on, and their papers with the date of their departure, one month away.

'Look here, Margherita. See the big ship? And here are our tickets. See, they have your name and my name too. Both together.'

Margherita takes a peep and is distracted by the cover with its blue and white line drawing of a ship with the waves curled around the pointed bow and the tall steam funnel rising above it. She notices a group of intended passengers carrying suitcases waiting on a dock. There is a couple with two young children. Margherita points to the woman and the girl holding hands and then points at Clementina and herself.

'That's right, darling. That's you and me. We'll be going on the big ship, on a big adventure.'

Margherita nods, this time looking at Mother Maddalena. She points again at Clementina and herself, then at the drawing of the ship.

'*Sì, cara.* That's right—you and Clementina are going together on the big ship to meet your Zia Linda in Australia. She sent you these beautiful gifts, and she's also written you a letter.'

Clementina stands and places Margherita securely in front of her. Her arms loop over the girl's head and her hands cross over her chest.

'It's time for bed, Mother Maddalena. I think Margherita has had enough for tonight. We'll come back another day for the box. But I'll take the letter, and we'll read it tomorrow. *Va bene, cara?*'

Margherita pulls on Clementina's hand and heads towards the door. But before she leaves, she turns back towards Mother Maddalena and executes a steady little curtsy.

Touched, the old nun walks towards the girl. Tilting her chin, she whispers, 'Thank you, my dear. You are a lovely, kind little girl and a very lucky one to have Clementina here, who adores you so much.'

Margherita nods and gives Clementina a wide, toothy grin, revealing two missing teeth in the bottom jaw. She takes Clementina's hand again and skips out of the room towards the stairs.

★ ★ ★

The next few weeks pass in a flurry of preparation. Mother Maddalena insists on Clementina and Margherita being measured for two new outfits each—a project which the convent seamstresses, Carolina and Maria, take on with gusto. For Margherita, they make two green checked dresses and sturdy navy smocks to wear over the top of them. They are easy to move around in, especially for an active little girl who would rather run and skip everywhere. And serviceable, the check pattern more likely to hide any potential stains. Carolina also fashions a sweet, lace-trimmed bonnet in soft green velvet, with cream and apricot ribbons. The grassy green works well with Margherita's fair skin, blonde hair and sea-green eyes.

For Clementina's outfits, there is disagreement between her and her roommates. At the convent, Clementina has continued to wear her 'widow's weeds', as the colourful musician, Luigina, disparagingly nicknamed them. Clementina has ignored the teasing, reminding them she is a widow and that it is customary in her town for widows to wear black for the first 5 years.

'I won't dishonour my husband's memory,' she firmly states whenever they broach the subject.

An appeal by Carolina and Maria to Mother Maddalena is their last desperate attempt to change Clementina's mind, but the nun does not side with them.

'By all means, you can update her style a little, but she is to be lauded for her faithfulness. In any case, she's going to be travelling a long way on her own, and her widow's outfits are more likely to afford her sympathy and protection.'

And so, Clementina packs the two new long black skirts, one in a fine wool and the other in linen, both gathered at the waist and falling to the ankle-length that she has insisted upon, with two high-collared pin-tucked black cotton blouses. A neatly fitting, short, black linen jacket with black beaded edging and large ebony buttons is her only nod to style. She has made herself a new shawl with the remnants of the fine wool and has embroidered the edges with the purple flax flowers of her childhood. Luigina wants to give her one of her own wide-brimmed straw hats, but Clementina is used to wearing her shawl over her simple headscarves and firmly refuses the kind offer.

When Clementina returns to Rapino to say goodbye for the last time, she insists Antonia take her remaining 300 lire.

'Use it for the children,' she insists, when Rosaria protests it is too much. 'Sister Maddalena has given me 500 lire for the trip, sent from Margherita's relative.'

With tears in her eyes, Rosaria nods and envelopes Clementina in a fierce hug.

'I've missed you so much already. You won't forget us, will you? I'll try to write too, even though I'm not so good with my lettering. But now that Netta has started school, I've started practising with her.'

That night, sitting at her window in the attic room, Clementina stares at the starlit sky. Her favourite Pleiades constellation is missing. She knows it will appear again for her birthday in October, and she feels a deep regret at the thought that she may never see it again. Nicola had first declared his love for her at its reappearance on her 16th birthday in 1914, just after she'd returned from the Guardiagrele convent. The childhood friends had missed each other terribly in the 4 years they had been separated. Memories of young Nicola come flooding back. Her mind conjures them as barefoot 4-year-olds, skimming stones when accompanying their fathers to the riverbed where the men prepare the pools in which to soak the flax reeds. Then, 10 years later, all dressed-up, when they danced at his brother Lorenzo's wedding, both red-cheeked and stiff, embarrassed by their growing awareness of their physical attraction to one another.

In the twilight, she can see the outline of her Maiella, still partially dressed in its winter snow cap. She recalls her grandmother telling her the legend of Maia, the eldest of the seven star-sisters of the Pleiades constellation, who brought her son Hermes to their land when he was wounded in battle. She came seeking the magic herbs to save him, but the deep snowy blanket impeded her quest. When he died, the distraught mother lay down on the crest of the mountain and fell into the sleep of despair. *La bella addormentata*, the sleeping beauty, the locals call the outline of the maid who lay down along the ridges of the mountain, her head cradled by her outstretched arm, forever to mourn her lost son. Clementina's heart swells in sympathy for the goddess Maia, as she understands too well the numbness and sense of defeat that invades you at the loss of your loved ones.

Before slipping into bed, she reminds herself she'll need to be brave. Lifting her rosary beads to her lips, she kisses the Mother Mary medallion at its centre, praying that the journey to Australia will go smoothly and that both she and Margherita will find happiness on the other side of the world, away from the misery of these last few years. And she prays too that she'll be able to fulfill her mother's dying wish of finding her errant brother, Francesco. Then maybe she too will finally shake off this bitter hollowness that accompanies her everywhere.

CHAPTER FIVE

Full steam ahead – June 1921

Mother Maddalena comes with them on the train from Chieti to Rome and then, after an overnight stay at a convent of her order, from Rome to Naples. The bishop's office has organised for someone to meet them at each train station to handle their belongings and make sure they board the correct ship at the dock in Naples.

Margherita, who is shaking uncontrollably at the sight of the colossal steamship sitting in the dock, its two silver funnels reaching beyond the clouds, tugs nervously at Clementina's hand. Freed by Mother Maddalena and the hired porter, who are looking after the bags and trunk, Clementina hoists the girl onto her hip, gently folding Margherita's head into the crook of her neck. She pulls at the edge of her shawl to shield the young one's eyes and ears from the chaos surrounding them. Clementina is equally overwhelmed and relieved by the respect Mother Maddalena's habit affords her. She's reassured when the nun charges towards the embarkation officers and people step aside to make way.

Papers sorted, Mother Maddalena doesn't just proffer her hand to be kissed, as she normally would, but engulfs Clementina, and Margherita still hanging off her, into an enormous bear hug. Clementina chokes out, 'Thank you, Mother. Thank you for everything.'

'The Lord go with you, my dears. You'll always be in our prayers. Don't forget to write. And Clementina, never forget, our doors will always be open to you, if you choose to return.'

Following the porter, Clementina takes a determined step towards her new life. Her eyes are filled with tears that she's valiantly trying to hold back, for Margherita's sake, but also for herself. She can't fall apart now. Too many people are relying on her.

Clementina and Margherita find themselves sharing a narrow cabin with two bunk beds pressed against each thin wall, with just enough room at the end of their beds to stow their bags. Their companions are Immacolata, a woman in her late 30s, and her 12-year-old daughter, Teresina. Having never travelled outside of Abruzzo, Clementina stands open-mouthed when Immacolata first speaks to her. She barely understands anything the woman says as she utters a rapidly fired missive. Her hand signals are the only clue that she means for herself and her daughter to take the bunks to the left of the door and for Clementina to take the ones on the right.

With her bags settled, Clementina sits at the edge of the lower bunk and draws Margherita protectively towards her. Teresina, perched on the top bunk opposite them, her legs dangling joyously, begins methodically brushing her long and lustrously dark wavy locks. Two ponytails with enormous white silk bows frame her freckled face. Seeing Margherita staring at her, she pats a space beside her, and the younger girl, forgetting her shyness, instantly clambers up the thin ladder attached to one end of the bed and crawls into a sitting position beside her newfound friend. With a nodded permission from the younger girl, Teresina pulls out Margherita's braids and gently combs her hair, parting it in the middle and re-braiding the thin blonde hair into tight tails that hang down her back. Pulling out a deck of cards, they begin a simple game of Snap.

Clementina and Immacolata adapt their language so that they can communicate better, foregoing their dialects for the standard Italian as best they can.

'I'm Immacolata Gallo, from Cosenza in Calabria, but in Australia, I use my husband's surname Esposito, as is the custom there. I've been in Italy for 3 months to care for my father. But now he's passed away, so I'm returning to my home in Australia.'

'Oh, I'm sorry for your loss. Please accept my condolences.'

For a moment, Clementina's head spins with images of her own family's graves, but she takes a deep breath and continues the conversation.

'I'm surprised to hear you've been to Australia before. I'm eager to hear of your experiences. This is my first sea voyage.'

Over the next 8 weeks, Clementina will find a kindred soul who helps her to unburden her heart and to look forward with more confidence to whatever is awaiting her in Adelaide. Having the older woman, also dressed in black, beside her, is a good shield from too many unwanted questions from other passengers when they go to the dining room or attend the small concerts and English lessons being offered on board. Imma compliments her younger companion on the progress she has already made after a year of weekly lessons in Chieti. Teresina, born and schooled in Australia, focuses on improving Clementina's pronunciation by listening to her read. By the end of her trip, Clementina hopes she'll be able to make herself understood and have an arsenal of key phrases to get her out of any difficulties.

'Do you plan to stay in Australia once you've settled the little one?' asks Imma.

'Mother Maddalena made it very clear to me that if I choose not to stay in Australia, my return trip will be organised immediately,' explains

Clementina.

'Trust me, *cara*, it's best you grab the bull by the horns and find yourself a job as soon as possible.'

'I hope that won't be necessary. Margherita's sponsor wrote that there is room for me at her house for as long as I wish to stay, and she has work for me in her sewing business too, if I'm interested.'

'That's very generous of her, but if it doesn't work out for you, I can assure you that there is plenty of opportunity for domestic work or in the city shirt factories, especially for someone with your sewing skills. I'd be happy to put you in touch with the right people.'

'I'm relieved to hear that. That's very generous of you, Imma.'

'Has this Linda woman given you any clue as to what she intends to do with the child?'

'Do with her? What do you mean?'

'Well, since she's mute, she probably won't be accepted at school. If this woman has her own business, she may not be able to care for her during the day. Will she be expecting you to continue to act as her governess?'

Clementina has wondered about this too, but has no answers, not having had any communication about this subject in any of Linda's letters.

About 10 days into their voyage, when all are promenading above deck after lunch, Clementina draws Margherita aside to wash her face and change her grubby smock. In the cabin alone, she broaches a sensitive subject.

'*Cara*, you know it won't be long before we meet your new *mamma* and *papà*?'

Margherita stiffens. Shaking her head, she reaches for Clementina's waist. She taps Clementina's face and then her own face and voicelessly mouths the word '*mamma*'.

Clementina bends down to Margherita's eye level.

'No, *bella*. I'm not your *mamma*. Your Zia Linda will be your new *mamma*. Do you understand?'

Margherita gives a firm shake of her head and stamps her foot. She wraps her hands behind Clementina's neck and whispers a raspy '*amma*' into her ear. Stunned at the sound, Clementina gasps and pulls away to better see into the girl's eyes.

'Say it again, darling. Say '*mamma*' for me.'

'*Mmmamma … Mmamma … Mamma.*' Margherita croaks.

Pulling her into a firm hug, Clementina lifts the little girl and swings her around the cramped cabin, the euphoria of hearing the child's first word making her forget the reason for its utterance. When Imma and Teresina wander down for their customary afternoon siesta, they find the two giggling wildly.

'What's going on here?'

Margherita stands proudly at Clementina's side, brings Clementina's hand to her lips to kiss it, then croaks her word again. '*Tina, mmm … amma.*'

One alarmed look from Imma is enough to bring Clementina back down to earth.

With a simultaneous sigh, both women sink onto the edges of their beds and stare at each other. Fat tears form at the corners of Clementina's eyes and roll down her cheeks. Hiding her face in her hands, a deep, long sob escapes. Clementina flings herself face down on the narrow bed, weeping uncontrollably. Margherita tries to jump into the bunk with her, but Imma stops her.

'Margherita, dear, you go up on deck with Teresina. Don't worry, I'll look after your Clementina. She's tired and needs a rest.'

Margherita refuses to move, yelling out a distinct, long 'Nooo … Rita stay.'

The shock of hearing more words come out of the little girl silences Clementina. She sits up again, facing her charge with her tear-streaked face and dumbfounded expression.

'Rita, what's this? Can you say what it's called in English?' Teresina asks, pointing to her shoe.

'Shoe,' Margherita replies with a grin.

Teresina continues the game, pointing out objects in the room. Margherita gives an accurate reply each time, stumbling only on a few words beginning with hard consonants. At each attempt, both Clementina and Imma shout with glee, clapping wildly and repeating each of the words. The game only ends when they hear loud knocking coming from annoyed passengers on both sides of their thin cabin walls, but the joy ends up in great cuddles for little Margherita, from each of her cabin companions.

Over the next week, Teresina, buoyed by her success, transforms into an earnest little teacher. Her loft bed becomes a classroom nest. She reads words and phrases from her English language school primer and has her friend 'Rita' repeat the words. Tracing her fingers over the words and the simple illustrations, her head nestled into the lap of her friend, Rita does as she's told, gaining confidence by the hour. Over the next 10 days, she learns to count to 20, identifies most of the letters of the alphabet and begins to form a few rudimentary answers to Teresina's basic questions, all in English.

A fortnight later, while Margherita and Teresina play hopscotch with some other girls as the adults, comfortably ensconced in deck chairs, watch on, Imma dares to ask the dreaded question.

'Do you think Margherita understands that you'll be handing her over?'

'I don't know …' wails Clementina, shaking her head and staring into the sky. 'What should I do, Imma? We've come so far with her regaining her voice, I don't want to frighten her and risk her losing it again.'

'*Mannaggia*,' sighs the older woman. 'I don't know how to advise you either. It's so complicated. But you know you have my support, and you can come and stay with me anytime. You have my address, and Adelaide's a small place. It won't be hard to find me.'

'Thank you, Imma, from the bottom of my heart. Your support gives me much more confidence to face whatever's ahead.'

CHAPTER SIX

Port Adelaide – July 1921

Everyone is up on deck watching intently as the tugs draw the steamer into the busy port. Clementina notices Imma has donned a plumed felt hat and stylishly cut camel-coloured wool coat with fur-trimmed collar over her black calf-length silk skirt, cut to show off her slim waist and hips. Her blouse is also in black silk, high-necked and lace-fringed and adorned by an enormous coral cameo in an ornate gold setting. On board, Imma had worn clothes very similar to Clementina's, so the young woman is momentarily mesmerised by her friend's modern elegance.

'*Papà! Papà!*' yells Teresina, who has dashed to the railing and is waving her straw hat wildly into the air. Pulling her mother to her, she points out two diminutive figures in black suits, standing on a horse-drawn cart, also waving their hats in the air.

Imma turns to her friend, beaming. 'They're here. My boys are here!' Her husband, Salvatore, and her eldest child, 17-year-old Filippo, are waiting to escort her home.

Clementina has both her hands fixed firmly on Margherita's shoulders, holding her close. She looks anxiously overboard to see if she can recognise Linda Scarpa from the grainy, sepia-tinted photo in her hand. There is a great swarm of people surging forward on deck, eager to leave, but Clementina holds back. Noticing the terror in her friend's eyes, Imma lifts her travel bag in one hand and hooks her free arm around Clementina's shoulders.

'Come down with us. We'll wait with you until you've been picked up.'

Teresina is jiggling and impatient. '*Jamù mamma.* Let's go, let's go.'

She grabs at Margherita's hand. 'Come meet my *papà* and my brother.'

But the little one pulls away, burying herself in the safety of Clementina's skirt. Conscious of not letting Margherita sense her fear, Clementina latches on to Imma's arm and with a few hearty encouragements, shepherds her charge down the gangplank. Teresina has raced ahead and returns with her father as the women reach the dock. Hugs exchanged and tears wiped away, Imma finally introduces Clementina and Margherita to Salvatore. The crowd on the wharf is still dense, as passengers and visitors mill about waiting for the trunks to be brought up from the ship's hold. From her handbag, Clementina fishes out her baggage ticket and gratefully hands it to Salvatore, who goes off to negotiate with the porters.

As the crowd thins, Clementina feels a light touch on her forearm and turns to find an older woman speaking her name. She has Margherita's sea-green eyes. Instinctively, they fall into a deep embrace, relieved to have found each other.

'I'm sorry, I didn't expect this enormous crowd! My husband is waiting with the dray further down the dock,' Linda bumbles nervously in halting Italian.

'*Signora* Scarpa, please allow me to introduce you to my shipboard friend Immacolata and her husband Salvatore Esposito.'

'*Piacere.* Please call me Linda,' she says to both Clementina and Immacolata as she proffers her cheek for a kiss. 'Here in Australia, I use my husband's surname of Walsh.'

She smiles warmly at Clementina, but then her eyes widen as she spots young Margherita.

'And you must be Margherita,' she whispers softly in Italian, bending down to the girl's height. 'You look so much like your mother,' she whispers, hungrily taking in every inch of the little girl.

Margherita, hanging back with Teresina, darts behind Clementina. Once again, placing an arm around her charge, she edges her forward, reminding her to use her manners. Timidly, the young girl eyes the lady's shoes and bobs a brief curtsey but doesn't look up, clutching tightly at Clementina's skirt. Reaching into her bag, Linda pulls out a cloth doll, holding it out for Margherita to see.

'I've brought you a little friend to welcome you to your new home. She doesn't have a name yet. I thought you could come up with one. What do you think?'

Margherita eyes the doll with curiosity. She looks around for Teresina, who steps in and takes it from Linda and makes a fuss over how beautiful she is until Margherita hesitatingly reaches for the gift. Still keeping her eyes fixed on the ground, Margherita gives Linda another little bob, uttering a warbled 'Thank you, Ma'am,' as Teresina has taught her.

Linda gasps. 'She speaks?' Her eyes swiftly turn to Clementina.

'Early days yet,' says Clementina. 'Her friend, Teresina, has been a wonderful teacher, both for Margherita and for me. I don't know how I would have managed the trip if it weren't for these two magnificent women,' she proclaims for the benefit of Salvatore, who beams at his wife and their daughter.

'Then allow me to thank you by inviting you and your family to our house for lunch next Sunday, *Signor* Esposito. Here is my card. We're at the last tram stop at Henley Beach.

'That's very kind of you, *Signora*,' replies Salvatore, searching his wife's face for approval.

'Yes, thank you very much. I'm sure Margherita will feel less anxious knowing she'll see her friend again soon.' Clementina speaks loud enough for Margherita to hear, relieved herself that she will only be parted from the sensible Imma for a few days too.

She still isn't sure what to make of this elegant woman with a thick coil of grey hair at her nape. Her stylish felt hat with a wide brim matches the colour of her fashionably heeled brown leather shoes and handbag. A slim belt cinches her burgundy wool overcoat which is fastened at the collar with an emerald brooch in the shape of a bow. Clementina notices that the woman's coat and skirt are at mid-calf length and that fine silk stockings in a pale beige cover the legs on show. Clementina has changed into her new black skirt, blouse and jacket, but her tightly pulled back hair is covered by her long wool shawl. Looking around, she sees that most of the women present wear more up-to-date clothes. Only a few, much older and obviously poorer women, are wearing the long skirt and shawl she favours. And even though hers are new and of good quality, she can't help feeling rather shabby in comparison.

Sighing in her confusion and fatigue, Clementina is relieved to see that her trunks have been delivered to the dock. A young man with a wooden handcart is swiftly commandeered by Linda and directed to the tall dray stationed further away. Seeing the lad approach, a nimble man in a bowler hat and brown striped suit clambers down the front wheel to direct them to the back of the dray. He lowers the back panel to form a ramp upon which the handcarts can be rolled.

Teresina engulfs Margherita in an enormous hug. 'Be brave, my little Rita, I'll see you in a few days.'

Margherita starts to wail, searching anxiously for Clementina.

'Come now, Margherita,' says Clementina sternly. 'I'm here with you, remember. There's no need to be afraid.'

Clementina shoots an apologetic look at Linda, who smiles warmly and pats her arm.

'I'm very grateful that you've both arrived safely. It's time to get you to your new home where you can rest from the voyage. Then we'll have plenty of time to get to know each other properly.'

Clementina nods, grateful that the woman seems as pleasant and kind as the person in her letters. She takes a deep breath before she follows Linda and the lad with her baggage to the seat of the dray and settles Margherita in between Linda and herself, under a thick woollen blanket to ward off the winter chill coming off the water.

CHAPTER SEVEN

Henley Beach – November 1921

'What if I sew three rows of these medium-sized pearls on the cuff and stagger them? Then I can thread some of this lovely thin silver embroidery silk through them to create a net effect,' says Clementina, as she holds up the shimmering thread.

'You mean like the pattern we saw on the hem of the gown at Miller Anderson's drapery last week?'

'Yes, the one you said would look nice on a coat collar. But what if we did the cuffs and used these smaller Japanese pearls around the neckline?'

'Yes, I think you're right. That could look quite spectacular against the navy silk.'

'Would you like me to create the same pattern on the girdle?'

'Oh, she's quite a stout woman. If we highlight the girdle, I think we'll draw attention to the hips. I was planning to add a slight gathering below and above a thin girdle, which will sit just below the widest part of her body. That will allow me to taper the skirt for a more streamlined look. Let's keep the decorative focus on the neckline and the cuffs and maybe make her a band that she can attach to her hat or wear in her hair of an evening.'

'You mean, keep the eyes looking up to her more attractive features.'

'You're a quick learner.'

'If I get started now, I should be able to finish sewing the cuffs before school finishes and Rita gets home.'

'Mrs Bell isn't coming in for her fitting until tomorrow afternoon, but we only need to give her an idea of what we're planning. Maybe just do a small sampler? Don't we have some large strips of that deep purple silk left over? The fabric we used for the lining of Mrs Bowes' coat?'

'Oh, yes. That would look good too, with the white pearl and shimmery silver thread.'

Clementina goes to the drawers where the fabric remnants are kept and finds what she needs before settling into her usual wicker armchair at the window of the sewing room, where the afternoon light is best. Linda is at the central table, converting her client's measurements, making a customisable muslin toile which can be cut and altered as needed during the first fitting tomorrow, before being transferred to the silk.

In the last 4 months, the two women have fallen into a comfortable routine. In the mornings, Linda gets up first and prepares breakfast for Eddie. He likes his toast and bacon and a sturdy cup of tea. She also packs sandwiches for him, as he rarely comes home at lunchtime, preferring to eat with his men at the building site. He is usually gone by the time Clementina has roused little Rita and supervised her morning cloth wash, helped dress her in her tunic and blouse and put plaits in her hair. When she sends her to Linda's kitchen to have her breakfast, Clementina gets herself ready, makes the beds, tidies the bedrooms and front rooms, and finally takes a coffee into the sewing room to begin the day with Linda.

On Mondays, however, Clementina walks Rita to school and stops at the little cottage which houses the Mercy Convent to visit with Sister Marie. There, she helps in the kitchen and practices her pronunciation and reading and writing in English while they wait for the dough to proof and the loaves to bake. Occasionally, on her way home, she spies Eddie Walsh, in the building site next door, where he works as a foreman, supervising the groundworks for the construction of a grand new convent and school.

Clementina is glad of this exercise, as the good food provided by Linda has certainly added weight to her slight frame. Within a matter of weeks, the sleeves of her jacket became so snug, she couldn't move her arms without fear of ripping the seams. Thankfully, the weather is warming, and the jacket isn't needed, even for her stroll along the seafront.

Linda, as a seamstress with over 30 years of experience in dealing with women's bodies, tactfully said nothing about her appearance when Clementina arrived. Clementina, though, had noticed Eddie's startled face the first time they met, when she was covered in her voluminous black shawl, but he too had never said a word. On the Sunday morning that they were expecting Imma and her family, Clementina had been surprised when Linda approached her with a short-brimmed black straw hat and hatpins, and a narrow black skirt, fitted at the hips, ending just below the calves.

'I thought we'd go for a walk along the seafront after lunch this afternoon,' Linda said. 'I wouldn't want you blown away like a balloon if the wind gets under your skirt.'

When she saw Clementina about to protest, she explained, 'They're mine, from when I was a widow. They've been sitting neglected in the cupboard for so long, I'm thankful to see them be of use.'

Even Rita gave her an encouraging smile, taking up the hat and trying it on herself. Clementina was hesitant, but once she'd cast off her wide skirt and heavy wool petticoat, she was surprised at the freedom of movement it gave her. Then Linda noticed her thick hand-knitted stockings and fetched a finer pair, also in black, along with a slim black satin petticoat so that the skirt sat more comfortably away from her legs. The final knell for her old look was sounded when Imma and Salvatore arrived with Teresina and their son Filippo. Teresina immediately remarked on how stylish she looked, and Imma simply smiled in approval as she wrapped her young friend in an encouraging hug.

A few days later, an old leather suitcase appeared at the foot of Clementina's bed, and Linda encouraged her to look through it to find anything else she might like. The two women are almost identical in size and stature—both lean and narrow-waisted with slim limbs and long fingers, ideal for needlework. Linda once had lustrous blonde hair, but only the bun worn at the nape reveals a few remaining gold strands. The rest of her hair is grey with a wide streak of sheer white at the temple. Clementina is her opposite, with her fulsome, dark wavy hair and dusky skin, but both women have a regal bearing, with firm chins, elegant long necks and forthright gazes.

When Clementina goes out with Linda to the post office or groceries and other small retail businesses huddled around the main square at the end of their street, many people nod or raise their hats in greeting. Even when she's on her own, some of the matrons stop her to enquire after her health. In the early days, her halting English made prolonged conversation difficult, but all know who she is—Linda's adopted daughter's governess. She senses she is afforded a certain amount of respect for her connection to Linda and Eddie, who are obviously well-liked in this small seaside town of Henley Beach. Linda, whose Italian dialect from the Veneto differs significantly from that of Clementina's Abruzzo dialect, made the effort to speak to Clementina in the standard Italian, even if she was quite rusty. But after the first weeks, they all decided it would be advantageous for Clementina and Rita to transition to English as soon as possible, so that they could better integrate themselves into the mostly

British community that surrounded them. That was a decision that proved sensible, especially now that Clementina has become an integral part of Linda's business and Rita is at school.

Clementina was assured right from the start that there was a home with Linda and Eddie for her too, for as long as she wanted one. She shares a room with Rita, which was a tremendous relief for both of them. Linda has never attempted to impose her own will upon them but allowed Rita to defer to her 'Tina' regarding all decisions. But now, the four of them have fallen into an easy routine. Without prompting, it was Rita herself who had started hugging and kissing Linda every morning and did the same with Eddie when he returned from work. In the evening, Eddie plays cards with the young girl after their dinner and checks her homework, praising her handsomely for her ability with arithmetic and her improving reading and writing. Then, once Rita is in bed, Linda insists Clementina joins them in the parlour as they read the daily papers and listen to recordings on their phonograph.

Not wanting to intrude on their private time, Clementina was initially hesitant, but Linda gently persuaded her, telling her it would help her English. And indeed, it has. The music too, especially the operatic arias in a familiar language, has soothed her longing heart and eased her transition to this new life. Between the music and snippets of the newspaper Eddie reads out, the couple entice Clementina into talking about her experiences in Italy, and in turn, they are frank about their own past.

By far the biggest surprise for Clementina has been her invitation to join Linda in the sewing room. From the very first day, Linda sought her opinion, especially about any embroidery embellishments she could add to an outfit.

'I'm getting too old for the fine needlework. My eyes just aren't what they used to be, and neither is my patience. If you're happy to take over that aspect of the work, I'll make sure you're fairly compensated.'

Clementina protested, saying that Linda's hospitality was enough compensation. But whenever she quoted a client for a job, Linda made a point of quoting a separate price for any embroidery needed and insisted that the client pay Clementina separately. Linda even encouraged Eddie to accompany Clementina to the local post office to open a savings account into which she could deposit her earnings. When Clementina protested or suggested she should pay something towards her keep, Linda wouldn't hear of it.

'I don't need the money, *cara*, but one day, you might. So, put it away or spend it on your own desires.'

Clementina, used to living frugally her whole life, has no needs. Not even trips to the city with Linda to the fancy drapers, where ribbons and laces, beads and buttons glitter before her eyes, entice her to spend. She's taken heed of Linda's words '*one day*'. One day she might need to fend for herself, so she is determined to save everything she earns, apart from the occasional treat for Rita. She enjoys taking Rita to the Wondergraph Cinema at Semaphore on a Sunday afternoon. Now that summer is upon them, she also allows Rita to take part in some of the foreshore games and rides with an ice cream treat for the walk home. And of course, she's grateful that every few months, there's enough to send a good sum of money home to support Antonia and the family.

The younger woman does her best to ease Linda's burdens, especially around the house, and has enjoyed planting vegetables in the back garden. The sandy soil is poor, but with a little help from Charlie the horse's droppings, she's harvested some fine carrots and summer salad vegetables. Eddie doesn't eat much apart from meat and potatoes, but he lapped up the simple tomato and cucumber salad with fresh basil she made one night. The only problem is getting hold of olive oil. But Imma has come through with her connections to some other Italians who live in the Adelaide Hills. Still, there isn't much of it, so it's reserved for salads, and she has become accustomed to using butter or the saved dripping for other cooking. This includes her traditional almond *biscotti*, which both she and Linda enjoy with their morning coffee.

Eddie, being a confirmed sweet tooth, also lavishes compliments on her whenever she prepares her traditional *pizzelle*—the ultra-thin, crisp waffles made with the special iron her family gifted her for her wedding. He and Linda had been baffled the day they were all out for a drive in the buggy, when Clementina spotted wild fennel growing at the side of the road. She'd startled everyone with her cry of 'Stop!' Jumping off, she ran back to examine the tall stalks, dancing excitedly and using her hat to collect the clumps of seeds still clinging to the dried flower heads. Whenever she made her *pizzelle* batter, she'd crush a tablespoon of seeds to add to her flour, for the highly perfumed and refreshing anise flavour. She'd also made sure to scatter a decent number of seeds along the fence in the back garden, looking forward to harvesting a proper crop next autumn.

The discovery of the fennel seeds had been a small turning point for Clementina. After 3 months in Henley Beach, when she'd worked so hard to understand and fit into her new home, she had succumbed to a bout of homesickness which derailed her equilibrium. She wasn't unhappy. It was more that everything was an adjustment—the language, the food, the weather. It never seemed to end. In addition, news from home took so long to arrive and added to her unease. She'd also been used to having company of her own age, both in the village and at the convent in Chieti, and she was surprised at how much she missed her roommates and their silly banter. Imma was not far away. Clementina saw her a couple of times a month, but she was busy with her family and their stall at the Central Market. Eddie had helped Clementina to find the Italian consul and ask for his help to find her lost brother, but there'd been no news yet. All this led to her feeling slightly adrift, especially as October and her birthday approached.

To celebrate her birthday, they'd gone for a stroll to the Pavillion refreshment rooms at the end of the jetty on the Saturday evening, where they'd met Mr and Mrs Connors, their neighbours. As they left, Clementina glanced at the horizon and gasped when she saw a familiar arrangement of stars. Was it possible that the Pleiades constellation was visible in the night sky of the southern hemisphere too? Mr Connors, an avid amateur astronomer, confirmed that she was not imagining their apparition. It was a lot lower in the sky and appeared throughout the summer instead of winter as it did in Europe, but it still appeared in time for her birthday. She'd just turned 24 years old. At her age, her mother had already given birth to three children. Everything was still too new and too raw for Clementina to know what she wanted her future to look like, but she took comfort in the constellation's familiarity, especially its connection to Nicola, and hoped that with time, more things would feel easier for her. As they began walking back, she laughed heartily at Rita, who'd managed to get chocolate ice-cream all over her face. Clementina was thankful that the young one was excited about going to school, where she had made some friends too, and she seemed to have settled into her new life without fuss. She marvelled at how quickly Rita had picked up English and had grown in confidence, her earlier speech affliction miraculously gone.

CHAPTER EIGHT

Popular Girl – 31 January 1922

'Oh Tina, do say you'll come to the dance next Tuesday, at the Henley Kiosk,' implores a cute blonde 16-year-old Nellie Smythe. She was one of the contestants for the 'Popular Girl Competition' being organised as a fundraiser for the Henley Beach Catholic Church Debt Relief.

Her mother, Henrietta Smythe, takes up the cause with Linda.

'My dear Mrs Walsh, you and Mr Walsh must come too. There's to be games and other entertainments, and Clarrie Young's Jazz Band will finish the night with dancing. We're hoping the whole of Henley and Grange Catholic Parish will be there, as well as young people from further afield. The girl who raises the most money is likely to be crowned Charity Queen next week at the Continental Fair being held in the Parish Hall.'

'Besides,' adds Nellie, 'I'm going to be the envy of the whole assembly once everyone sees me in this divine dress. They'll all want to know who made it.'

Nellie makes a final twirl and curtsy in front of Linda's full-length cheval mirror before slipping behind the folding screen to remove the baby-blue taffeta dress with a three-layered ruffle skirt. A matching pale blue chiffon overlay with slashed pagoda sleeves, held strategically together with tiny silver buttons, ends at the lowered waist with sweet bows whose edges have been detailed with scallop stitching in shimmering silver thread. Clementina has beaded the chiffon torso in varying lengths of fine silver bugle beads, pearls and clear crystal beads to form starbursts of multiple sizes all over the loosely flowing top, so that as she moves, Nellie spangles bewitchingly. To match the dress, Clementina has embroidered a peaked headpiece, studded with more bugle beads and clear crystals. It's designed for Nellie to wear on her forehead, tied behind her head with soft silk ribbons to sit above the bouncy, blonde curls she plans to create for the evening.

Linda had explained the purpose of the Popular Girl Competition, which had been advertised in their parish for several months. Clementina quickly understood that under the guise of fundraising, it was also a way for ambitious mothers to promote their daughter's charms. She and Linda spent several weeks deciding on suitable designs and sourcing appropriate fabrics and notions for their client, which included requests for dresses for the mother, two grandmothers, an aunt and three cousins. They'd been working non-stop since November, and there'd been no time to think about attending balls themselves.

'I'll talk it over with Mr Walsh this evening,' says Linda, bringing an end to the discussion and young Nellie's excited imploring.

When Linda brings the subject up again that evening, Clementina is quick to suggest the couple have a night out.

'Eddie and I are far too old for such frivolities, but you are just the right age, *cara*. I know that the Neilsens from across the road are looking forward to attending. I'm sure they'd happily have you join their set.'

'Oh, no, I couldn't,' blurts Clementina immediately. 'Besides, I'm not interested,' she confirms, resolutely shaking her head.

'Why is that, Tina?' enquires Linda in a gentle voice, yet fixing the young woman with a pointed look, determined to get an answer from her. 'It's 5 years now since you were widowed. You've done your best to honour your husband's memory. Isn't it time to open yourself up to new experiences? I'm sure your family in Italy would wish that for you.'

Clementina shifts uncomfortably in her chair. Her eyes lock helplessly on a floral patch of carpet at her feet. She feels like crying but does not want to embarrass herself or her dear friends. Linda has never broached the subject of her widowhood before. Now it seems, everyone is coming at her. First Imma, who'd invited them all to lunch last Sunday and had also conveniently invited a very eligible bachelor of their acquaintance. Clementina was mortified at the way he looked at her like a piece of meat, and his distasteful, insistent comments on her appearance. Then a letter finally arrived from Rapino with lovely news, but Antonia had scrawled a message at the bottom of Rosaria's letter, reminding her that her childbearing years would not last forever and that if she were still in Italy, she'd be encouraging her to seek a new marriage.

Clementina is saddened by her mother-in-law's pragmatism. While she appreciates Antonia loving her enough to give her permission to move on, she herself is not ready. It has taken her so long to get used to the idea of her widowhood that to suddenly be expected to entertain the idea of a new relationship leaves her confused and anxious. And then Antonia reminds her about having children. In all honesty, she can't even recall having that conversation with Nicola. They'd just assumed that children would come along, as willed by God. She remembers being upset when her courses arrived a fortnight after Nicola had left for the war front, because she'd fantasised about being pregnant and giving him the surprise of a child when he came home. When she learned he was never coming home though, her first thought had been one of relief, thankful that she wouldn't have to bring up a child on her own. But then she had been immediately regretful that he had not left a piece of himself behind to cherish. Lost in this whirlwind of thoughts, Clementina automatically stands when Linda tugs at her arm.

'Come to the sewing room, *cara*.'

Once inside the room, Linda opens a wardrobe and pushes aside the half-finished dresses hanging there to reveal a large cardboard box at the bottom. She has Clementina pull out the box and remove its lid. Inside are a long bottle-green silk skirt and a matching fitted bodice, adorned with exquisite fringe beading. At the bottom of the box are a pair of long silk, bottle-green gloves and a beaded headband with a large peacock feather, and even a small silk drawstring pouch with matching fringe beading.

Clementina silently picks up the pieces and lays them on the cutting table, mesmerised by the intricate beading, and its purple, gold and blue shimmers. The swish of the long, beaded fringes is like firm sand being rippled by the breeze. Clementina can see a few patches where some mending needs to be done and looks inquisitively at Linda, thinking she's being shown the ballgown to see if she can make the necessary repairs.

'This is the dress I wore to a ball 2 years after I'd been widowed. You know my story. I was the same age that you are now. I was not ready to go out, but my parents forced me, for my younger sister's sake, so that she would not miss out on making a match. It was the night I met Eddie, and even though I was not even remotely interested, he waited patiently for me for three more years, until I knew it was time to move on.'

Clementina nods, not trusting herself to speak. Linda has told her the story of losing her husband to a workplace accident and the dire financial straits she discovered they were in, which left her with no assets. Luckily, she had her parents to turn to, but they were concerned for her younger sister and could not afford another dowry for Linda. Her only assets were her sewing and design skills. Clementina realises that this is the famous 'advertising dress' as Linda had labelled it—the one which Linda used to show her skills to all of Castlemaine society, so that she could attract the sort of custom she needed to support herself.

Linda draws Clementina towards her with both hands on her shoulders and looks deep into her eyes.

'You have Nellie's dress to be your advertising. We can whip up something simple for you, that you'll feel comfortable in, but you need to show your face at that ball. I feel my sewing days are coming to a close. My eyes are failing me, and I'm tired. I'd like to teach you to take over. But to be successful, you have to be out there, showing your support for your clients. Do you understand?'

Clementina, feeling overwhelmed by the myriads of thoughts cramming her head and the emotional rollercoaster of the last few days, nods slowly and wraps her arms around Linda. She places her head on her friend's shoulders and finally lets out the sob she has been holding in.

'*Perché piangi, cara*? There's no need for tears. I don't plan on going anywhere for at least another 10 years, but I'm tired of coming up with the designs. That's what I want you to take over.'

Clementina nods, but her mind is a blur. 'How?' she utters.

'Oh, we'll do it slowly, and no-one will be bothered. After seeing Nellie's dress, I'm sure most new clients will hope to be consulted by you. I'll still be here to tend to my older ladies looking for serviceable frocks, but you can take over the evening and bridal wear.'

Clementina's eyes finally light up. 'Do you think I can really do that?'

'Of course you can, and I'll be beside you every step of the way, so there's no need to be afraid.'

She hasn't thought about her own business before, but she has certainly enjoyed becoming more and more involved in Linda's business, particularly in the design and execution of the special occasion wear.

Clementina loves getting lost in thoughts about colours and patterns and the hunt for special trims and fabrics. Several fancy drapers in the city have already come to know her by name and as soon as she enters the store, they immediately direct her to new stock they have secreted away just for her.

'And we'll have to think about building a legacy for Rita too. She's just the right age to learn some more advanced skills. I love that you've taught her to hand sew and do some basic handkerchiefs, but she might like to be given some more important work.' Linda looks pensive for a moment, bringing her hand to her chin until an idea comes to her.

'She might like to learn how to do beading. I notice that beaded evening bags are back in fashion again. They are quite simple to run up, and if we say she can keep the profits from the sales, she might be encouraged to take care with her work. She enjoys her mathematics. If you give her a pattern to follow, she may surprise us.'

In bed that night, Clementina plays out the scenario that might face her at the social next Tuesday evening. She doesn't have a suitable evening dress, but she has her wide linen skirt made by her friend Carolina. There is plenty of fabric there to run up a simple shift under Linda's Singer sewing machine—a skill she's proud to have mastered with relative ease. It would have to be decorous, suitable for the occasion and, most importantly, she should blend in. There is nothing worse than drawing attention to yourself by being different. Linda is right. It's time for her to venture out of her little cocoon. Just thinking about it, though, gives her the jitters. Yet, the idea of building her own business and security for her long-term future is the right motivation. Linda and Eddie have been very generous, welcoming her, a stranger, like a daughter, but it's time for her to stand on her own two feet.

The possibility of paying back Linda and Eddie's generosity in this way also appeals to her. She worries about the extra burden her presence means to them. She is especially appreciative of having avoided a separation from her little Margherita, not so little anymore. The good food, the fresh air and daily walks, the thrill of being at school, learning and making friends with peers, and the undivided adoration from three adults at home have seen Margherita blossom. She has just turned 7 years old and is almost shoulder height to both Clementina and Linda. Her hair has grown longer and thicker, and now that her face has filled out too, she is turning into a little beauty.

Drifting off to sleep, as she does every night, Clementina's thoughts return to the mountain backdrop of her village. She can still hear the call of her friends when they were all Rita's age, as they played barefoot in the street or traipsed through the fields behind the sheep on the way up the Maiella to the summer pastures. Clementina is enthralled by the ever-changing seafront here at Henley Beach and never tires of the soothing sound of the waves, especially on stormy nights. But she misses the fragrance of home—the lush carpet of wildflowers, the moss and lichens along the edges of the streams, the pungent oil released by the olive leaves in the hot summers, the sweetness of the lemons, and the earthy woodiness of the chestnut and almond kernels once they've cracked open. Most of all, she misses the people. She still hasn't come to terms with the fact that she'll never see Nicola, her parents and grandparents, or her two siblings again.

The 5-year anniversary of Nicola's death has crept up on her. With so much newness and activity, she's hardly had time to think about her past. But tonight, with all this talk of moving on, she's started to wonder about her appearance. Linda is probably right. It's time to add some colour to her wardrobe. Certainly, a white cotton shift would be most welcome in the dry summer heat, the likes of which she's never experienced before. She bought a bolt of crisp white cotton poplin for Rita, who has outgrown most of her clothes. During the school term, she mostly wears her uniform. During the summer though, when she was home every day, it was clear that the fussy little girl clothes were no longer suitable. Clementina has observed Rita's local friends. They are dressed in simple, short-sleeved frocks, with minimal embellishments, certainly very few frills and flounces.

'Tomorrow,' she thinks, 'tomorrow I should get started on those.'

Focussing on the sound of the waves coming through the thin glass of her bedroom window and Rita's soft slumber in the bed beside her, Clementina finally relaxes into her own deep sleep, ready for another busy day.

CHAPTER NINE

Heat wave – Tuesday 7 February 1922

The temperature gauge had been hovering around the century mark for several weeks. When Rita started in the third grade on Monday, the nuns at the Mercy Convent, following convention, allowed students to go home at lunchtime before the searing afternoon sun really sets in. But dear little Rita came home exhausted and on the verge of tears and slept most of the afternoon on the front verandah in her short cotton bloomers, soothed by a damp towel around her neck.

Eddie too had told his workers to stay home. The sun was too strong to labour in the open air on a building site. 'I won't risk anyone succumbing to sunstroke.'

'I think it'll just be omelettes and buttered bread tonight. There's a half watermelon left, and I'll put a jug of mint tea in the icebox,' suggests Linda, fanning herself furiously.

It's bearable in the larger, airy sewing room, on the southeastern side of the house. It has its own door to the front garden, so clients can walk straight in rather than traipse through the family's living quarters. The bay window at which Clementina does her embroidery provides beautiful sunlight in cooler weather, but these last couple of weeks, the light has been almost too intense. Clementina has resorted to sitting at the wicker table and chairs under the deep front verandah too, protected from the glare by a large eucalyptus. Mercifully, she has finished all her client work, and even her own little outfit has been run up under the sewing machine. She just needs to finish the ribbon embroidery at the hem. Fearful that her sweaty hands might leave stains, Clementina puts on some short cotton gloves to complete the task.

Neighbours, 18- and 19-year-old siblings, June and Henry Nielsen, who work with their parents at the General Store, have agreed to collect her for the ball on Tuesday evening. They have reserved a table for themselves and three other young friends who Clementina knows from church. Clementina feels positively ancient compared to them, but they'd all been friendly, especially in the early days when her English had been quite limited.

There is to be a concert first, followed by supper. Then Clarrie Young's Jazz Band is scheduled to start at around 9 o'clock. Eddie has suggested he'd saunter down to the jetty at around that time, and if Clementina felt she'd had enough, she could come home with him. She'd nearly cried at his fatherly concern, the offer helping her to feel more positive about participating in the unfamiliar evening event.

She had just stepped out of a cool bath and was tying her hair up in muslin strips, so it would curl as it dried, when a light tap sounded at the bathroom door. Slipping on a silken kimono, another gift from Linda's wondrous wardrobes, Clementina tentatively opens the door to see who is knocking. Rita is standing there with a wide grin on her face and her hands behind her back.

'Uncle Eddie and I stopped at the chemist before we came home.'

'Are you unwell?' Clementina gasps in alarm.

'Nah, I'm fine, but we wanted to get you something special for tonight.'

And with that proclamation, she pulls out a paper bag from behind her back and holds it out, almost hitting Clementina in the nose. Belting her kimono more securely, Clementina opens the door fully and reaches for the packet. It's heavy, and from its weight and shape, she suspects there is a bottle in there.

'What have we here, then?' She asks coyly, tapping Rita's nose in a playful gesture.

'Look inside!' Rita squeals. She rocks from heel to toe, her hands waving from side to side like the follies dancers they've seen on the movie screen.

Clementina reaches inside to pull out a faceted glass bottle with a cork stopper and a large gold bow attached to the neck. Tilting it back, she can see a pale gold label adorned with purple violets, swirling leaves in various shades of green and the words *Eau de Toilette-Violettes* outlined in black and gold.

'Oh, my goodness. Where has this come from?'

'I told you, at the chemist. Uncle Eddie lent me the money. He says I can work it off by feeding Charlie some oats every evening this week. I wanted to surprise you, so you'd have something new to wear tonight.'

'I have my new dress!'

'But you made it yourself, and from your old skirt. This is brand new and a complete surprise! Did I choose the right one? It's the same flowers as your talc, isn't it?'

Clementina doesn't say another word but pulls Rita to her in a tight hug.

'Thank you so much, my darling,' she whispers into her ear. 'You've been so thoughtful, I'll treasure it always.'

'So, you like it then?'

'I love it,' she reassures her.

At that, the little scamp rushes off, calling out, 'Uncle Eddie, she loves it! I told you she would!'

The whole family was sitting on the front verandah with Clementina when June and Henry and their party arrived. Clementina's nerves were getting the better of her, so she jumped up immediately, barely giving anyone time for a greeting before she'd reached the front gate and started the short trek to the whimsical Kiosk with its castle-like turrets dominating Henley Square.

The ballroom on the first floor was festooned with fairy lights. Once up the stairs, Clementina gasped when she saw the decorations. Nellie and Mrs Smythe were not exaggerating when they said the decorations would match Nellie's dress. Baby-blue crepe paper streamers were scalloped across the walls with a tin star, shaped like the design she had created on Nellie's dress—a central circle surrounded by four short stems and four long stems to create the starburst effect. The tall stage had an apron of baby-blue flounces with similar tin stars attached. Each table had a baby-blue balloon on a slim stand with sparkling silver paper ribbons and the table numbers written on little silver star-shaped cards.

Clementina wondered how much all this effort cost. Surely the Smythes could have donated the money they spent directly to the Church's Debt Fund and avoided all this fuss? She leaned in to make this observation to June.

'But isn't this so much more fun for all of us? If they didn't organise these amusements, there'd be nothing to do, and life would be so dull.'

'Besides, what would we have to talk and gossip about?' added Frances, June's school friend.

'Not to mention the extra business it generates,' says Henry. 'You have no idea how many extra supplies I've had to deliver this week. I can assure you that supper will be grand!' He pronounced confidently, slapping his quiet friend George firmly across the shoulders as he strutted ahead of the group.

The four girls took their seats at the table, eager to look about them at what everyone was wearing, while Henry and George went to the bar for some fruit punch. The drink was a tad warm, but tangy with the added slices of lemon. Clementina appreciated being able to wet her nervously dry throat.

Given the weather, Clementina decided against a jacket and ran up a simple tunic top cut to below the hip. She crafted a square neckline with wide sleeves finishing at the elbows. The skirt, stopping at mid-calf, featured a tapered, double-tiered bottom with an inverted sunray pleat at the back for ease of movement. She'd used an ultra-thin shimmering silver ribbon to produce a long stem stitch around the collar and edge of the sleeves and added a similar treatment at the end of each tier of her skirt. She'd packed away her clumsy country lace-up boots at the beginning of summer and was wearing an elegant pair of black leather sally-pumps with a neat silver buckle on the side. She'd chosen black silk stockings, thinking that they looked more elegant than fawn or white ones and made her legs look longer. Back home, she always considered herself of average height, but in this British land, she felt quite short, surprised that she often had to crane her neck to look up at people when talking to them. Linda had insisted she be fitted for a proper corselette with attached garters for her stockings, so, adding to her nervousness tonight was the feeling that her stockings might slip down her legs with any sudden movement, despite the saleswoman's assurances.

She'd curled her hair, and when it was dry, she parted it on the side and swept her fringe low over her forehead. She'd gathered the tail with the rest of her hair into a soft plaited coil at her nape, leaving some tendrils at the side to curl and paste against her right cheek. She'd read in the women's pages of the Sunday Mail about how to do this with a little whipped egg white to smooth the frizz and keep the curl in place. She had also made herself a wide black headband with the same shimmering silver ribbon stitching, which she attached with hidden hair grips to form a sheath over her forehead, ensuring her hair stayed neat for the evening.

There'd been plenty of fabric left over to make herself a matching purse with a little handle and a shiny silver button and ribbon loop to keep it secured. In it, she carried a handkerchief dabbed with some of the delicate violet fragrance Rita had gifted her. She'd never worn the new trend of face powder, but she had borrowed some of Linda's lipstick which she had lightly rubbed into her lips and onto her cheeks to give her light olive skin a hint of colour. Tonight, she was wearing her red coral necklace, the one she'd worn since she was a child, and which now fitted snugly along her collarbone. In the south of Italy, young children were commonly adorned with red coral bead necklaces at birth. The red colour, being the colour of blood, was believed to be a protector of the life forces, ensuring the child grew up strong and safe from illness. The nuns at the convent, both in Guardiagrele and Chieti, did not believe in these pagan superstitions, preferring to replace them with scapulars, saint medals or rosary beads, so Clementina had always kept her red beads out of sight. When she was young and away from home, tracing them with her fingers and feeling their warmth against her skin, she imagined receiving a little caress from her dear mother, who had first tied them around her neck. Tonight, she was proud to wear them in the open.

June, Frances and Claire were all wearing white. June's cool-white crêpe de chine dress had a simple round neck and slim sleeves ending three-quarters of the way down her arm. At her hips, a wide taffeta sash tied in an enormous bow on one side suited her fashionably slender, boyish figure. The short blonde fringe accentuated her gamin-like large blue eyes. The rest of her hair was neatly slicked back into a low bun.

The plumper Frances had opted for a light silk dress with a boat neck and wide slashed sleeves, secured at the wrist with diamante buttons. Her bobbed, curly dark hair, highlighted with a thick band of white ribbon and a diamante pin worn low on her forehead, was very eye-catching.

Their friend Claire, wearing a sturdier white linen shift dress with a pastel, rose-printed asymmetrical organza overlay starting at the waist, had tied her long russet hair into a ponytail at one side and threaded some of the same rose-printed organza fabric through it, creating a generous bow just above her left ear. Claire's dress was daringly sleeveless, and above the elbow, one of her slender arms sported a thick filigree silver bangle, shaped like a serpent, studded with tiny pink sapphires for eyes. Clementina noticed that there was only one other young woman in the gathering who was wearing a sleeveless dress. She had seen such ideas in the *Vogue* magazine, imported from Paris, but none of Linda's clients had been audacious enough to try such a trend. Claire's translucent white skin, green eyes and red hair turned many heads as they'd walked in. June and Frances seemed a little miffed at all the attention she was getting, but Clementina was glad to walk alongside them, almost unobserved.

The gentlemen in their party were wearing the uniform of all the young men present. The standard seemed to be tapered stovepipe trousers made in a soft, lightweight fabric, in beige, brown or grey. Shirts had small, soft collars, and thin silk ties in diagonal stripes seemed all the rage. Very few of the younger men wore jackets, opting for waistcoats with plain silk backs but whimsically patterned fronts. Plaids in a wide range of colour combinations seemed popular. Given the heat, Clementina was not surprised to see this option so widespread. Two-toned brogues were also very much in style as footwear, and without exception, hair was cut very short at the neck with a longer front, slicked backwards or to the side with hair oil. Both young men immediately rolled up their shirt sleeves once they sat down. Glancing around the room, Clementina saw that even Father Kenny, their parish priest, had done the same.

The ballroom was on the first floor, and the concertina glass doors all around the room had been opened to allow for a cross breeze to flow through. The chaos of young people shouting greetings from one table to another, the bright lights overhead and the press of the growing crowd felt overwhelming. She wished she'd thought to bring a fan with her, both to give her some relief from the humidity of the room, but also to hide behind when her eyes crossed someone else's uncomfortably intense regard.

CHAPTER TEN

New amusements – Tuesday 7 February 1922

Soon there was little opportunity to talk to her table mates as the room echoed ferociously with the noise of over 200 patrons. Clementina relaxed. Not being able to talk made it easy for her. She could simply sit back and watch. Their table was near the balcony facing the sea, for which she was immensely grateful, because the sea breezes, meagre as they were, at least afforded them some cool air. Turning to look behind her, Clementina was surprised to see a very tall older woman in an immaculately starched white nurse's uniform and a prominent long white veil with the symbol of the Red Cross on the front. She was with three men in uniform. One had his arm in a triangular bandage, and under the lights, Clementina could see there was a leather-clad stump where a hand should have been. A younger man was wearing a patch over an eye, and the other was seated in a wheeled wicker chair with his bandaged leg propped up on an attached rest. Having not seen a soldier in this area before, Clementina noted the elegance of their broad slouch hats worn at a tilt and secured with a leather tie at the chin. A small feather was attached to the band with a brass brooch featuring a rising sun.

'I wonder where they've come from?' she leant over to ask Frances.

'Oh, they're from the Red Cross Hospital at Henley South. Have you never been down that way?'

At Clementina's shaking head, she continued, cupping her mouth with her hand against Clementina's ear to be better heard.

'Lady Galway, the last governor's wife, started it up during the war as a Cheer Up Club for any servicemen home on leave, but after the war, the Red Cross Society took it over as a Convalescent Home for wounded soldiers. I think it houses around 30 men at a time. They're big on retraining to equip the men with new skills so they can find work, especially those who have been physically injured.'

Clementina was concentrating hard to understand what Frances was saying, thwarted by the noise and the unfamiliar words.

'My mother and my aunt volunteer there. They provide afternoon tea once a week with some of the other ladies from our church. The men like a good feed, but they like the company too. I must admit, I'm surprised to see them here. From what my mother says, I didn't think the crowd and the noise would be suitable for them. I guess that's why the Matron is here.'

Father Kenny hopped up on the stage and motioned for silence so he could introduce the lady of the hour, Nellie Smythe, accompanied by her parents, Mr and Mrs Thomas Smythe. They were newly returned to the area, having moved back a year ago, when Mr Smythe was appointed manager of the Commonwealth Bank in Grange. The priest was well-liked in the district and didn't mince words when it came to asking for participants to be generous in buying raffle tickets and signing up for the various games out on the balcony. Nellie gave a very charming speech too, thanking all her friends and members of the parish for their help in setting up earlier today. Much to Clementina's embarrassment,

Nellie asked her to stand, so that all assembled could applaud her beautiful design and needlework, which Nellie gladly pirouetted before everyone.

The first act of the evening was Nellie. She performed an admiral piano solo and accompanying sweet song. When she finished, the room erupted with applause and whistling from the young men. Next, a ventriloquist with his doll 'Jim' was also well received. Then came a series of instrumental performances by pupils from the local music schools, followed by a troupe of young Irish folk dancers, all garnering generous acknowledgement. At 8 o'clock, the dimmed electric lights were reanimated, and Nellie and her mother's friends brought platters to the tables for supper. There were dainty teacakes and biscuits, and mini meat pies served with a sweet tomato sauce, which Clementina still found most strange. The pies were tasty, but she avoided the tomato sauce with the vinegary and sugary aftertaste that burnt the back of the throat. The plump cheese and ham sandwiches were wolfed down by the two lads. As usual, there was a copious amount of tea to drink, which Clementina found bitter and over-steeped. Despite the two spoonfuls of sugar she'd added, her cup remained untouched.

'How about a bit of Scottish sweetener for that tea of yours, Mrs Vitale?' winked Henry.

'Henry, don't be foolish,' hissed his sister. 'You'll get us all thrown out. This is an unlicensed event.'

Clementina looked from one to the other trying to understand what was going on. The confusion must have been written all over her face because young George, sitting to her left, leant over and whispered, 'He's hidden a flask of Scotch Whisky in his pocket.'

Clementina's eyebrows shot up immediately, confused by Henry's action. Eddie occasionally had 'a dram' as he called it, and she and Linda joined him for a wine at dinner, or a small port on a Saturday evening.

Eddie had offered her a taste of whisky, and while she found the smoky smell pleasant, the small sip she'd taken proved too harsh for her palate. She quickly put her hand over her teacup to dissuade Henry, who was now slumped morosely in his chair after another furious look from June. Clementina was slightly baffled by the harsh condemnation of alcohol consumption. In Italy, she'd been drinking their family's home-made wines and liqueurs since she was a child, but this practice seemed very much frowned upon here.

During supper, their table was visited by some young women and their mothers, keen to compliment Clementina and enquire about how to book an appointment with her. Luckily, Linda anticipated the interest and suggested Clementina take a bundle of calling cards with the name 'Castlemaine Couture' and their address and business hours neatly stamped on the front.

When supper ended, a long list of raffle prizes was drawn, one of which was a lovely set of simulated tortoiseshell hair combs, won by a blushing George, who said his mother would love them. With the arrival of the jazz band, it was time to clear the tables and chairs. An army of young men, as if conjured by magic, entered through the open glass folding doors of the four balconies around the ballroom to remove cups and plates, bundle up tablecloths, move stacked tables out to the balconies and reposition the chairs to the extremities of the room, making way for a large dancing space. The overhead lights were once again dimmed, leaving only the twinkling fairy lights strung up on the balconies for illumination.

Clementina stood back, wondering if she should leave. George looked shyly at her and held out his hand. She shook her head. 'I'm sorry, I don't know how.'

He bowed stiffly from the waist with one hand behind his back, then moved to ask for June's hand. Frances and Claire had been whisked off by two other young men, and Henry had disappeared. Clementina was mesmerised by the frenetic and jerky movements of the dancers as they skipped and hopped their way around the floor. From behind her, the Matron, who had been on the balcony, asked to pass, followed by the gentleman with the eyepatch. They were both very tall and stiff, and Clementina twittered at their attempts to follow along with the jaunty music as they hopped around the dance floor.

'Looks ridiculous, don't it?' suggested a voice from behind her.

Startled, Clementina swung around to find the soldier with the stump hand. Pulling aside some chairs, he made room for the soldier in the wheeled wicker chair to get a better glimpse of the dance floor. He doffed his hat to Clementina as he came to stand alongside her.

'I'm Private John McLeod, Ma'am, and my friend is Private Andy Sloane. Do you mind if we keep you company?'

'Please,' answered Clementina with a kind smile.

'Ah, I hear a slight accent. Where are you from, may I ask?'

'From Italy, from Abruzzo, sir.'

'Well, I've seen some of France, but I never got to Italy,' he said and then trailed off as recognition dawned. 'Oh, wait … You're the lady who made Nellie's dress, aren't you? She's my niece.'

Surprised by the connection, Clementina searched the man's eyes and face for a resemblance.

'Only, me and Andy here, we do some embroidery ourselves, you see. It's part of our rehabilitation. She's been telling me all about how clever you are with a needle.'

'You do embroidery?' replied a perplexed Clementina as she glanced automatically to the leather cover where his left hand should have been.

'I'm pretty good, even if I say so myself,' he laughed mischievously, flapping his bandaged arm.

Before the conversation could continue, the Matron and the tall soldier returned, and the older woman declared, 'I think I've done my duty for the night, Private McLeod. If you don't mind, I'd like to get us all home before I risk falling asleep on my very tired feet.'

'Of course, Matron. But may I first introduce you to this lovely lady, whose name I've completely forgotten, but whose embroidery skills I've admired all evening.'

'Matron Heritage,' said the nurse, holding out a hand to shake.

'Mrs Vitale, Clementina.'

'Matron Heritage, I believe this talented lady should be invited to inspect some of our embroidery work. She may be able to offer us some tips for improvement?'

'What a capital idea. With your permission, Mrs Vitale, I'll send a note to invite you to visit our workshop on a Sunday afternoon. I assume you live locally?'

'Yes, thank you. That would be most interesting. I live on Main Street, just past Military Road, with Mr and Mrs Walsh. May I have them accompany me?' asked Clementina, fishing out another of Linda's calling cards.

'The more, the merrier, I always say.'

Taking firm control of the wheeled armchair, Matron Heritage led the other men down the ramp installed at the end of the balcony.

Waving goodbye to June and George as they passed her, Clementina followed the Matron and was relieved to see that Eddie was in the square, chatting with some other older men who had most likely also happily escaped from the new-fangled jazz music.

Seeing her approach, Eddie extended his hand to the small group of gentlemen and then turned to offer Clementina his arm for the short stroll back to their cottage.

'How did you get along, my dear?'

'Oh, it was all quite amusing, but I think I'm going to need June to give me some lessons on how to dance. I've never seen anything so extraordinary before.'

CHAPTER ELEVEN

An invitation – March 1922

From her window seat in the sewing room, Clementina heard the side gate open and saw a diminutive woman gliding up the path. She was in a white nurse's uniform and was shading her face under the cover of a bright red Chinese parasol. A neat, white cap with the emblem of the Red Cross was pinned down on a head of thick, light brown, wavy hair rolled away from her face. Her white, shirt-waist dress was covered by an ample bibbed apron with the same Red Cross logo. Linda welcomed her, introducing herself and Clementina. The young nurse, who looked to be in her early 20s, reached into the small brown leather satchel she was carrying across her torso and handed Clementina an envelope.

'I've come to deliver an invitation to our Afternoon Tea Fundraiser for the last Sunday of the month on behalf of Matron Heritage. She apologises for not having invited you last month, but there were already too many scheduled guests for that one. Our afternoon teas and craft sales are very popular.'

'Please, Nurse Harrison, do sit. May I offer you tea?'

'That would be delightful, Mrs Walsh, as I've come on a mission of my own. I need an outfit for my sister's wedding in May.'

Linda kept a samovar of hot water on the sideboard and quickly transferred the silver tray laden with teapot, cups and saucers and a decorative tin of homemade biscuits to the tea trolley tucked in beside the cabinet. It didn't take long for Cynthia Harrison to outline her request, agree to a date for a first fitting and have her measurements properly recorded.

'I heard about the outfits you made for Nellie Smythe and her family,' Cynthia gushed. 'Of course, I couldn't wear anything so bold. My mother would have kittens! But I'd love something stylish that can't be found in any of the stores. I'd be mortified if I turned up in the same gown as a guest.'

'Naturally. It's a very important occasion for your family,' sympathised Clementina. 'The weather in May should allow us to create something that incorporates a jacket for the ceremony and wedding banquet, but which could be removed to create an evening silhouette for dancing.'

'Oh, that sounds ideal. I won't be able to go home to change for the evening event.'

'Do you have a hat already or would you like us to supply one for you?' asked Linda.

'I haven't bought it, but I saw a divine one in a little hat shop on Hindley Street just last week. It was a pale gold light wool felt, with a spray of autumn leaves across the front.'

'Was it wide or narrow-brimmed?' asked Clementina.

'It had a small brim at the back with a turned-up brim at the front. I feel I'm too short for wide-brimmed hats. They make me look stunted.'

'That's very sensible,' reassured Linda. 'You have a good idea of what would suit you. I think a pale gold would brighten your colouring, and adding some autumnal highlights would work well with the season.

'Do you know what colour your sister's bridesmaids will wear?' asked Clementina.

'Oh, it's a second wedding. My sister lost her first husband in the war. I'm to be her matron of honour, and my brother's little 4-year-old daughter will be the only other attendant. She'll be wearing white. One of the men at the Convalescent Home has made me a sweet little straw basket for her, which I thought I could adorn with a ribbon to match my dress.'

'Well, that makes it very easy for us,' Linda reassured the young woman.

While Cynthia had been taking her tea, Clementina had already drawn up some sketches with ideas for her new client's outfit.

'Oh my. That's incredible,' gushed Cynthia 'I think this one appeals the most.'

She was pointing to a straight dress with a lightly flared, plain skirt and a matching long-line jacket.

'I recommend we make the dress sleeveless to avoid bulk,' explained Clementina. 'I'd put some contrasting trim at the armholes, around the collar and at the edges of the lapel-less jacket.'

'Maybe something floral?' suggested Cynthia.

'If we make it in a soft jersey, I can put some small gathers at the shoulder so that the jacket falls gently around your figure and won't overwhelm you. I'd use one button, down low, to create a long V at the front of your jacket, which would elongate your figure. We can put a vent in the back of the jacket to allow ease of movement, especially when sitting, and I would add some darts to taper the bottom of the jacket to give you a narrower silhouette.'

'Then, for the evening,' continued Clementina, 'you could remove the jacket and pop on a light chiffon, loose-sleeved cape, short at the front, tying just below the bustline to give you extra length. I'll add a gathered back that ends in a flounce at your hip, maybe in the same floral fabric which we use as the trim. I suggest something peachy-coloured to add softness.'

'Ooh, yes! You've worked out that I'd like to hide my big bottom and bosom. How very discreet of you, Mrs Vitale. I understand why people have been talking about you with such enthusiasm. We barely know one another, and yet you've understood my needs exactly. You are as clever as they say.'

Linda, who was standing behind Nurse Harrison, lit up with pride for her protégé. She flashed Clementina a discreet smile and clasped her hands together at her chest, barely able to contain her glee. The many hours she'd seen Clementina patiently tracing and copying the drawings of women's fashions from the local newspaper and the *Home* magazine fashion pages were paying off. Being able to provide a quick sketch helped the clients visualise the proposed outfit and saved much time and disappointment, avoiding crossed communication.

'When is your next day off, Nurse Harrison?' asked Linda.

'Actually, I'm free tomorrow. I'd like to go into the city to fetch that hat.'

'Well, may I suggest we accompany you so we can take you to our draper? The importers, Davis & Browne, on the corner of Hindley and Blythe Street had a good stock of jerseys and printed chiffons the last time we were there. If we are with you, they'd give you a much better price.'

'Oh, Mrs Walsh, that would be wonderful. The little hat shop I saw is only a few doors down from there.'

'Is it a small, red-framed window with a single red door?'

'Yes, yes. That's it. But I don't remember what it's called. I've been berating myself for not stopping in and buying the hat when I saw it. Only, I was on official business and didn't want to be carrying around a bulky package.'

'That's Miss Delaney's shopfront. We send many clients to her, so she'll give you a good price if we go in together. And there's no need to fret—she makes everything herself, so if it's been sold, I'm sure she can produce another one for you and to your exact size. She'll also let us have a swatch of felt to match the colour,' Linda explained.

'Oh, you are both such darlings. I'm so glad I had the courage to drop in. I was afraid I wouldn't be able to afford your services.'

'We understand. But set aside your fears. We'd be quite happy to pay for the hat and fabric upfront, and you can pay us in instalments if you prefer.'

'Oh, that won't be necessary, Mrs Walsh, but thank you for the kind offer. My father has sent me a decent sum, which will be enough to cover the expenses. But any possible discount would be a bonus. I'd love to get some new shoes too.'

Once Nurse Harrison left, with promises to meet up at the tram stop the following morning, Linda and Clementina tidied away the projects they were working on before stopping for a brief lunch. Linda had long ago instituted the practice of keeping her mornings free and scheduling fittings or new appointments in the afternoons. Today, there was a final fitting for the Wickins wedding to be held in a fortnight at the Congregational Church. The bride had opted for a simple white pin-striped georgette suit. Two little flower girls would be dressed in froths of pastel pink. Mrs Wickins and her married daughter were also to be decked in toning shades of pink—one in dusky rose and the other salmon. Both dresses were quite plain, but the mother had asked for a matching jacket, and the elder daughter had asked for her fox fur stole to be lined with a matching salmon silk. Linda and Clementina worked together and managed to cut and sew the five items in less than 10 days. Without the need for any embroidery or other embellishments, and with the help of their sturdy Singer sewing machine, they could offer good prices, which made them very competitive in this tight, mostly middle-or working-class community.

Nellie's success brought Clementina attention from further afield, and Linda had always attracted custom from wealthier clients holidaying in the area, or from Glenelg where there were more substantial mansions. Her only stipulation was that she would not go to a client's home. If the client wouldn't come to her, she wasn't interested. Eddie suggested they might like to buy a motor car, which had become increasingly popular, but both Linda and Clementina were terrified by the idea. It was bad enough that the seaside was crawling with them in the summer. They just didn't feel the need for one. They easily walked everywhere in their local community or caught the tram to the city. And when the Henley Beach Road flooded from time to time, there was always the train along the seafront to Grange and then Woodville and into the city from there.

Later in the week, Linda left Clementina to deal with her clients and headed out to meet Rita returning from school. The girl was old enough to walk home on her own, but Linda liked to surprise her. She knew Rita was ravenous after school and loved a visit to Mr Badenoch's Refreshment Rooms in cooler weather or Lenny Bowes' Confectionery and Cool Drinks shop for some sweets or an ice cream soda. If she left the house at around 2 o'clock, Linda could drop into the large drapery on Seaview Road, Whibley & Ferrier. Miss Gill, who worked in the dress fabrics section, was stocking some of the newer fabrics. Linda was pleased to give her custom to a local business which saved a trip into the city. Clementina instead liked to visit Imma, using a shopping trip as an excuse to see her friend who lived at the western end of Hindley Street. It was an area with quite a few Italian families. However, Linda's first order of business today was to stop and make an appointment at Mr Cluse, the optician. She'd been in denial for too long. She really couldn't see well enough anymore to continue sewing. Eddie looked at her askance last night when she had the newspaper held out at almost arm's length and was still struggling to read more than just the titles. He'd quietly slipped off his own reading glasses and had handed them to her, and she'd been shocked at the difference they'd made.

While Rita and her friend Eva were sitting on a bench, finishing their ice cream sodas, Linda stepped into the Post and Telegraph Office to see if there was any mail. Mr Reynolds handed her an envelope for Clementina. She could see that it had come from Mr Patterson, the gentleman who performed the duties of the Italian Consul. Securing it carefully in her handbag, she hoped there might be some good news this time. All enquiries Clementina had made after her long-lost brother, Francesco, had come to nothing so far.

CHAPTER TWELVE

Afternoon Tea – Sunday 26 March 1922

The letter from Mr Patterson revealed little. He'd written to let them know that he had advised other Italian consuls around Australia to be on the lookout for a Francesco Enrico Vitale whose last communication had been via a postcard from Adelaide in 1912. Clementina had followed Mr Patterson's advice and also placed a small advertisement in all the major newspapers and the Italian—Australian Newspaper printed in Melbourne, which was widely distributed in Italian communities around Australia. But again, no news had been forthcoming.

For the moment, Clementina was preoccupied with the invitation to the garden party at the convalescent home. Linda reminded her it was a formal affair and that it was customary to wear white and wide-brimmed sun hats to these sorts of events. This would be a significant departure for Clementina, who'd worn only black for the last 5 years. She was nervous about the radical change to all-white, but she didn't want to embarrass Linda and Eddie, nor cause any gossip. This type of dress-related transgression could harm Linda's excellent business reputation, so Clementina steeled herself to this fresh development. Linda suggested Clementina look through her cupboards to see if there was anything she might like to borrow. She found a choice of hats with wide brims, some short white gloves and a plain white purse. She even found a pair of white shoes that fit nicely, but Linda's clothes, while elegant, were more suitable for a mature woman. Clementina had seen a drawing for a simple shift dress with a drop waist and a sailor collar which she thought could be easy to run up. What attracted her most was the handkerchief hem of the skirt, made up of panels of longer lengths at the side, falling elegantly to mid-calf, while the rest of the skirt reached to just below the knees. She'd been thinking about this pattern for a while after having seen it in the *Vogue.*

'It sounds like an ideal dress, Clementina. And if you perfect the cut, I'm sure you'll receive requests for similar outfits soon. I believe these events draw in a couple of hundred people, so your dress might even attract some new, younger customers for you.'

It was such a godsend that Clementina was the same size as her, Linda reflected, but she was delighted to see that Clementina was now embracing a new, more modern aesthetic of her own. Linda had offered to adopt Margherita, hoping to find a daughter in her, but she'd been doubly blessed to find the daughter figure in Clementina and a precious granddaughter she could spoil in Margherita. What did it matter that she and Clementina were not officially related? They had the same passions and similar life experiences that had bound them together from the first days they had written to each other, long before Clementina and Margherita had even arrived in Adelaide. Like any mother though, Linda was concerned for Clementina's long-term happiness and security. She fully understood Clementina's need to shut herself off and protect herself after her harrowing experience of loss and near famine. However, Linda knew instinctively that Clementina was almost ready to face the world again. She just needed a gentle nudge to get her started.

On the last Sunday afternoon of the month, the four of them set off in the buggy for the half mile distance down Seaview Road to the Red Cross complex. It was made up of a convalescent home, recreation and training rooms, kitchen and dining rooms, a library, military offices and a separate nurses' cottage that fronted the foreshore. A man in uniform came out to meet them and offered to take Charlie to the barn for a rubdown and refreshments too. Eddie lined up the buggy alongside several others while eyeing the shiny motorcars parked on the other side of the street. The gentlemen were in top hats and tails, with soft wool grey trousers. Eddie had even added his gold fob watch to his waist pocket. As Linda had forewarned, most of the women and girls were in white dresses, with only a few elderly women in navy or black.

Holding onto Rita's gloved hand, Eddie stepped back so that Linda and Clementina could go ahead of him to the front door of the converted mansion. In the foyer, there were several small groups milling about, but they were immediately approached by Nurse Harrison, who greeted them warmly. She gushed admiringly at Clementina's stylish new dress, making Clementina feel more confident about her choice.

'Captain Dixon, would you be a dear and take the Walsh family on a tour of the premises, please? It's their first visit here. And also, do make sure to stop with Private McLeod in the Sewing Studio. He's waiting eagerly for them.'

'This way please, ladies and Mr Walsh.'

'By golly, Captain, what an array of works happening here. I had no idea of the extent of the skills being taught,' admitted Eddie Walsh. 'I'm a building works supervisor myself. I'm always on the lookout for skilled cabinet-makers. Who would I contact to engage such services?'

'Ah, well that's my role as the Liaison Officer. The Red Cross is in charge of the premises and the activities here, but the Armed Forces choose suitable candidates and subsidises a rehabilitation program for them, to transition the men back to civic life. Here's my card, sir. My office is here, and I would be at your disposal anytime to discuss potential employment opportunities.'

'Thank you, Captain. I'll make sure to get in contact soon.'

Linda purchased a cane basket from one of the trading tables to hold the items that Rita had picked up. She'd found a family of four palm-sized wooden mice with articulated limbs attached with leather ties and dressed in cute hats and clothes which were removeable. A delicately carved small black lacquered wooden box was chosen to hold a necklace made from sea glass that had been smoothed to even-sized beads. A stained leather book cover with a painting of a delicate seashell on the front, and three attached leather thongs to act as page markers, was deemed just the right size for her dictionary. At each trading table, the man responsible for the items proudly talked about the technique used and how much time they had spent working on the item. Linda made sure to ask the men where they were from. She discreetly avoided talking about the war, yet still remembered to thank them for their service, wishing them success in finding an income with their newly acquired skills.

As they entered the Sewing Studio, they were captivated by the array of machine and hand-stitched quilts hung in double rows along the walls. Many of the quilts had patriotic words and symbols. Some had scenes of home, with sheep and farm buildings, sheaves of wheat and even stock horses. Tables were laden with towels, tablecloths and duchess doily sets, in both white and coloured work.

Clementina's eyes shone when she spotted the small loom tucked into the corner, but she was dismayed to see it was not in use. Private McLeod finished talking to another couple and approached them, eyes fixed on Clementina, who was caressing the contraption and had even dared to sit on the stool and run her feet briefly over the pedals.

'Unfortunately, we don't have anyone to show us how the loom works at the moment. Have you ever seen one in use?'

'I come from a family of linen-weavers,' was all Clementina could say, overcome by the emotion of seeing this extraordinary reminder of her childhood. Remembering her manners, she recovered quickly and introduced the Private to Linda, Eddie and Rita before they moved towards his trading table.

'Oh, my goodness, Private. Where did you learn to do such outstanding work? You certainly weren't exaggerating your skills,' enthused a surprised Clementina, eagerly inspecting the wooden framework set up to enable him to work one-handed. He'd made cushion covers, armchair covers and book covers all using ribbon work on a velvet background, fashioning intricate bouquets of flowers in a riot of colours.

'Thank you, Ma'am. That compliment means a great deal coming from you. It was my granny who used to do this sort of work. She copied the flowers in the garden, and as a lad, I was always interested in watching her as she transformed a design on a flat surface and made it look so lifelike.'

'The velvet works beautifully as a backdrop,' added Linda. 'Do you take commissions, Private? I have a mind to order four new covers for our parlour cushions. I could supply the materials for you. I think I'd like a background in a pale apricot. Do you think that would work?'

'Certainly, Mrs Walsh. It would be my honour,' said John, standing up even taller and prouder, if that were at all possible.

Clementina flashed a grateful smile at Linda. She knew very well that the cushion covers in their parlour really did not need replacing. And if they did, the two women could have easily run up some covers in less than a day. But she recognised Linda's generous nature at work—she was a kind soul who was eager to encourage the dapper gent who'd beamed so proudly at her words.

'And once you've sent word that you've finished, I'll fetch you myself for Sunday lunch, so you can see with your own eyes how spectacular they will look in the parlour,' added Eddie, shaking the man's good hand.

Rita was observing silently for once. She'd been a little intimidated by John McLeod's leather-clad stump, but when the adults were about to move off, she whispered her question in a grave voice.

'Your hand—does it hurt?'

'Not much. I've gotten used to it,' said John, pinching her cheek and giving her a slow wink.

'How did it happen?'

'Well, I got an infection, you understand? Got bit by a nasty rat, and by the time I got it seen to, the gangrene had set in, and they had to cut off my hand to save the rest of me.'

Rita's mouth was hanging wide-open, and she had no retort for John's gruesome account. She continued staring, first at the hand and then back at John's face, and finally at Linda and Clementina.

They were saved by the 3 o'clock bell which Captain Dixon told them was the signal for all guests to move to the garden for the speeches from the guest of honour, Lady Bridges from the Red Cross Society and the Mayor of Henley Beach and other local dignitaries. This would be followed by refreshments.

'I think there's even ice cream for patient little girls,' he added for Rita's sake, distracting her finally from John's hand.

Captain Dixon settled the Walsh family at one of the tables scattered across the narrow strip of lawn below the verandah, then took his leave. Another group was being ushered to the table next to theirs, and Eddie recognised one of the men. Soon, introductions were being made all around. The gentleman was Dr Lewis Muirhead, one of the local physicians and a prominent member of the Star of the Sea school board, where Rita attended. The board had contracted Eddie Walsh's building company to construct the new convent and school. As the men drifted off to discuss building development, the ladies began chatting. Mrs Muirhead seemed frosty to Clementina, answering their questions with curt responses. She had not met the woman but had seen her sitting in the front pews at church services. Clementina and Linda were in unison in preferring to sit unobserved at the back. The woman's daughter, Clarice, sliding in beside her with a baby boy in her arms, dressed in a blue and white sailor suit, broke the ice.

'Dear Mrs Walsh, so lovely to see you again. I can't thank you enough for your contribution to our Christmas hampers. The families we distributed to were touched by the thoughtful gifts.' She turned to her mother. 'Mrs Walsh was the lady who fashioned the kimono-style dressing gowns we added to the hampers.'

'Oh, you were the lady responsible for those,' replied Mrs Muirhead, finally deigning to meet their eyes. 'Clarice showed them to me before her committee packed them. I did admire them so, they were very well made, and so stylish. It was a thoughtful idea,' she added with more warmth.

Linda smiled and nodded.

'And mother, this is Mrs Vitale, who lives with Mrs Walsh and works in her couture business. Don't you remember—Mrs Smythe was in raptures over Mrs Vitale's creations for her family, especially young Nellie's outfits?'

'Oh, of course, now I remember where I've heard your name. You're from the continent, is that right?'

'Yes, I'm from Italy. From Abruzzo.'

'Oh, my own dear mother and I went to Florence when we toured the continent, probably before you were born. It was such a delight. Well, at least the art. I cared little for the food. Thankfully, some other British tourists we met at the Uffizi suggested we move to their Pensione which was run by an English lady, and she knew how to cater to our needs.'

Catching Clementina's eye, Clarice, otherwise known as Mrs Reginald King, the dentist's wife, let an arched brow and the tiniest smirk cross her face.

'I had hoped to do the same with my darling Clarice, but of course the wretched war put a stop to any travel plans,' continued the older woman in an unnecessarily loud and affected voice. All the while she swivelled her head about, trying to catch the eye of other, possibly more socially interesting acquaintances.

Clarice quickly jumped in again to prevent more clueless pontificating from her mother.

'And have you met my dear friend, Miss Caroline Thomson? We're here to support her brother, Lieutenant Albert Thomson, who works here representing the Navy.'

'Thomson?' repeated Linda. 'My goodness, are you Emmeline's daughter?'

'Yes, do you know my mother?'

'I know both your mother and your father. I haven't seen you since you were 6 years old, so you probably don't remember me, but we were neighbours in the city.'

'I'm terribly sorry, Mrs Walsh. I've been with my grandmother in Sydney and only recently returned home when my brother Albie came back from the war.'

'And your mother, is she back too?'

'Yes, she is. She's been unable to move about as she had a fall, but I'll let her know we've spoken.'

'And you say your brother works here too?'

As if on cue, the brother in a dazzling white uniform approached with Captain Dixon. The captain was possibly in his 40s, but the lieutenant was considerably younger, perhaps only 30. He wore a jovial smile but relied heavily on a sturdy walking stick.

Again, introductions were made, and the lieutenant made them all laugh when he bent down with a flourish to plant a kiss on Rita's hand and that of her friend Eva, who'd wandered over from another table.

'Peg-leg Albie Thomson, at your service, mademoiselles.'

Further conversation was prevented by the beginning of the speeches. After a brief interlude during which scones with cream and jam, finger sandwiches, shortbread and Anzac biscuits were served, accompanied by the usual over-steeped tea, Lieutenant Thomson suggested a game of croquet. Captain Dixon and Miss Thomson were eager. Passing the baby, now in his perambulator, to her mother, Mrs King quickly convinced her husband to join them.

'And how about you, Mrs Vitale? Would you like to come with your charming daughter?'

'Oh, Rita's not my daughter,' blurted a surprised Clementina.

'Rita's my adopted daughter, and Mrs Vitale is my wonderful friend and business associate,' piped up Linda. 'Why don't you take Mrs Vitale for a game, Lieutenant? I'll go for a nice walk with Rita and Eva. I noticed the ice cream cart has arrived.'

'Forgive my blunder, ladies,' said Albie with a mischievous wink. 'Come along, Mrs Vitale, let's not keep them waiting.'

CHAPTER THIRTEEN

Easter Sunday – 16 April 1922

Clementina was surprised by how solemn Easter services were at their local church. There were no processions or even bells rung to mark the day. There were almost triple the number of people present than the usual weekly churchgoers. Some people must have been down on holidays, probably staying at one of the many hotels and guesthouses in the area. Sundays, especially on good weather days, or for special events, meant their little community became quite crowded now that transport by rail, electric tram or even as a passenger in Mr Abbott's Motor Coaches allowed for day trippers.

Eddie spotted the very tall Captain Dixon over by the side gate and threaded a path through the crowd towards him. Clementina gripped tightly onto Rita's hand, fearful of being separated from her in the throng. When they reached the captain, they discovered he was with Caroline Thomson and her family. Eddie and Linda immediately greeted their old acquaintances, Captain Francis and Mrs Emmeline Thomson, and introduced Clementina and Rita.

'So lovely to see you again, Emmeline,' said Linda. 'We met Caroline at Lady Galway's garden party last month. And we met your charming son Albert too. Is he not here this morning?'

'Both Albie and Freddie are involved with entertaining interstate visitors for the Regatta being hosted by South Australia this year. They're spending the day at a reception at Government House.'

'Emmeline, dear, why don't we invite Mr Walsh and his family to join us for the Regatta tomorrow morning,' said Captain Thomson, looking for his wife's approval.

'Splendid idea. Linda and I will relish the opportunity to catch up. We lost touch while I was away in Sydney.' She reached out for Linda's hands and gave her a wide smile.

Clementina noticed that the older woman was relying on a walking stick, which she had tucked in behind her when she sat down on the bench under the tree.

Taking their leave, the Walsh family headed home, stopping every so often to greet other local acquaintances. They were hastened by Rita, eager to get home to sample one of the eggs she had collected from the garden that morning, left to her by the mysterious Easter Bunny.

Neither Rita nor Clementina had heard of this mythical creature before arriving in Australia but had marvelled at the chocolate creations in the window of Mr Bowes' Confectionery in the lead up to the holiday. Rita's friends had assured her it was a rabbit and not a chicken who brought the eggs, and Uncle Eddie had confirmed that indeed this was true.

'I imagine that if you are extra good at school and at home, you'd be sure to receive a generous gift from the Easter Bunny,' he'd suggested a few weeks previously.

She'd had to look very hard in the back garden and had eventually found four palm-sized eggs. Two were in chocolate and covered in shiny foil, and two were in pink sugar paste, decorated with white marguerite daisies and her name. The excitement in her eyes at these exquisite creations led to effusive kisses for all three adults. At 7 years old, she hadn't been fooled about who the real benefactors were.

The previous afternoon, Clementina had kept Rita occupied with some baking, making the traditional Abruzzese Easter *pupi*, the shortbread doll and horse into which were nestled a boiled egg. She also made batches of her almond biscuits and some sweet *taralli*—baked shortbreads shaped into dainty wreaths and dipped in a thick lemon glaze. She sighed, remembering these were Nicola's favourite as a child, and she'd always ask her Nonna for a few extra to bring to him when they played in the street. She would have liked to make her favourite sweet ricotta pie, but had not seen any of the cheese available, not even at the Central Market she and Linda had visited during the week. Knowing the cheese could easily be made at home, she reminded herself to ask for a recipe in her next letter to the convent in Chieti.

They'd had fish supplied locally for Good Friday. They had their usual Tommy Ruffs, which was a type of herring, which Linda had deboned and battered before frying. And Eddie had gone to the bakery early in the morning and had come home with warm hot cross buns, another novelty for Rita and Clementina.

Today's meal would be their usual Sunday fare—roast beef with roast potatoes, some of Clementina's garden carrots which Linda suggested could be boiled and tossed with a pinch of sugar, butter and nutmeg to finish. Linda had planned to serve a light broth for starters, and Clementina had suggested adding '*scrippelle*', ultra-thin, lacy crêpes, filled with a sharp grated cheese and chives, and rolled into long sausages in the bottom of the plate before being doused with a clear chicken broth. Dessert would be a vanilla custard with some stewed plums from their backyard tree which they had bottled in sugar syrup and cloves at the end of summer.

They were lunching alone because, despite their many friends, Linda and Eddie had become distanced from their families when they married. Linda had already told Clementina that she had grown up in Castlemaine, Victoria. She had migrated to Australia as a 10-year-old with her mother and two older brothers. They joined their father and his brother, who'd migrated earlier from the Veneto region to try their luck during the gold rush. The brothers hadn't found the millions they'd dreamt of, but over 8 years they had accumulated enough money to set up a home and a cartage business. That's when they brought out Linda, her mother and her brothers. Pietro, Linda's father's younger brother, brought out his fiancée, accompanied by her widowed mother. Another sister and brother were born to Linda's parents in Australia, and her aunt and uncle produced seven cousins.

Eddie and his parents had grown up in Melbourne, but at the turn of the century, they had worked on a rural property near Castlemaine. Linda had said they'd met at a dance, but today, she admitted Eddie had been their driver. He'd been hired by Linda's father in his cartage business, but had become the family's coach driver, mostly because he didn't speak Italian, so Linda's family could talk freely in front of the hired help.

Linda explained that around a year after the ball, Linda's older brother had done the unthinkable. He'd promised Linda's hand in marriage to a widowed business acquaintance without consulting her. When Linda complained to her parents, they were surprised but not perturbed. The man had enchanted her family with his fine manners and generosity. A local grocer, he had built up a substantial business in Castlemaine.

They'd known his young wife, a frail, delicate woman, who'd come as a proxy bride. However, only Linda had seen the bruises the woman had tried to cover when she'd done her dress fittings. Everyone sympathised with the grocer when his wife had been found fully clothed, drowned in Lake Augusta in the Castlemaine Botanic Gardens barely a year after their marriage. Rumours about her unstable mind circulated wildly. Linda had said nothing at the time, out of respect for the woman's memory, but she had no intention of becoming victim number two. She'd tried to tell her mother about her suspicions, but they'd been dismissed as ridiculous. Because he was only recently widowed, she convinced the grocer it would be unseemly to remarry only a few months after his wife's death. She prayed that he'd lose interest, but when he'd become insistent, she'd gone to Eddie for help, hoping simply that he'd find a way to get her away to Melbourne. Over the last two years, they'd become firm friends and often confided in each other when Eddie took Linda to appointments at her client's homes.

They'd caught the train to Melbourne, but Eddie convinced her they should set off again to Adelaide, knowing too well the reach of Linda's father's business acquaintances. Linda knew too that her brother would react badly to having his plans thwarted. Linda suspected he owed the grocer a considerable sum of money, because her brother loved a flutter on the horses. She was certain that he had been behind the mountain of debt her first husband had accumulated and couldn't shake the suspicion that her first husband's 'accident' might have been tied to those mysterious debts.

In Adelaide, they married as soon as they arrived, and the priest they had first approached had helped Eddie find work on a construction site while Linda slowly recommenced her dressmaking business. After a few months, Linda sent her mother a letter. She'd received a response telling her that her actions had disgraced the family, and she was not to communicate with them anymore. Over time, when children had not come, Linda expanded her business and built a formidable reputation. Eddie also built a reputation as a fine builder and was eventually entrusted with the role of foreman. Eddie was sympathetic to the foreign workers on site and was able to read and write in English. These attributes made him well-regarded by workers, bosses and customers alike. After 20 years in Adelaide, they decided to move to the less crowded area of Henley Beach. Eddie could see construction was booming here, which enabled him to start a branch business. At Henley Beach, they could also afford a home large enough to enable Linda to set herself up. Clients could come to her, instead of her wasting hours of time traipsing about with her heavy work basket.

Before their move, they made a voyage to Europe, a long overdue honeymoon. Linda reacquainted herself with her childhood haunts and reconnected with family in the Veneto, and Eddie visited his grandparent's origins in Ireland for the first time. When war broke out a few years later, they were already close to their 50s and so were unaffected by the development. That was until Linda received a letter from Rita's mother, her first cousin, asking for assistance for her family who'd been made refugees because of the war. Linda had been very generous, distraught by her cousin's circumstances. Linda's letter had been found amongst her cousin's things when Rita had been orphaned. It had been the Italian Red Cross who contacted Linda and apprised her of Rita's situation.

'Thank you for trusting me with your story, Linda.'

Clementina had heard snippets of the tale, but this was the first time Linda had entrusted her with the full story. Eddie was softly snoring in his armchair and Rita had set up a schoolroom for her dolls and stuffed toys in her bedroom, happily ensconced in her make-believe world.

'Tell me now how you came to know Captain Thomson and his family then?'

'Oh, that's simple. Eddie was the foreman for the build of their house here, right on the sand dunes, when the captain retired from the merchant navy. But we knew them well before that. Emmeline and I were the same age, in our late 30s. She had six children. The newborn, her youngest son, was very poorly. We were neighbours in the city, so I offered to take in the other children when she needed to suddenly get the youngest one to the Royal Hospital. It was a tragic time in her life—he died of scarlet fever a week later. With her husband often away at sea, her two older sons had been placed in boarding school, so they were safe. Albie was the middle child, with Caroline and Frederic following him, all three of them under ten years old. Eventually, when we realised they were safe from the disease, Eddie and I helped get the children settled with family in Semaphore for a few months, so that Emmeline could return home to rest after her ordeal.'

'And the walking stick?'

'I'm not entirely sure. I heard she'd had a fall in Sydney. She was there to be with her second oldest son. He'd been at Gallipoli and had sustained burns to a large part of his body when the boat in which he'd been rowing into shore was blown up by enemy fire. He'd eventually been transferred to a Sydney hospital in late 1916, but he'd died of his wounds. And I heard that the eldest also died on the battlefront in France.'

'And it looks like her son Albert has suffered too.'

'Yes, I had no idea she'd returned from Sydney. Today was the first time I've seen her at church.'

'What an enormous sacrifice the family has made,' whispered Clementina. She thought of her own losses, more acutely felt on these special days, and understood the woman's need for privacy to grieve.

'I was very surprised to receive that invitation for tomorrow from Captain Thomson. I hope he didn't force his wife's hand. We'll have to tread carefully when we get there to see how she's faring. But you'll love her house. The parlour and dining room open up directly onto the beach. And we'll have a splendid view of the sailboats as they compete in the

Regatta, as the house is set quite high from the beachfront.'

'Will we be expected to bring something for morning tea?'

'Emmeline would have said if she expected anything, but some of your delicious, glazed lemon *taralli* wouldn't go astray, I suspect.'

'The smaller Menz Yo-Yo tin Mrs Watkins gifted us is nearly empty. Perhaps I could clean that and line it with some muslin?'

'Perfect. But have you seen the time? If we want to get a seat at the rotunda to hear the Tramways Military Band playing, we'll have to get moving.'

'To be honest, unless you're desperate to hear them, I'm happy to stay home. Given the crowd at church this morning, the foreshore is going to be crawling with sightseers.'

'You're right. Let's move out to the front verandah. If the wind comes from the right direction, we might hear the orchestra from there, in the comfort of our own home.'

'I'll go check on Rita, then I'll join you. Shall I make a coffee?'

'That would be marvellous.'

Clementina peeked in on Rita from the doorway of the bedroom and suggested some milk and biscuits on the front verandah when she wanted to take a break. Clementina also picked up her little bundle of mail to indulge in again—a new letter from home, and a special one from Mother Maddalena at the convent, and a card from Imma.

CHAPTER FOURTEEN

Regatta – Monday 17 April 1922

The Thomson family and their few guests were on their back verandah, nestled high on the sand dunes with a fabulous view of the gulf before them. Other guests were local acquaintances, known to Linda and Eddie and mostly around their age. But there was also a little girl from Rita's school who'd come with her grandparents, so it promised to be an easy, relaxed morning. Clementina was not surprised to see Captain Dixon amongst the gathering, much more obviously attentive to Caroline, the daughter of the house.

'Mrs Vitale,' said Captain Dixon, inclining his head in a stiff bow.

'Oh, please call me Clementina, or Tina if you prefer.

'In that case, I'm Reggie.'

'Reggie, I'm pleased to see you here as I have a proposition for you.'

Both Reggie and Caroline looked at her, raised eyebrows flying in unison.

'I believe you have volunteers who work at Lady Galway's. I was wondering if I could volunteer in the Sewing Room, maybe to set up the loom?'

'Goodness, this is a wonderful coincidence, Tina. Private McLeod suggested I approach you about becoming a teacher for the younger lads in the Sewing Studio. He's done his best to impart his own knowledge, but he only knows one form of embroidery well, and he says that there are a few new arrivals who could use some specific training from an expert.'

'I'd be delighted,' exclaimed Clementina. 'I already volunteer at the Mercy Convent one morning a week, so I'll need to have a discussion with my business associate, Mrs Walsh, before I can give you a definitive answer.'

'Of course. We'd be proud to have someone of your skill level on board, but if it's not possible, I'll put a call out to the Red Cross ladies next week. Will that give you enough time to decide?'

'Thank you. I will let you know either way in a few days.'

There was a croquet set laid out on the side lawn, and Rita and her friend Constance were having a wonderful time with Eddie and Constance's grandfather.

'I'm sorry my brother Albie isn't here today to partner up for a croquet re-match,' said Caroline. 'He's down on the Jetty as an official for the start and finish of the race. But we'll be cheering for my younger brother, Freddie. He's sailing on one of the Henley Beach dinghies—the Radiant, representing South Australia.'

'I'm afraid I know very little about these competitions,' confessed Clementina.

'It's an interstate competition. There are three races for the 14-foot dinghies. One was held on Saturday at Port Adelaide. The second one is here at Henley Beach today. The third one will take place at Glenelg tomorrow. And finally, on Wednesday, there'll be a full sail yacht race at Brighton. That's quite a beauty to behold. Father has secured an invitation to a private party at the Brighton Jetty Hotel, which has a large cast iron balcony from which we'll have a spectacular view of the harbour.'

'And how are Freddie's sailing skills? Do you expect him to be successful?'

'I'm afraid he and his team of mostly university lads don't have enough power in the dinghy class, but we're hopeful of a win in the yacht race. The weather will have a much greater influence, and it's predicted to be quite breezy on Wednesday, so they may just get the help they need.'

'Do you sail too, Reggie?' asked Clementina.

'I'm afraid I'm a total landlubber, Tina. Until meeting Caro here, I had never attended a regatta. My interest is purely in athletics, and I'm not a confident swimmer. Though, seeing Caro so animated in the water and under sail, I could grow to love it too.' He'd addressed his last statement to Caroline, who was lapping up his attention. Clementina slipped away discreetly to give them some private space, admonishing herself for feeling a little envious of their blossoming relationship.

Clementina and Linda were given a pair of binoculars, which meant they could immerse themselves in the festive atmosphere and frenetic cheering coming from many groups in nearby houses. The Henley Beach Jetty's Pavillion, well out on a spur from the main jetty, was so full it looked like it might tumble into the water any minute under the weight of the patrons. At some point, the crowd had swayed wildly, and a hole had opened up amongst the throng, but the women were too far to see what had happened.

'Maybe someone's fainted,' suggested Linda when they saw the horse-drawn ambulance arriving and two gentlemen carrying a stretcher being cleared a path by uniformed police. Two wet, bedraggled figures were eventually spotted being carted down the jetty to the waiting horse-drawn ambulance.

The Walsh foursome took their leave and sauntered down the road on their way home. Eddie suggested that if the crowds weren't too bad, they could stop at the Pier Café for fish and chips to take home for lunch. While Eddie was waiting in the queue and the ladies were over the road in the shade of Mrs Nicholls' Ramsgate Hotel balcony, they heard rumours aplenty about what had happened on the jetty. The most consistent one was that a young boy had fallen off the jetty into the water and an older lad, a member of the newly formed Life Saving Club, hadn't hesitated to jump in to fetch him. They were calling him a hero for his decisive action, which saved the boy's life.

★ ★ ★

By late afternoon, Eddie and Linda were snoozing in the parlour armchairs, and Rita was lying quietly on the sofa absorbed in her book, so Clementina decided it was time to answer her letters. To the family in Rapino, she tried valiantly to describe her activities of the last couple of months and her growing confidence in being able to handle all the new experiences and also the new language. Antonia, her mother-in-law, had been delighted to hear that she'd been able to integrate herself into Linda's business and that she had a stable roof over her head. She reassured them of Linda and Eddie's kindness and that she was slowly getting to know more people. For her friends, Rosaria and Sabia, she included drawings of the dresses she had designed and the reactions to them. She added snippets about the wonderful stores she had visited and the extraordinary experience of living in a seaside resort, including the fast cars and daring fashions on show by Adelaide's elites. Finally, she reported on her quest to find her brother and the lack of progress made in that regard.

To Mother Maddalena, she wrote of Margherita's progress, with her speech and her studies. She emphasised the little girl's now complete acceptance of Linda and Eddie as her guardians and how much the couple doted on her. In particular, she took the time to reassure the nun of how much they had done for her too, especially for her integration into Linda's business, giving her an opportunity to provide for her own long-term future and that of Rita's, if it became necessary. She also wrote about her contact with the Sisters of Mercy and about the incredibly generous Argentinian benefactor who'd paid for the construction of the new school and convent, which Eddie said was on track to be finished in around 6 months.

She explained how different it was to eat the mostly bland British fare because it was so difficult to find Italian ingredients. She also remembered to ask for the *ricotta* recipe she knew the convent kitchen often made. She described how Christmas and Easter had felt topsy-turvy because of the difference in the seasons. She'd been quite shocked at the almost unbearable heat they'd experienced on Christmas Day which had left them all lethargic and dispirited. She reassured Mother Maddalena that she had not forgotten her prayers and that, thanks to her Catholic school, Rita would soon be ready for her First Communion. With both letters, she included a postcard featuring a photograph of the four of them taken at a seaside booth on New Year's Day. They all looked healthy and happy. Linda and Eddie had been placed in chairs with Rita wrapped in Linda's arms and Clementina standing between them in her fashionable new attire, including a silk hat, borrowed from Linda. It was Clementina's first ever photo. She and Nicola had planned to have one taken on their wedding day, but the itinerant photographer was not in their area that month and then, worries about the war had become a greater priority.

An answer to Imma's greeting card was more difficult. Apart from the usual Easter salutations, Imma had also invited them to a ball being organised by a Mr Carlo Bodoni, a well-known city businessman of their acquaintance who claimed that he remembered Clementina's brother from the time that young Italian men of conscription age, living in Australia, had been forcibly repatriated to Italy to fight in the war. He'd told Imma that they had all been on a ship to Italy together in early 1918, but they'd been separated along regional lines, and this man had not seen her brother again.

If this information were true, Mr Patterson, the vice-consul, would have had his name on a list for repatriation. Also, her brother Francesco would have ended up in a battalion with other men from Abruzzo. But if he'd been in Italy in 1918, why hadn't he tried to contact the family? If he'd perished, surely the Army would have let them know? She was dumbfounded because no-one here or in Italy seemed to have come across him. Clementina's relationship with this mysterious brother was quite remote, as he had left home when she was still a young girl. However, she was feeling quite burdened by her duty to her deceased parents to solve the mystery of his disappearance.

Imma wanted her to come to the fundraiser ball to meet the gentleman who claimed to have travelled with her brother. Clementina was wary after her experience of Imma's matchmaking with the odious Giorgio just last month. He'd certainly be at the ball too. Linda left the decision about attending the ball to Clementina but said she and Eddie would happily accompany her if she wished to attend, to act as a buffer between Clementina and Imma's overenthusiastic suitor friend.

Clementina finished her letter to Imma, wishing her and the family well. She was profuse in her thanks for her friend's attempt to uncover her brother's whereabouts and asked her to continue in this endeavour, which was much appreciated. She decided she would go to the ball to meet this gentleman, taking up Imma's offer to stay with her for the night, so that she wouldn't need to trouble Linda and Eddie further.

Imma and her husband, the easy-going Salvatore, manned a stall at the Central Market, selling fruits and vegetables. They also stocked many items sought after by the small group of Italian immigrants in Adelaide, especially pickled olives and olive oil, cured meats, some types of cheeses, dried mushrooms, beans and seeds for vegetable varieties common in Italy, but unobtainable here. The couple were a pivotal source of news, both from Italy and locally. However, Imma enjoyed gossip a little too much, and Clementina was not keen to have her own private affairs spread willy-nilly. So, she opted to tell Imma carefully curated details about what was going on with her life in Henley Beach, despite still cherishing her friendship dearly. She would have to be firm and make Imma promise to abandon her matchmaking though. Clementina also reasoned that the opportunity to meet other Italians might give her the opportunity to get more people involved in the search for Francesco's whereabouts, and perhaps even attract a new line of customers to Castlemaine Couture.

CHAPTER FIFTEEN

At Lady Galway's – May 1922

Clementina came to an arrangement with Linda, about taking Mondays off. She would continue to help Sister Marie at the convent on Monday mornings and then, after lunch, would spend 3 hours at Lady Galway's, supervising the work in the Sewing Studio and teaching the men whatever techniques she could coax out of them. She hoped she remembered how to set up the loom. Her mother and her grandmother were the weavers, though they had taught her the rudiments, and she'd been watching them do it since she was a child.

On her first visit, she planned to bring a basket of sample work. They were the items from her glory box. As she was choosing which items to pack, she ran her hands lovingly over hand-crocheted lace borders and the simple embroidery patterns. Assailed by the nostalgia of these familiar items, tears sprang to her eyes. Linda had taught her the English names: cross-stitch, stem stitch, long stitch, running stitch and chain stitch. There were also the knots and rich overlays used to create flowers, birds and little field and forest animals, motifs commonly used in her village. Then, there was a range of background stitches used to fill an area. She was especially pleased to show off her precise satin stitches and feather stitches which gave texture, and the tiny, evenly spaced blanket stitches used to secure edges.

Most of all, she was proud of her drawn-thread work. This was produced on white linen, using the pulled thread to fill the open holes created when the threads were removed. This space was then filled with an endless variety of geometric shapes. Her tablecloth had a field of stars pattern running all along the border, and then she had used cutwork in the centre to create an elaborate pattern of swirls, mimicking the night sky she loved so much. She'd even incorporated some raised cord covered in tightly packed satin stitch to give more body to the design.

Clementina had been taught all this at the Franciscan Convent in Guardiagrele from when she was 12, deemed ready by the nuns because her mother had already taught her all the basics so well. As the only daughter, she'd spent all her time with her mother and grandmother, observing and copying, listening to all the advice given to the older girls who came to show them the problems they were having with their own embroideries. She visited the women working at the looms when her mother was called in to inspect the work before it was removed and the edges were finished by hand.

At home, she'd grown up with the smell of wet grass in the barns when her grandmother would scutch the soaked flax stalks. Her grandmother would bang and crush them under a wooden press to break open the bark, leaving the cellulose interior of the stalks ready for carding between the ever-finer grades of the metal teeth of the paddles, forming long, soft filaments. Moistening her fingers with her tongue, her grandmother needed only a flick of her wrist to fuse the ends together to form a single thread.

Clementina remembered with fondness the rapid clacking sound of the spinning wheel as her grandmother rocked the pedal backwards and forwards. She would make the wheel turn at an even speed and use her calloused but sure fingers to stretch out the filament, teasing the knots out and feeding the smooth thread onto the wheel. After this process, Clementina would be implored to sit patiently by the fireplace, with her hands spread evenly, listening to her grandmother's stories as the older woman wound the thread around Clementina's hands. At the end she would magically twist the bundle, creating a tight, figure eight skein to be hung at the top of the loom with the many others needed.

Then there was the equally laborious work of her mother, whose role was to draw down those skeins to set up the network of single threads needed as the base. The loom had been made by her great-grandfather, from the local oak wood, and even after decades of use, it still creaked and groaned, moaning at being torn out of the ground. She could still hear her mother singing as she worked, the whoomph of the pedals which separated the threads, the soft swish of the shuttle as it was sent flying between the alternately raised threads and finally the hard bang of the batten as it moved forward and backward to push the weft thread firmly into place, creating a dense and even fabric.

These memories rushed back to her as she fingered one of the older linen bath towels in her dowry. This was the work of her ancestors made especially for her. Then there was the evidence of her own time spent embroidering her initials with a simple geometric pattern of her fancy. What had she been thinking as she'd been sitting on the stoop of their stone house to take advantage of the natural light? She could still hear the chit-chat of the older women who'd brought their chairs out into the afternoon sunshine too. She remembered the stories fed to her and the other children, of charming princes and magical castles, but not in her wildest dreams would she ever have imagined her life as it was unfolding before her now.

★ ★ ★

'Now lads, listen up. Mrs Vitale here has generously agreed to come see us every Monday afternoon to help you with your work. I know you'll make her feel welcome and appreciated.'

'Thank you, Captain Dixon, for this opportunity.'

As Eddie had advised her, Clementina continued with the little speech she had rehearsed. He'd suggested that being open about her background would stop speculation and afford her more respect. Eddie was currently standing in the corner, smiling encouragingly at her, here to support her, just for this first afternoon.

'My name is Clementina, but you can call me Tina,' she began in a clear voice. 'I come from Italy. My husband died in battle. After the war, I was an embroidery teacher in an orphanage and came to Australia as a governess for a young child related to Mr and Mrs Walsh. I've been here for 10 months now, working with Mrs Walsh in her couture business. I'm looking forward to getting to know all of you, and to being of assistance here where I can, and I hope you will help me when I forget my words or need to improve my accent.'

Eddie gave her a wink and quietly followed Captain Dixon out of the room. Private McLeod offered her his good arm to escort her and introduce her to the other seven men present. Clementina examined each man's work with seriousness, asking him what skills he thought he might need to work on. Then, when her tour was finished, she pulled from her basket only the examples that she thought might apply to each man, chatting with them again, one by one, as they settled down at their tables.

The men had been polite and very quiet. Even the very chatty Private McLeod had been concentrating hard on his work. The last 3-monthly

Afternoon Tea and Open House events had netted him several commissions, so he had plenty to keep him busy. His motivation in asking for Clementina's help was mostly because he had no time to devote to the others. Clementina had met Private Andy Sloane at Nellie's fundraiser, in the wheeled armchair, but was now moving around with crutches. He installed himself at the sewing machine and got busy joining small lengths together to create a quilt. He was a jovial fellow and knew his artistic limitations, explaining to Clementina that he was happy to put together plain blocks of colour in simple geometric patterns to create cheerful quilted bedspreads.

'They're popular with mothers looking for something festive for their children's rooms,' he explained.

There were two other men, also with lower limb issues, who were working on finishing larger projects at sewing machines. They indicated that once they had finished their quilt projects, they would like instruction on how to start some tablecloths or doilies for the small tables and breakfast trays other men were making in the Woodwork Studio. Clementina promised to think about how to get them started in a few weeks.

The three newbies were the ones that needed Clementina's dedicated attention. Two were very young, still in their early 20s. Reggie Dixon had told her that they'd both had multiple fractures which had required resetting, so they moved both legs and arms stiffly. One had lost an eye, and another had a leg chopped off at the knee. They'd only just arrived at Lady Galway's, having been discharged from Keswick Hospital, and were put in the Sewing Studio because they hadn't shown interest in much else. He'd suggested that they probably found the advanced skills of the mostly older men in the other workshops intimidating. He hoped Clementina could muster some enthusiasm in them.

'How would you like to help me set up the loom? It would be something new that no-one else knows how to do.'

When they nodded enthusiastically, she took them over to sort and organise the large box of threads that had been delivered, accompanied by a useful book with detailed drawings and instructions, upon which they immediately pounced.

The third chap, possibly in his early 30s, seemed physically intact, but he had a lost, vacant stare, barely aware of his surroundings. When Clementina approached him, he gave her a beautiful smile and stared intently at her lips while she was talking. She wondered if he were perhaps hard of hearing. He answered basic yes and no questions with a shake or nod of the head, but he wouldn't or couldn't speak. She suggested he try a cross-stitch, but when he lifted his hands from under the table, she saw they were shaking uncontrollably. Clementina was relieved when the matron arrived and sat next to him, holding his hands to help him pick up the threaded needle and begin making small green x marks along one edge of the fabric. Matron Heritage murmured low, encouraging words, keeping him focussed. After a half hour of this slow, steady activity, she gently helped him stand.

'I think Alfred here's had enough for today, so we'll go out for a walk around the garden now. Shall we say thank you to Mrs Vitale, Alfred?'

Alfred smiled brightly, but his eyes did not meet hers. Still, he nodded politely before the matron shepherded him slowly out of the room.

As soon as he left, the others broke out into regular talk, calling to each other across the room, enquiring about progress. Clementina looked to John.

'Alfred has the shell shock and loud noises set him off, so when he's in here, we use hushed voices. We know it won't be for long, so we do our best for him. Some of us others were like that when we first arrived, and our mates helped us to recover.'

Clementina was touched by their kindness and understanding. She instantly felt her heart physically expanding in her chest for these beautiful, thoughtful men who'd served their country and were trying to do their best to avoid being a burden to their families. Meeting them, though, inevitably triggered memories of her husband. What if Nicola hadn't died in battle, but had returned home damaged, physically or mentally, or both? What would she have had to do to support him? What if he hadn't been able to return to his trade as a ceramist and could not contribute to the household? How would he have felt at this impotence?

She was left wondering about her village and the way it had been decimated by war and disease. She remembered that so many families had silently and mysteriously moved away. Was it because of the shame of a loved one's infirmity? Or had they gone to the big cities for the type of support unavailable in their remote village? Clementina had been too lost in her own grief and the daily struggle for survival to pay attention, but now her mind travelled back to those years when everything she knew and expected of her world and her future had been forever overturned.

Before she realised, it was nearly 4.30 pm and time to wind up activities. She was satisfied that all the men had enough ideas about what to continue with during the week, and she promised she would be back the following Monday afternoon. Linda had decided that she and Rita would come pick her up in the buggy, so she didn't have to lug her heavy basket home. Tina was relieved to see them waiting outside the complex, eager to fall into the comfortable seat and release the tension that had settled onto her shoulders.

'We've started setting up the loom!' was the first thing she reported.

CHAPTER SIXTEEN

Dazzle Days – June 1922

It seemed all of Henley Beach was getting married or attending a wedding in the months of May and June. Linda reminded her that these months had the best weather of the year, apart from September to November, when there would be another surge, as Clementina had already noted last year.

The requests were generally straightforward, with the colours and styles demure, as befitted this semi-rural community. The straight lines of the previous year had continued, and ornamentation by adding beads or embroidery was still popular. Clementina created extra handmade embellishments only for their more discerning clients who were prepared to pay her for the time and attention required, otherwise she and Linda had sourced decorative ribbon and lace strips in a variety of widths to match the range of fabrics they bought.

In mid-June, a definite trend in requests for feathers to embellish gowns was noted. Clementina had been approached by a young woman making her debut at the University of Adelaide Ball, where she was to be presented to Lady and Sir Archibald Weigall, the Governor and his wife. The spirited 18-year-old wished to stand out amongst all the other girls wearing white and had requested silver tipped white feathers as epaulettes to her sleeveless shift and an overskirt made of longer white feathers attached to a band of silver silk, tied low at the hips. A keen ballet dancer, the girl wished to emulate her idol, prima ballerina Anna Pavlova. Clementina satisfied the girl's whim, creating the desired swan-effect, complete with a ruffled white tulle skirt under the feathers to prop them up. A write-up of her gown and a photograph in the *Observer* newspaper, with the name Castlemaine Couture favourably mentioned, brought in even more enquiries from other aspiring debutantes, which seemed to be a very popular event on the social calendars of all classes, held in a wide range of venues across the city.

Clementina found the concept of a debutante very amusing, guessing that it was no different to the special feast days she'd attended in her hometown. She remembered the *Festa della Madonna di Carpineto* held in her village on the 8th of May every year, where one young girl from each family was dressed as the Virgin with a long white dress covered by a blue mantle. Onto the white dress was sewn all the gold jewellery the family could rustle up, with necklaces forming glittering arcs. The girls, followed by all the villagers, walked from the main church in the village square to the small church at the edge of the forest. They walked in procession behind the men carrying a wooden float on their shoulders with the statue of Mary in her blue mantle. The statue was believed to have been received by a desperate shepherd as a miracle for the village, whose prayers to the mother of Jesus had saved their agricultural community from an extended drought.

Clementina remembered that in her 16th year, she was deemed too old to join the girls at the front of the procession, but her parents made sure she had a new outfit for the feast day, including a pair of traditional half-moon gold dangling earrings, a matching heavy gold chain with a pendant of the Madonna and a thick gold bracelet. It was a symbol to everyone in the village that she was no longer a child. Before leaving the house, her parents reminded her to act decorously and stay close to them because today was the day where all the families from near and far would be looking at her, to assess whether she would make a good match for a young man in their household. She had said nothing on the day, but she already knew that the only person's eye she wanted to catch was Nicola's. It was important for him to notice.

Briefly, her reminiscences stirred a pang of regret. She'd sold all her gold when her parents and the rest of her family had died, because she needed the money for their graves and modest headstones. Family and survival were more important than objects, she reminded herself, shocked that the sale had only happened 3 years ago. It felt like it was a century ago. Again, she was reminded of how grateful she was to Linda and Eddie, who'd given her this opportunity for an unprecedented future, and she resolved again to do everything she could to bring in more business opportunities.

Linda interrupted Clementina's reverie when she too finished reading the newspaper article.

'*Cara*, I'm so thrilled you're making a name for yourself. You've worked very hard, so focussed on learning about the latest fashion techniques, and you deserve the accolades. But we may have to consider hiring another seamstress if this pace continues. You can't keep working these long hours without a break.'

'But didn't you say that July and August are quiet months?'

'Quiet for weddings, yes, but particularly busy for Debutante Balls and the Winter Balls, which will start up again along the coastal communities. And since you've attracted a steady stream of these clients, I'm guessing there won't be any let-up.'

'I see. But how would we find somebody?'

'We could start with an advertisement in the *Port Adelaide News*. It seems to cover many local stories, so maybe an announcement in the classifieds would attract a local girl, which would be preferable. We'd have to make sure to ask for someone with several years' experience of using a sewing machine, as we wouldn't have the time to train her.'

Clementina agreed, and when they mentioned their discussion to Eddie that evening, he suggested that they also advertise for someone to help with the chores around the house, especially the weekly washing and ironing, which he noticed was wearing them both out. They decided it would be best to begin by asking Father Kenny about someone reliable, as they wouldn't want just anyone wandering about their home while they were busy in the sewing room.

* * *

A few days later, Linda and Clementina were surprised to see Father Kenny pass the sewing room window, accompanied by two women. It seemed Eddie had already put in a word with the priest for them.

'Mrs Walsh and Mrs Vitale, allow me to introduce Mrs Florrie Booth and her daughter Annie,' he began. 'Mrs Booth is a relative of one of our long-time parishioners, Mrs William Graves in Marlborough Street. They've recently come down from Burra and are looking for employment in the area. Annie here has a merit certificate in machine sewing, and Mrs Booth would like to pick up some housekeeping work.'

Sitting around the sewing table with cups of tea, Linda gently enquired about the ladies' backgrounds.

'So, Annie, you've had experience with the sewing machine? What about hand-stitching?'

'Yes, Mrs Walsh. I've brought some samples of my work to show you.'

The young girl, just turned 16, uncovered the basket she'd been carrying and pulled out a baby's layette set she said had won first prize at their local agricultural show. Both Linda and Clementina examined the items carefully and complimented the girl on the fine stitching and the charming embroidery at the collars and cuffs, and at the edges of the bibs. But most impressive were the crochet lace borders around the quilted blanket, showing a steady hand, attention to detail and a flair for following instructions.

'She's been making clothes for me and her two younger sisters since she was 12,' said a very proud Mrs Booth.

'You have younger children, Mrs Booth?'

'Yes, Millie and Helen have been enrolled at the sisters' in the second and third class. My husband, Tom, went to war just after Helen was born in 1916, but he suffered from gassing and hasn't been able to return to working in the mines. He's been transferred to Lady Galway's Red Cross Home nearby. His great-aunt, Mrs Graves, has generously offered to let us stay with her for the duration of his treatment. My husband's pension doesn't stretch very far, so I'd like to find a couple of days' work myself.'

Having clearly understood each other, the newcomers were offered work immediately. Mrs Booth would come on Mondays and Tuesdays to handle the washing and ironing and to give the bathroom and outhouse a good scrub. Annie would come Tuesdays to Saturdays from 10 until 4. Father Kenny discreetly broached the subject of wages, and a satisfactory price was agreed upon, subject to a one-month trial.

The arrangement turned out to be ideal for all parties. Mrs Booth was the model of efficiency, happy and able to work without direction or supervision, coming and going unobtrusively. Annie proved willing to take direction and was eager to learn, always curious about what new ideas Linda and Clementina came up with. She quickly became invaluable for finishing hems and seams and even cutting some of the fabric to the required pattern, leaving Linda and Clementina more time for consultations and design, and giving them back their free evenings, which they were able to spend with Rita and Eddie. Clementina had heeded Linda's advice about giving Rita lessons in more complex embroidery and beading, which the young girl relished, pleased to regain her closeness to Clementina once again.

'Tina, when I grow up, I hope I'm going to be as famous as you and Zia Linda.'

'Famous? I'm not famous!'

'Yes, you are! All my friends say so! Their mothers are always talking about you, and their older sisters are hoping to come to you for their debutante dresses.'

'Well, Rita, darling, it would be my greatest joy to see you join us in the business one day, and I hope you'll be even more famous than us when the time comes for you to take over.'

Rita smirked, but tucked Clementina's words away, determined to prove herself useful to her adopted mothers.

⋆ ⋆ ⋆

During the school term, as soon as Rita came home, she'd remove her uniform and carefully fold her tunic and jacket over her bedroom chair, ready to be worn again the next day. She would change into her house clothes and then drop into the sewing room. Sometimes, Zia Linda would ask her to peel the potatoes for their dinner and leave them to soak in a pan of cold water, but most of the time, she'd find a free corner of the sewing table and settle down to do her homework. She loved the camaraderie of the sewing room, especially now that Annie had joined.

Annie would always ask what she had learnt that day and was keen for Rita to show her the arithmetic she was studying, saying that she had been no good at it when she was younger, but when Rita explained things, it all made much more sense. Often, Clementina and Linda would look up from their projects and listen in awe too.

On Saturday mornings, she was very dutiful about doing her indoor chores while Zia Linda and Clementina were preparing to receive clients in the sewing room. She'd begin by bringing the two smaller tin tubs in from the outdoor laundry and half filling them with cold water and topping them up with hot water from the kettle, taking care to stand well back so she didn't splash any on herself. Then she would take the grater from the laundry and grate the Velvet soap flakes into the tub. Finally, she would check her uniform pockets before dunking the five pairs of fawn socks and her two fawn shirts in one tub and her navy tunic into the other tub, ready for Zia Linda or Clementina to rinse when they came in for lunch.

Next, she dusted the parlour. She would carefully lift away Linda's precious pair of Italian apricot Capodimonte porcelain vases with their delicately crafted floral blooms in vibrant colours. These were always positioned on either side of Uncle Eddie's green brass and enamel pagoda-shaped mantel clock, the one he would wind and reset every night. Standing on her special stool, she'd aim the long-handled feather duster over the top of the curved brass-framed mirror hanging over the mantelpiece, before using some lemon-scented beeswax to polish the jarrah and tile surrounds. Finally, she'd use the floor sweep, with a handle taller than her, to run over the carpet. Rita would finish by plumping up the pillows, folding the lap rugs and polishing the side tables. She liked to hum as she worked, favouring the new songs and hymns she learnt at school.

Close to lunchtime, she would head back to the kitchen, unwrap the bread rolls which had been delivered that morning and pull out the cheese, ham, butter and piccalilli from the icebox. Kneeling carefully on a chair at the table, she would pull apart the soft rolls, generously butter them and add the fillings. Arranging the filled rolls on the cream ceramic platter with the green ivy border collected from the sideboard, with a clean tea towel over the top, she would return everything to the icebox, ready for when Linda, Clementina and Annie came in for lunch.

But it was Sundays she loved the best. That's when the whole family would spend the day together, sometimes going out on excursions further afield from their little corner of the world. She loved going to the cinema best. Sometimes Clementina would ask if she'd like to invite a friend, and while she always had a good time if Ava or Grace came with them, she much preferred it when she and Clementina were alone and they could chat about nothing and everything on their way to Semaphore or Glenelg, or sometimes even into the city if the road over the Reedbeds wasn't flooded. They would always sit on the top deck of the omnibus, looking out in awe at the fields and then the rows of houses as the bus neared the city, fiercely holding on to their straw hats to prevent them from being blown off.

Rita had very little recollection of her first family, as she liked to refer to them. She was only a baby when her mother and her siblings had been evacuated to Chieti, something she was too young to remember, though there was often talk in the refugee camp of the harrowing experience they'd endured during their trek south. She vaguely remembered her older sister Anita singing to her and her brother making her giggle with his silly faces. When the Spanish influenza decimated the camp, she'd only just turned 4. She had no photos of her family and could no longer recall any of their faces. For this, she sometimes became quite sad, and that's when she would go to her room and play with her dolls, whom she'd named after her mother and her siblings. Talking to her dolls and pretending they were all still there with her always comforted her.

Her earliest clear memories were of the orphanage, of finally having something good to eat and a warm place to sleep, and of Clementina holding her and coming to her little bed at night to say her prayers with her, reassuring her that all would be well. She remembered being too frightened to talk because she didn't know the unfamiliar dialect the children used in the orphanage. Then there was the noise and the chaos of all those girls together, all that screeching and flapping, just like the hens in the backyard. In the classroom, there were so many of them squished together in the one room, she had to take turns to look at the picture book and try to understand what Sister Addolorata was teaching them. She had more success with the numbers, because Sister would write those on the blackboard at the front of the room, where she had been seated because she was so small. She still loved numbers today.

Her next clear memory was of their time on the ship—of Teresina combing her hair and playing cards with her and being on deck in the salty air and playing quoits with the other children. She was popular at school, especially when she pulled out her 'elastics' to play with at lunchtime. With her long legs, she had a definite advantage in the game and loved to compete against the older girls, especially Sally Caruthers from the fifth class, who thought she was the boss of everyone. She was also good at running games and had won several ribbons at the Parish Sports Day Running Races, even beating some of the boys!

When she said her prayers at night, she gave thanks for her blessings, for Tina, for Zia Linda and Uncle Eddie, for Charlie the horse, for having enough to eat and a warm bed and toys to play with. In her own way she acknowledged she was now immersed in a privileged life—one that could easily have been so very different.

CHAPTER SEVENTEEN

Remembrance – Monday 24 July 1922

'Mrs Vitale, many of us will be attending the opening of the Henley & Grange Soldiers' Memorial this coming Sunday. What about you?'

'Yes John. I've been reading all about it in the newspaper and I'm planning to be at the official opening on Sunday afternoon. I've had a couple of clients come in for new outfits for the Saturday evening's grand ball at the town hall and all of them have been very excited about the event, and very proud of the township's efforts in organising the memorial so quickly.'

'The men from this area who perished in the war will be remembered with photographs, and all of us will have our service records listed, including Andy and me and some of the other local lads,' continued John, pensively. 'My mother and sisters have been part of the women's committee to raise money for the stained-glass window. I haven't seen it yet, but it was commissioned from Clarkson's, the glass people, and Mr Williams there is famous for having done many churches and other important buildings in the state. I hope it lives up to expectations.'

'So, you've always lived in this area then?' asked Clementina quietly, as she approached.

'Yes, my father was a saddler and did a bit of woodwork too, mostly to fix buggies and carts.'

'Did you lose many friends from here during the war?'

The normally jocular John was almost morose this afternoon, unable to concentrate on his work, and not leading the usual banter with the other men.

'Today would have been my mate Bert's 30th birthday. We were neighbours, went to school together, got our first jobs at Hart's Mill in Port Adelaide together, and joined up together in 1915.'

Clementina remained silent, watching John's face contort in pain and working hard to hide his distress. She reached out to put her hand on his stumped arm and bent down so she could be at his height while he was seated at his worktable.

'How did you lose him?' she whispered.

'At the Somme, in 1916, only a few months after we'd arrived.'

'That's the same year I lost my husband Nicola,' mumbled Clementina, her voice catching as she said his name. She lowered her eyelids for just a moment but quickly returned to look at the Private, sensing he needed to unburden his thoughts.

'Bert got married a week before we shipped out. Evie … she was lovely, but very young. She'd only turned 17. She moved on fairly quickly … married again just 2 years later. I don't blame her. They barely knew each other. We all got caught up in the propaganda and the great romance of it all.'

'Are you married, John?'

'Nah, I was my mother's only son. My father had already passed. I had to keep supporting her with my Army pay. Whether I lived or died, she would be covered. If I married, my pay or my pension would go to my wife.'

'Is your mother still alive?'

'Oh yes. She's 72 years old and lives nearby. She usually volunteers with the morning tea ladies on Tuesdays, with my sister Ruth … you've met my mother, and my sisters Ruth and Henrietta. Henrietta is Nellie Smythe's mother.'

'Oh, of course. I remember Nellie. And I remember your mother too, though it was my friend Linda who made her dress for Nellie's fundraiser. That's where the two of us first met, wasn't it, John … at Nellie's concert earlier this year?'

'Nellie's a smashing girl. We're very proud of her. She's going to be singing the national anthem at the ceremony on Sunday. I've heard that the Premier, Sir Henry Barwell, is coming to officiate.'

'Oh my goodness. That's quite an honour for such a young person. I'll make sure I don't miss it, and I'll look out for you.'

'I'd be honoured, Mrs Vitale. You're doing a wonderful job here, especially with the young lads.'

'Please, my friends call me Tina. And I'd like to think we are well on our way to being friends, aren't we, John?'

Clementina stood up again and beamed back at John, whose more cheerful demeanour had returned. She guessed he was probably in his early 30s. He had straight jet-black hair, which showed no signs of grey, yet was thinning at the temples, made more obvious by the pomade he used to keep the longer fringe slicked back. Warm brown eyes were close set and surrounded by a spidery trail of crease lines, but the skin of his prominent cheeks was polished smooth, underscored by the dark stubble of his shaven rounded chin below. His mouth, thin lips which framed a wide smile with a crooked upper front tooth, matched his comical attitude, and was accompanied by two deep laughter lines on either side, almost like two apostrophes encapsulating his regular quips.

'Most of my friends are either dead or have moved on with their lives. I'm lucky to still be standing, with my family nearby, and to have found friends with the lads in the centre here. We all understand each other, and we help give each other hope for the future. But I could use a good-looking friend,' he said, winking. 'Most of this lot are an ugly bunch.'

Clementina blushed at the compliment.

'You're such a card! Aren't you John? That's a new English phrase Sister Marie has taught me, and I think it describes you perfectly.'

'I certainly like to keep an ace up my sleeve.' He winked again.

Clementina chuckled as she moved off to check on the other men, especially the boys at the loom. They'd taken to their project of making small colourful cotton rugs with gusto, and hearing the familiar swish of the shuttle and thump of the batten transported her back to her childhood home, bringing her a sense of comfort she couldn't explain.

When she finished with the lads in the Sewing Studio that afternoon, Clementina was still pensive. The sky had turned grey, and the wind was fiercer than when she had arrived. As she walked along Seaview Road, she struggled to hold on to her hat, and the front of her skirt clung to her legs, making it difficult to walk at her usual brisk pace. Looking out to the sea, she saw it was covered in large, choppy waves, their white crests like open mouths ready to swallow up all before them. The water, so crystal clear and vibrant blue in summer, was murky with the silt being dredged up from the bottom. The noise of the wind whistling in her ears and the cold slap against her cheeks made her wish she'd thought to bring her woollen shawl instead of the flimsy soft velour hat which threatened to fly away at any minute.

She continued up the slight incline towards the central Henley township. She was so lost in her thoughts that she jumped at the sound of a car horn. She stopped and moved over to the furthest side of the rudimentary path to let the motor go past her. To her astonishment, the large shiny black car came to a halt.

'Mrs Vitale, may I offer you a ride home?' yelled the driver.

'Lieutenant!'

'You look like you might be swept out to sea at any minute. Please allow me to escort you home,' shouted Lieutenant Albert Thomson over the roar of the waves.

Clementina hesitated; she'd never been in a motor car, yet the prospect of getting home quickly and out of this threatening weather was enticing. Noting her hesitation and startled eyes, the Lieutenant slipped out of his side of the car and hobbled around to open the front door for her. Reaching out his hand, he encouraged her up the step and onto the plush red leather seat at the front.

At first, Clementina's feet dangled on the front bench seat, and as the car lurched on start-up, she put both hands out to reach for the dashboard, inching herself forward on the seat so that her feet could reach the floor. Albert Thomson let out a hearty laugh.

'Relax, Mrs Vitale. You're quite safe,' he shouted as he shifted gear and sped up the road.

Clementina's stomach did another somersault, her olive skin turning grey. She continued to clutch the dashboard, eyes glued to the road ahead. She was never so glad to see the familiar buildings of Henley Square approach within a few minutes of their travel. Albert finally slowed down.

'Where can I drop you off, Mrs Vitale?'

'Here's fine. The Walsh house is just at the beginning of Main Street, after Military Road,' waved Clementina.

Instead of stopping, Albert Thomson put his hand out of the

window to indicate his intentions and turned off Seaview Road onto Main Street, coming to a jerky halt when Clementina pointed out the house. Rita was at the sewing room window, waiting for her return. She stared open-mouthed to see Clementina step out of the flashy car with Lieutenant Thomson's help.

'May I come in to pay my respects to the Walsh's?' he asked brazenly.

Embarrassed by her awkwardness, and still shaken, Clementina motioned him forward to the parlour entrance. She settled him in an armchair, and hastily retreated, going in search of Linda. Sending Rita to put the kettle on and call Eddie, Linda took Clementina by the arm and escorted her back to the parlour.

'My dear Lieutenant Thomson. What a pleasure to see you again.'

Standing up as the ladies entered the room, Albert bowed slightly.

'Mrs Walsh, the pleasure is mine. I'm afraid I've startled Mrs Vitale, even with such a short ride in the motor car,' he exclaimed, grinning cheekily at Clementina. He was amused by her reaction.

'I thank you very much for getting me out of the weather. I was struggling to walk against the wind,' replied Clementina, recovering her senses.

Eddie and Rita walked in together, and Clementina made her escape again, murmuring something about fetching the tea. Linda sent her a curious look, but Clementina scurried away. In the kitchen, she finally paused to catch her breath. Was it the trip in the motor car that had discombobulated her so? Or was it the presence of the dashing lieutenant that had shaken her? Taking a deep breath and standing up to her full height of five feet, Clementina scooped tea leaves into the teapot, fetched the cups and cutlery, set out some homemade almond biscuits on a pretty china plate and wheeled it all into the parlour on the wooden trolley they kept for the purpose. Eddie had taken the liberty of serving himself and the lieutenant a whisky, so they declined the tea, but Albert was keen to try the biscuits when Rita explained she and Tina had made them together the day before.

The impromptu visit was brief, and the conversation was stilted, concentrating on the exchange of social information about their common acquaintances. But as he took his leave, Albert Thomson addressed Clementina specifically.

'Mrs Vitale, may I be bold and request the pleasure of your company Saturday week, for the Henley Sailing Club's Annual Awards Dinner? My family will all be in attendance. It's being held at the Ramsgate Hotel. I promise not to come collect you in the car!'

They all laughed at his joke, given that the Ramsgate was only a few feet away on the corner of Main Street and Seaview Road. Taken aback, Clementina just stared at first, but with a subtle nudge from Linda, finally answered.

'Thank you very much for your kind invitation, Lieutenant. What time should I expect you?'

'Just before six should give us plenty of time to saunter down the road.'

With those last words, he scooped up his peaked cap from the armchair and thanked his hosts. He shook hands all around, including with Rita, who giggled and made him a wobbly curtsy. Linda chose not to say much, but behind Clementina's back, a knowing look passed between her and Eddie. Clementina, her face flushed, offered to start preparing dinner, and ushered Rita and the tea trolley into the kitchen, keen to get away from any unwanted questions.

By the following Sunday, the threatening storms had passed, and the day dawned cool but sunny. After church, they had a light breakfast, sitting around the kitchen table, sharing news and discussing plans for the afternoon's event at the town hall.

'I've promised to look out for the boys from the Sewing Studio. John was quite upset last week, remembering his childhood friend. His friend will be one of the fallen soldiers to have their portrait on display.'

'I caught a small glimpse of the window from the street the other evening. It's quite spectacular when illuminated from inside. It's a wonderful tribute,' added Eddie.

'I think I forgot to tell you that Henrietta Smythe, Nellie's mother, is John's sister. Remember the dresses we made for Nellie's fundraiser?'

'Ah yes, the one you designed. Your advertising dress!' Linda mused. 'That seems such a long time ago now, yet it was only in February this year. How far you've come, Clementina. You should be very proud of yourself.'

She beamed at Clementina, stretching out her hand to clutch the one reaching for hers.

'I couldn't have done anything without you,' she said with emotion, squeezing Linda's hand.

Tears came to Clementina's eyes as she searched lovingly into all three pairs of eyes sitting around the kitchen table with her.

'It's we who've been blessed by your presence,' added Eddie, lifting Rita onto his lap. 'Weren't we a pair of old fuddy-duddies before these two bright young things came into our lives?'

'Yes, Mr Walsh, we've certainly found a new lease on life,' smiled a satisfied Linda. She reached out to squeeze his hand too in acknowledgement.

The family left early to ensure they would find a spot for the official unveiling ceremony. A section of the road had been roped off and closed to traffic. The Boy Scouts and their parents had set up tents around the perimeter of the cordoned-off space, acting as a buffer against the light but chilly wind blowing in off the water. Refreshments would be served inside the tents at the conclusion of the ceremony.

Standing sentinel to the imposing red brick of the town hall was a tall pair of Ionic sandstone columns flanking the protrusion which housed the arched window of the Soldier's Memorial. A cream cement beehive-shaped roof with a classical funerary urn at its peak crowning the cream cement triangular pediments of the memorial, formed a majestic façade. The construction of the town hall had only been completed a few months earlier.

In front of the main body of the single-storey town hall, a high platform, festooned with Union Jack flags and red, white and blue bunting, had been set up for the dignitaries. The Walsh family stood at the back, behind the rows of chairs set up at the front for the ex-soldiers and their families. Soon they saw the contingent from Lady Galway arriving. John looked about for Clementina, waving in acknowledgement. She saw him moving once again when his mother and older sister's family arrived, accompanied by Henrietta and Thomas Smythe.

A middle-aged gentleman positioned himself on the stool of the piano on stage. A small band lined up on either side of him. The dignitaries turned up, at first shuffling around on the chairs set out for them. Then, when the Premier arrived with the mayor, proudly sporting their regalia, everyone on stage stood. Nellie, who'd been standing in the front row of the choir positioned to the left of the stage, waltzed up the side stairs to the microphone. The band began to play the overture to 'God Save the King' and Nellie launched into her rendition, with an unfalteringly clear, bell-like voice. There was silence when she finished, no-one wishing to interrupt the solemnity of the proceedings. The Methodist pastor, Reverend Clarke, led the prayers of blessings before the speeches from the various dignitaries began.

Much praise was offered to the specially formed committee of the Henley and Grange District Council that in 3 years had raised £1,800 for the construction and interior of the Shrine of Remembrance and to the Ladies Committee who fundraised a further £300, which was the equivalent of 2 years' wages, for the specially commissioned window. Members of the press had come to document the proceedings in words and pictures.

It was a long afternoon, but it was made enjoyable by the number of locals who stopped to chat with them. Eventually, it was the turn of the Walsh foursome to file into the small memorial room. A copper plaque, listing the names of the 148 men from the district who had enlisted, was prominently displayed in an alcove above the altar, where laurel wreaths with purple ribbons had been placed. The names and photographs of the 28 men who had fallen were displayed around a polished wooden signboard with the list of the battles in which they'd fought stamped in gold.

'It's so grand!' exclaimed Clementina, staring open-mouthed at the imposing stained-glass window which cast a mesmerising glow over the reverential space.

The gloriously coloured glass painting depicted a kneeling soldier in khaki uniform, complete with the distinctive slouch hat. The Union Jack and the Australian flag, with the striking Southern Cross star pattern, flanked the soldier, whose hand was on the rifle placed before him. A wooden jetty and the swirls of green and blue hues representing the sea were depicted in the background. A Christ figure in royal red robes and a golden crown soared above the waves, dominating the scene.

John caught up with Clementina as she was moving from his name among local servicemen listed and was looking for his friend's portrait.

'Which one is Bert?' she asked, speaking softly to respect the solemnity of the space.

'This one. Herbert Edward Roberts,' choked out John.

'So, so young,' muttered Linda, shaking her head at the sepia-tinted headshot of a young lad in uniform, proudly wearing his slouch hat secured at the chin.

Clementina had no words but nodded in acknowledgement and turned to the Christ figure in the window, making the sign of the cross against her body. Distressingly, her thoughts flew to her husband, Nicola. Would he ever get the respect he deserved for his own supreme sacrifice? No letters from home had ever mentioned a memorial. Some of the returned soldiers from her village, who would have fought alongside him, had taken the trouble to seek her out to reassure her he had fought and died in honour. But they had never said a word about where he was buried, if indeed he had been buried, so far from home, or was simply lost in the mud of the northern Italian battlefields. Certainly, no such news had ever come from the Italian War Office. Clementina held her stomach, churning now in sympathy with her thoughts, which were a whirlwind of regret and guilt.

'How could I have left Italy without even making sure he was properly buried?' She slumped onto a bench. She braced her left arm against her body and with her right arm shielded her tightly closed eyes. The first time she'd heard anything about a war pension was from her conversations with John. What about all the Italian widows? Were they entitled to anything? Or were these women just too many in number to be effectively dealt with by a country crippled economically by war, disease and constant natural disasters?

Linda came to sit beside her, gently placing an arm around Clementina's shoulders and whispering, 'Are you unwell, *cara*?'

Clementina slowly shook her head from side to side, and turning to

Linda, grimaced her sorrow. 'This all reminds me of Nicola.'

On the walk home, she barely spoke. She decided she must write home tonight to ask about such things. She would write to Father Ernesto. He would be the only one who might have any idea. Any monies that she might be entitled to wouldn't be for her, but for Antonia and her sister-in-law Rosaria, and her niece and nephew, for whom she continued to worry. She sent money every 3 months and knew from the letters received how much that meant to her family. But that money was just for survival. There was little for any extras, or for the proper education of her niece and nephew. Obtaining an education was the only hope for the future, now that the flax-growing and weaving activity of the neighbourhood had disappeared. The large cotton and wool mills in Lombardy had seen their fortunes rise thanks to the requisition of uniforms and bandages for the war effort, leaving the more laborious cottage industries that produced linen, like Clementina's little village, stranded. Rosaria had explained that with materials imported from other, larger producers, especially those in France whose recovery had been boosted by American money, there was no market for their linen. Many families had opted to migrate to these larger holdings to find work.

Sleep did not come easily that night. She spent a long time staring at Nicola's photo, allowing silent tears to trickle down her cheeks. It had been a year since she'd left Italy, and in her haste to adapt to her new situation, she'd deliberately pushed thoughts of home and her previous life aside, not wanting them to poison her progress. She couldn't shake the overwhelming sense of shame that had suddenly assailed her today. How could she have forgotten her Nicola? And worse still, what right did she have to feel happy and settled, when Nicola was still caught in limbo?

CHAPTER EIGHTEEN

Society Pages – Saturday 5 August 1922

Feeling sullen all week, Clementina had suggested to Linda that she should cancel the plans made to accompany the Lieutenant to the awards dinner. Linda hinted it would be impolite, unless she were truly ill. She'd reminded Clementina that she'd be with the Thomson family, whom she knew, so she'd be well looked after.

'Your family wouldn't want you to give up on life,' Linda had encouraged.

Still, Clementina couldn't muster much enthusiasm. Linda had given Annie the task of adding embellishments to a plain black silk shift. Annie had chosen another black silk fabric of similar weight, but with small white polka dots to create a contrast effect. She added a flounce at the bottom, some side panels starting at the hip and some long sleeves.

'You've done a marvellous job, Annie. I'm very proud of you,' said Linda.

Last month, Clementina had unpicked her woollen skirt from Italy and laid it on the bias to create a cape jacket with long, slim ties at the neck. Something a little more stylish than her woollen shawl, but just as easy to wear. Annie had offered to embellish the neck and the ends of the ties with some pearls to create the same polka dot effect as her dress, and both Linda and Clementina had been very impressed with her initiative and invisible stitching.

Hats were not worn with evening attire, but Linda suggested a black silk band for around Clementina's forehead, embellished with a tulle fan, and a few more pearls, to create a little drama. Linda had also encouraged Clementina to borrow a long string of pearls from her jewellery box.

The lieutenant turned up with a small arrangement of pink carnations, which he tied to her wrist. She was surprised to see him out of uniform. He was wearing a black tuxedo jacket and matching trousers with a black bow tie and white shirt with a stiff collar and front. In his hands, he carried a top hat and a slim black cane to help him walk. He proffered his left arm to escort Clementina, so that he could use the cane in his right hand to balance his posture. Clementina was impressed with how he managed with his wooden leg. Beneath the trousers, she could see that he had donned a matching pair of shoes, disguising the artificial leg entirely.

They ambled up the road, careful not to lose their footing on the rough footpath. The yellow, gas-fired streetlights on Seaview Road weren't of much help, but as they approached the hotel, its own electric lights spilled out liberally, and the footpath had been cleared and smoothed around the building. The dinner was being held in the grand ballroom on the first floor, so they took the stairs in a leisurely fashion.

'Thank you for your support and understanding, my dear. Stairs are still quite tricky for me.'

'Of course, Lieutenant. There's no need to apologise.'

'Please, won't you call me Albie tonight?'

'As long as you drop the Mrs Vitale. I'm Clementina or Tina.'

'I love the sound of Clementina. Very juicy!' he smirked.

It took Clementina several seconds to understand the reference. She blushed furiously.

When they reached the entrance to the ballroom, Clementina was not expecting the obvious stares directed at them as they walked through the crowd. Worried that something was amiss with her outfit, she looked nervously down at her feet until they reached their table. She was relieved to be warmly greeted by Albie's parents and his sister Caro, who was accompanied by Captain Reggie Dixon from Lady Galway's. Albie's younger brother Freddie, with their young cousin Alice, were also seated at the table. All were eager to chat with her so that she soon forgot her reservations.

After the welcome from the club president, a small band played unobtrusively during dinner. The awards and speeches were given between courses. Clementina was taken aback by the elegant presentation of the dishes, but she felt it all tasted quite bland, perhaps because of her nervousness. Even the dessert, a puff pastry marvel, was filled with too much plain whipped cream and accompanied by a thin sliver of insipid poached pear, staring pale and insignificant at her from her plate. They had some fine wine on her table, but she noticed other tables were drinking tea. She asked Albie if it were normal to serve tea at these types of formal dinners.

'Oh, that's the Protestants. Some of them are teetotallers. They don't believe in drinking alcohol,' he added when he realised Clementina was unfamiliar with the term. 'Luckily, we Catholics have no such scruples.'

Both Albie and Freddie were called up several times to receive recognition for their efforts in various sailing competitions held in the previous season. The brothers, looking so similar even though there was at least 10 years difference between them, spent much time talking to their teammates at other tables, returning to their own table to deposit trophies and medals on colourful ribbons and to apologise for being called away. Clementina didn't mind. It excused her from having to make small talk and allowed her to watch the crowd.

She greeted three ladies, Linda's long-term clients, who stopped by to say hello. One of them, though, was very curious about how long she and the lieutenant had been an item. Clementina was quick to set her straight but was mortified by the reply she received.

'That's good to hear. I find it strange that the lieutenant is keeping company with a working girl, when there are so many available girls of his own class.'

Clementina was uncertain that she had properly understood the woman. But the barb was soon confirmed when she noticed Emmeline and Caro's flushed faces. Emmeline tried to reassure her that the family did not think that way, but the encounter left Clementina confused and embarrassed.

After the meal, some couples, including Caro and Reggie, got up to dance. Fascinated by the jaunty music and the rapid movements, Clementina watched on eagerly, trying to decipher the steps. Alice helped her by pointing out the shifts in the movement and counting the beat. While she didn't think she'd be ready to try the dances, she was slightly perturbed that Albie hadn't returned to their table and didn't even seem to be in the room anymore. She didn't want to embarrass his parents by pointing out his absence, but when Freddie came back without him and took Alice off to the dance floor, she did feel quite foolish sitting alone on her side of the table. She kept a quiet smile plastered to her face, but she was tiring of the pretence. The captain and his wife looked tired. Learning that they had come in their own buggy, which they'd left on Main Street, Clementina suggested she could walk with them on her way home. The captain, catching his younger son's eye, motioned to him to return to the table and sent him to fetch Albie from wherever he'd gone. Alice was invited to dance by another young man, so the threesome were left alone again, the captain looking grim, and his wife fighting to keep her eyes open.

It was at least another 10 minutes before Albie and Freddie returned. Freddie was tugging on his arm, steering him carefully through the tangle of tables. Albie's face was flushed, his bow tie was gone and his collar was loose. When he reached their table, he apologised profusely and loudly. Clementina was shocked to see him so obviously intoxicated. His parents could barely disguise their fury. Caro and Reggie, alerted to the irregularity of the situation, suggested that it was time for the family to all go home. Caro helped her mother off her chair and, with her father, headed towards the stairs with Freddie and Alice following. Reggie gallantly picked up Clementina's cape and placed it on her shoulders, offering her his arm to escort her from the room.

'Let's see your guest home, old chap,' he said, grabbing hold of Albie's other arm and forcing him into a standing position. A gentleman from the next table, one of Albie's teammates, came to the rescue, hooking his arm under Albie's and practically dragging him to the doorway.

'Tina, I'm terribly sorry that you had to see Albie reduced like this. I don't understand what's come over him this evening. I've never known him to be so rude. Please accept my apologies.'

They'd reached the footpath outside the hotel, and Clementina untangled her arm from the captain's.

'Thank you for looking out for me, Reggie, but I am merely a few doors across the road. See—the verandah light has been left lit for me. I'll take my leave here and allow you to see the Thomson family home.'

Clementina couldn't hurry across the road fast enough, up the front steps and through the front door, extinguishing the verandah light as she entered. Linda and Eddie were still in the parlour, but both were fast asleep. She gently woke Linda to let her know she had returned but quickly scooted out to her own room before the older woman began asking questions.

Of course, agitated and confused, sleep evaded her. She tried to reconstruct the evening, wondering if she had said or done something wrong that might have chased Albie away from the table, but no matter how often she reviewed the situation, she could not understand how the charming and polished Lieutenant Albert Thomson had been reduced to a tiresome bore in such a short time. She shouldn't have gone. The sting of the comment made by that odious woman came back to her. Had someone said something similar to Albie? Was that the reason he'd kept away from her? She was mortified to think that others felt she had stepped out of line.

The next morning, she struggled to get out of bed. Linda came in to her with their usual coffee and suggested she could sleep in a little longer while she and Eddie took Rita to church, then if Clementina felt up to it, she could go to the later service.

'No, no, I'm fine. Thanks for the coffee. I'll get ready and join you soon.' She didn't want to risk running into the Thomsons or any other revellers from last night at the later, and more popular 10 o'clock service.

In the afternoon, Eddie volunteered to take the energetic Rita for a walk to see the matches at the Grange Bowling Club, leaving Linda and Clementina a chance to talk freely.

'My darling, what an awful experience for you. I'm so sorry to hear this news. It sounds like Emmeline and the Captain were embarrassed too, both with that silly woman's comments and their son's behaviour. Would you like me to call on them this week to see if they can shed any light on what's going on?'

'No! Please don't! I think the whole night is best forgotten. I don't normally come across the lieutenant, so there's no need to drag the situation out. He clearly can't hold his liquor, and if that's the case, I want nothing to do with him,' said Clementina firmly, crossing her arms and pursing her lips, still wounded by her unpleasant experience.

'I'm going to the sewing room. I need to cut out the Dempsey wedding outfits so that Annie will have something to start with on Tuesday,' said Clementina to curtail any further discussion.

'Good idea. I'll put a pot of coffee on, then I'll join you.'

As they were leaving the parlour, there was a knock on the door. Linda looked through the window and saw Freddie Thomson.

'Master Freddie, this is a surprise.'

'Excuse me, Mrs Walsh,' he said, removing his cloth cap, 'but I've come with a note from my mother.'

No sooner had Linda accepted the envelope, Freddie rushed down the steps and out the gate, hurrying off towards the square.

'Oh, my goodness,' muttered Linda in his wake.

The envelope was addressed to Clementina. Linda handed it to her and made to leave.

'Please, Linda, stay. You read it. I'm too tired to concentrate.'

The letter apologised to Clementina for any embarrassment caused by her son. His mother explained that since Albie's return from the war, and losing his two older brothers, he had not been himself. Emmeline and her husband had only realised last night the extent of the physical and emotional pain he was carrying and trying to blunt with alcohol. The letter said they had decided, after discussion with Captain Dixon, that it would be best to book Albie into a clinic in the country and away from the improper influence of his sailing mates. They hoped some quiet time away would help him reconnect with his true self.

Linda was dismayed for her friend. She clarified to Clementina what a blow to her pride it would have been to write this letter, emphasising Emmeline's ingrained kindness in wanting to make sure Clementina understood she was not to blame for anything that happened last night.

Seeing it from Linda's perspective helped Clementina. She moved to the sewing room with a lighter heart. Linda re-read the letter. She would send a reply to her friend, letting her know Clementina was fine, and that they both hoped Albie would get the support he needed. Most importantly, she would reassure Emmeline of their continued friendship and discretion.

The following Saturday, Eddie pointed out Clementina and Albie's photo in the *Observer Newspaper*'s social pages. Together with Caroline Thomson and Captain Dixon, the four of them made a handsome and glamorous set. Clementina's large dark eyes and dark wavy hair, her slim, chiselled jaw and regal bearing stood out against the paler, flatter features of her companions.

'Fortunately, it was taken at the beginning of the night,' quipped Clementina, barely glancing at the photo.

'And Castlemaine Couture is mentioned too,' added Rita, who'd asked permission to cut out the article and photo. Wouldn't her friends be envious when she showed them her movie star Tina on Monday!

CHAPTER NINETEEN

Celebrations – Friday 25 August 1922

Linda received a note from Emmeline Thomson requesting an appointment to discuss outfits for Caro's upcoming engagement and wedding. Linda was delighted for Caroline, who, a few weeks ago, had invited Clementina to a fundraising Croquet Tournament for the younger set of their church. Clementina was reluctant to go, but Linda had persuaded her to attend and had been relieved to hear that Caro had discreetly avoided any mention of her brother Albie. Clementina had been able to relax and get to know some lovely people, including some mothers of Rita's classmates.

This Friday afternoon, therefore, Linda baked her special sultana cake in anticipation of the Thomson's visit. Clementina had produced a few drawings of ideas for engagement and wedding dresses which she thought would suit Caro's figure. She had also bookmarked ideas in magazines which might interest both the older and younger woman. Excited chatter of engagement and wedding preparations dominated the visit, but in a quiet moment, while Caroline and Clementina were rifling through the drawers of buttons and notions, Linda discretely asked about Albie's progress. She was relieved to hear, for his mother's sake as much as for his own, that he was making good progress, and a return to Adelaide was expected for his sister's mid-January wedding.

The following afternoon, both Linda and Clementina were invited to accompany Rita to an 8th birthday party for a little girl in her class. Celebrating birthdays was not a custom familiar to either Linda or Clementina. Clementina remembered only that her parents had once celebrated her name day, when she was around Rita's age, on the Feast of Saint Clement. In late November they had set off on a family pilgrimage to the Abbey of Saint Clement near Pescara on the Adriatic Sea, about 40 km northeast of their village. She had a vague recollection that her father had wrapped homemade salami and sheep's milk cheeses in vine leaves to offer to the monks, and that she and her mother had picked some wildflowers to lay before the altar, in gratitude for Clementina's continued good health. Too many children still died in infancy in the little rural villages of her region.

On the way to the party, they stopped at the florist for a posy of sweet-scented blue hyacinths for Mrs Murphy. For her daughter Janice, Clementina had run up a soft jersey cape, also in pale blue with a detachable white collar, onto which she had embroidered some pink hearts. Rita had used some white lawn fabric to make her friend a matching handkerchief with a neat blanket stitch edge in blue silk thread and a corner adorned with a similar bouquet of pink hearts. She'd taken great care with this project, anticipating the joy both she and Janice would derive from seeing the handkerchief retrieved from her friend's pocket. She savoured too, the praise she received from Linda and Clementina for her neat work.

The party was being held on the front verandah of a house in North Street, which was festooned with pink crepe paper twists. As the guests arrived, Janice's two older sisters, young adults of around 13 and 15, took charge of the friends, swapping serviceable straw or cloth hats for coloured cardboard cones decorated in coloured foil and secured under the chin with fine elastic. Games on the front lawn included a three-legged race, an egg and spoon race and the great peanut hunt, which saw the guests nearly knock each other out as they scrambled through the bushes in search of the elusive peanuts in their hairy brown double-barrelled shells. Pauline's skirt had deep pockets which gave her a distinct advantage—she collected 79 peanuts and was declared the winner. She was encouraged to take them home in a paper boat, skilfully folded from the previous day's newspaper.

Eventually, the young guests joined mothers and grandmothers on the verandah. A prettily iced two-tier sponge cake with eight candles appeared. The birthday song was sung, charming little speeches were made by the sisters and the birthday girl, and sandwiches, currant buns and toffee apples were wolfed down with glasses of cold Ovaltine chocolate milk. Each little guest left the party with a brown paper package tied with a pretty pink ribbon. It contained a slim bar of pink and white coconut ice, which they carried home in their inverted party hats.

Linda, without children of her own, was as nervous as Clementina at the outset. But once she recognised most of the mothers and grandmothers in attendance as locals, she could relax and enjoy the tea and scones on offer for the adults. As they walked home, they discussed what reciprocal arrangements they would be expected to make for Rita.

'Is it expected that a child has a birthday party every year?'

'Oh, not at all. I believe it depends on the circumstances of the family. Mrs Murphy did say it was Janice's turn this year and that, because she has five children, she wouldn't be having another party to celebrate her birthday again until she was 13,' relayed Linda.

'I see,' sighed Clementina in relief. She hesitated before asking, 'And how do you feel about such arrangements? Do you feel it would be expected that we hold a party in return?'

'I think if we accept invitations, we would be expected to hold our own party at some point. But since Rita will have her First Communion a few weeks prior to her 8th birthday, perhaps we can wait for a proper party. We could always invite a couple of her little friends to an ice cream tea at the Ozone Café, and a ride on the merry-go-round, don't you think?'

'Oh, that sounds very reasonable. I'd be much more comfortable with that,' sighed Clementina, balking at the idea of having to host a party for a high-spirited crowd of little girls. 'I think we should be prepared for other types of requests, though. Now that she's familiar with the concept of a birthday party, we may be bombarded with ideas. It would be best we three adults presented a unified front.'

Linda smiled benevolently, both at Clementina and at Rita, who was skipping ahead. 'Listen to the two of us,' she chuckled as she took Clementina's arm. 'Neither of us natural mothers, but learning to be good ones, nevertheless.' Clementina beamed back at Linda and tucked her friend's arm even tighter into her own elbow. Matched in height and stature, they found it easy to keep in step. As they neared the collection of shops around the Henley Beach Jetty and the turnoff to Main Street, they were stopped several times by local traders and their customers, all eager to greet or exchange a few words with the well-known elegant ladies and their animated 'daughter' who always had an amusing observation to make, despite her young age.

Back at home, Annie was just finishing the last hem of the bundle she'd been left to complete. Out of her bag, Linda pulled a neatly wrapped package of peanuts and coconut ice that she'd discreetly requested of Mrs Murphy. It transpired that Annie and her little sisters, like Linda, had never been to a children's birthday party. Annie gushed in appreciation of Linda's thoughtfulness. Although it was past the time for her to go home, Linda could see she was desperate to ask Rita questions.

'Why don't Mr Walsh and Rita accompany you home in the buggy, since it looks like it's about to rain, and Rita can tell you all about the party,' suggested Linda.

Within minutes, Eddie had been roused from behind his newspaper, and the three had set off, giving Linda and Clementina quiet time to retreat to their kitchen for reminiscences of their own.

'I spoke to a Ruth Jones, little Lucille's mother. Do you remember her from Nellie Smythe's crowd? She's Henrietta's older sister. I made her the periwinkle blue crepe two-piece,' said Linda.

'Yes, we greeted one another, but I didn't get a chance to talk to her.'

'She was very friendly. Asked me many questions, though. Not only about myself and the business, but about Rita and my connection to her and to you, too.'

'Did that upset you?' asked Clementina, her eyes narrowing in curious concern.

'Oh no … I just thought it was strange, especially since everyone else mostly engaged in polite small talk. She was very curious about your long-term plans.'

'My plans?'

'If she's Henrietta Smythe's sister, then that makes her your John's sister too, doesn't it?'

'Oh, of course. I keep forgetting about his connection to the Smythe's. They're so different. But he's not *my John*—we're merely acquaintances through my work at Lady Galway's.'

'Are you sure about that? He was very taken with your interest in him and his lost friend at the Soldier's Memorial Opening Ceremony.

He followed you with his eyes everywhere, from the moment we stepped into the room.'

'It was a very emotional day for him, and he'd shared his friend's story with me the week before.'

'So, he expected you to be there?'

'Oh yes. I'd promised him I would attend. I'd said we were all planning to be there.'

'Do you think he may have mentioned your interest to his sister?'

'My interest? What do you mean?'

'Do you think he has some expectations of you, given your interest in him?'

'Oh, my goodness!' Clementina dropped the paring knife she'd been using to peel the potatoes and put her hands to her face to cool her cheeks which felt like they were on fire. She picked up the folded newspaper Eddie had left on the chair to fan herself.

'You don't think …' she stammered, 'that the family thinks … that they might think … that I have designs on him?'

Linda's arched eyebrow cocked in her direction was all the answer she needed.

'*Mamma mia*. How embarrassing! I've never entertained any such ideas about him. And I can assure you, he's been nothing but a proper gentleman when I'm at Lady Galway's! What do you think he's told them?'

'Given how much the sister was questioning me, I'd say he hasn't told them very much at all. But they've obviously made some assumptions, maybe based purely on the way he acted around you at the unveiling.'

Clementina plopped herself back on the chair and took up the paring knife again. She didn't say anymore, but didn't dare look at Linda either, pretending to be absorbed in coring the eyes from the potatoes before slicing them into the pan of cold water in front of her. Wisely, Linda pretended to get on with trimming and seasoning the lamb chops.

Clementina pondered this news. John McLeod, hmmm … He's a wonderful mentor to the younger boys, and he always looks out for me—protects me like an older brother. No, surely Linda's mistaken. Lost in her reverie, she was startled when Linda interrupted her thoughts.

'What about those cushion covers I commissioned from him? Has he finished them yet? Remember, Eddie promised to have him for lunch when they were done. Perhaps you can check on their progress on Monday?'

'Cushion covers? I don't think I've seen him working on them, but I'll ask,' promised Clementina.

★ ★ ★

When Clementina arrived at Lady Galway's the following Monday afternoon, she was feeling apprehensive, hoping Linda had been wrong about the motivation for John's interest in her. She wondered if he'd bring up his sister Ruth's encounter with them at the party. To Clementina's dismay, John was not in attendance. Discreet inquiries of the other men elicited little information. They hadn't seen him since the previous Tuesday, and he hadn't explained a potential absence, so they couldn't enlighten her.

The workshop continued in its usual vein, but without John's humorous banter, the mood was a little subdued. About halfway through the afternoon, Matron Heritage popped in, as she always did, eager to see developments in the output and workmanship of the Sewing Studio, and also to check on the welfare of the men. Clementina was busy helping Samuel tack a binding to the edge of the quilt he was working on and didn't want to blurt out her curiosity about John's non-attendance to the whole room. The matron just smiled, exhorting them all to 'carry on,' saying nothing about John's absence before she left.

CHAPTER TWENTY

A Mystery – Monday 28 August 1922

Normally, when her time with the men came to an end, Clementina would just leave and head out through the front doors to walk home. Today, she lingered a little in the main entrance hallway, hoping she might catch someone who could enlighten her regarding John's absence. To her relief, Reggie Dixon walked out of his office with his leather briefcase, ready to leave for the day.

'Tina, how lovely to see you again,' he said, doffing his hat.

'Reggie, I believe congratulations are in order for your coming engagement.'

'I'm a very lucky man to have met Caro and to have persuaded her to marry me.'

'We've been discussing dress patterns, and I can assure you, she feels very lucky to have met you too.'

'Thank you for your reassurance, Tina. That's very kind of you to say. But have I come across you on your way home? My motor car is out the front, and I'd be happy to give you a ride.'

Clementina balked at the thought of the motor car but gathered her courage because she knew this might be the only way to find out whether John's disappearance meant he was avoiding her.

'I'd be delighted.'

Captain Dixon's car was much smaller than Albie's and lower to the ground. She sat comfortably in the front seat, her feet able to touch the floor of the cab without having to grip the dash to stop her from sliding. Captain Dixon was also a more careful driver, motoring at an even pace, slowing down at obvious potholes rather than trying to fly over them. Soon Clementina's fear subsided, and her curiosity re-ignited.

'I was surprised not to see John McLeod at the workshop today. Do you know if he's ill?'

'Oh, did nobody tell you? That's strange. He's not ill. In fact, it's wonderful news. It's what my work is all about.'

Still none the wiser, Clementina persevered. 'Oh, what news is that?' She tried to ask as nonchalantly as possible.

'He's left Lady Galway's to set up his own workshop.'

'His own workshop … Really? And where is this new workshop?'

'He's opened a shop front on the corner of Main and East Terrace here in Henley Beach. It's his mother's house, and there is a large woodworking shed out the back. He's gone into business with Private Sanderson from the Woodworking Studio to make small items of bespoke furniture. They've produced some amazing examples. I'm sure once word gets out, they'll gather plenty of business.'

Clementina was floored. John had never once mentioned going into business for himself.

'That is wonderful news,' she uttered. 'Wish him well for me the next time you see him, won't you?'

'I'm on my way there now, why don't you come with me? I'm sure he'd be chuffed to show you around.'

Before she could think, she'd already blurted out, 'Thank you for the kind offer, but I'm expected at home. I'll have to see Private McLeod another time. If you could deposit me on Main Street, just down from the Ramsgate, that would be very kind.'

In a few seconds, Captain Dixon had smoothly turned the car into Main Street and had slowed down in front of the Walsh residence. He quickly hopped out to open the door for her and assist her from the vehicle. He doffed his hat as she opened the gate and went up the steps to the sewing room entrance where Rita was sitting in the window, looking out for her arrival, as she always did. Clementina was never so glad to see her as she came out onto the verandah. Turning at the door, with Rita firmly planted in front of her, she waved the captain goodbye with a fake grin plastered to her face.

'A package came for Zia Linda and a letter for you,' announced Rita as she pointed to the sewing table.

'Where's Zia Linda?'

'She's in the kitchen, but she's baking, so she told me to come do my homework in here.'

'And have you finished your homework?'

'Yes, all done. I'm just waiting for Uncle Eddie to get home so he can check my sums and my spelling.'

'Well, right then. Let's go see what your Zia Linda is up to. It's not like her to bake during the week.'

'Oh, Tina, you're home early. I could use some help!'

'What's going on?' asked Clementina as she took in the flour spread all over the table and mounds of shortbread dough waiting for the rolling pin. A delicious smell of brown sugar and ginger wafted from the oven, as Linda turned to remove one tray and insert another.

'I went to the monthly Catholic Women's League meeting in Port

Adelaide this afternoon, and we were asked to bake for their fundraiser picnic on Sunday. I thought I'd better get to it today since we're booked out with appointments for the week ahead. If I get them finished, Mrs Booth will package everything for me tomorrow, and I'm hoping Eddie will drop them off to the Port Adelaide parish later in the week.'

Linda was speaking at breakneck speed, and her voice was raised at least an octave. It seemed she'd taken on more than she could handle. Clementina promised to return in a few minutes. She changed into her house clothes, washed her hands and popped on an apron. When she returned to the kitchen, she saw that there was no sign of dinner anywhere and Rita was quite jumpy, echoing Linda's frazzled nerves.

'Run up the road to the Nielsen grocery, Rita dear, and ask for a tin of ham and a loaf of bread if there's any left. Tell them to put it on the Walsh account. Can you do that, *cara*?'

Rita didn't need telling twice. She relished opportunities to show how grown-up and responsible she could be.

On her return, Clementina had the little one wash her hands and break half the eggs they had left on the counter into a bowl and beat them with a pinch of salt. She then sliced and fried up the ham, followed by a few thick slices of bread to soak up the grease from the pan. Then she fried some onion and turned the eggs into an omelette by grating some cheese over it just before flipping it. Distributing everything across three plates, she sent Linda and Rita into the cosy parlour to eat there, while she made some sense of what was left in the oven and on the table. Linda had already produced four trays of ginger biscuits, and the dough on the table smelled of lemon. Forsaking the rolling pin and biscuit cutter, which took too much time, Clementina used both hands to roll rounds of dough into thin snakes, cutting them into even lengths and then twisting them into little coils. In the space of thirty minutes, she had filled four trays, ready for Linda to put into the oven.

'You sit here, Linda. You can watch the oven while I tidy up. And Rita, see those lemons on the sink with their peels removed? I need you to juice them for me.'

With orders given and chaos averted, Clementina sat and ate her dinner too, quietly returning to the shock of John's news.

By the time Eddie returned, the floor had been swept of its film of flour, and the table was filled with coils of dough sitting safely under a tablecloth, waiting to cool. In a big pan, a sugar syrup made with the juiced lemons was simmering, and the frypan was ready to make an egg and ham dinner for Eddie too. He was also sent to the parlour with Rita and her homework, and a storybook to calm her down.

Linda was sitting, staring vacantly into her cup of chamomile tea.

'I'm sorry to have alarmed you, *cara*. I keep forgetting how old I am and that I can't do the things I used to do as a girl. I got all excited and made way too much dough. I should have stuck to just one lot.'

'Never mind, Linda. We've managed together,' reassured Clementina, squeezing her shoulders.

'I got back at 3 o'clock, just as Mrs Booth was leaving, and I thought I could get a couple of batches done by the time you got home. I completely forgot about dinner and poor Rita. I think I scared her. She was so eager to help, but I sent her off to the sewing room and told her not to come out until you'd gotten home.'

'No harm done. It's good for her to see how much effort it takes to make biscuits in such quantities,' she laughed. 'I'm fine to finish glazing these on my own. You go join Rita and Eddie in the parlour and put your feet up.'

'Alright, Tina. Thank you for coming to my rescue. I'll make sure Rita gets to bed.'

Linda planted a kiss on Clementina's forehead, and with another sigh, dragged herself to the parlour.

★ ★ ★

The next morning, the biscuits were nestled in layers of white tissue paper in the large Arnott's biscuit tin they usually used for storing their baking equipment. Clementina had wrapped the tin in brown butcher paper, securing it with twine and labelling it with Linda's name and the words 'Henley Beach Parish'.

'Thankfully, it's still winter,' she mumbled, 'and we won't have to worry about ants.'

The kitchen floor had been mopped just before she'd fallen into bed at midnight. But, once again, sleep had eluded her, partially from an excess of fatigue, and partially from trying to understand her reaction to not seeing John. Surely the news that he had been well enough to leave the Convalescent Home and had set himself up in business should have made her happy? Part of her swelled with pride at the thought of his endeavour, but the other part of her was disheartened that she would no longer see him every week. She had to admit she would miss his company very much, especially as he did so much to improve the mood of the Sewing Studio. But she would continue to work with the other men, at least until the end of the year, as she had made a commitment to Captain Dixon and Matron Heritage.

The next morning, stumbling into the sewing room, a little bleary-eyed, Clementina came across Annie, who'd arrived punctually and immediately started the jobs Clementina and Linda had set aside for her.

'If you're looking for the package and letter, I've moved them to the sideboard.'

Linda had just entered with the kettle of hot water to fill their samovar for tea.

'Oh, I'd forgotten about yesterday afternoon's delivery. I had Rita answer the door and put everything in here. Is it the grey lace fabric I ordered from Whibley & Ferrier? Miss Gill promised she'd send it over as soon as it arrived.'

Clementina picked up the package addressed to Linda, but there was no other identifying mark on it. The envelope next to it was addressed to her, and in the top left corner, she saw the addressee was John McLeod. For the briefest moment, her heart missed a beat.

'The package is for you, but it doesn't say where it's come from. The letter is for me.'

Clementina went to her wicker chair under the window and rifled in her basket for something to use as a letter opener. A pleat maker would have to do. Sliding the ebony blade under the seal, she opened the envelope and gingerly pulled out a thin blue card. It was an invitation from John McLeod to the opening of his new business. On the back, he had written a note, apologising for not being able to tell her about the news in person. The official opening was to be on the first Saturday in September, only a few days away. A flush of hope reanimated the weary Clementina. John had not forgotten her.

As she looked up, Clementina saw Linda opening her package. She unfolded four exquisite peach velvet cushion covers. The covers were enhanced by John's unmistakable ribbon embroidery to suggest a carpet of wildflowers. But in the centre of each cover was a delicately hand-stitched and distinctive reproduction of a clementine orange tree with its deep green, glossy oval leaves covered in plump, brilliant red-orange fruit.

'Oh, Clementina, you remembered to ask John for my cushion covers.'

'Actually, I didn't, because he wasn't at the studio yesterday. He's left. That's why he had them delivered.'

'He's left? What do you mean?'

But Clementina wasn't listening; she was too wrapped up in stroking the plush velvet covers with the knobbles of soft ribbons giving texture at the bases and the silky satin feel of the trees in the middle. Trees created for her. She lifted one cover to feel the caress of the silk ribbon against her cheek.

Annie and Linda looked on, amused. Linda watched Clementina's face, full of wonder at this unexpected treasure. She motioned to Annie to keep working and went to the kitchen to continue getting the tea service ready. When she returned, the glow on Clementina's dreamy face told her everything she needed to know. But alas, they were feelings she was sure Clementina wasn't ready to admit to yet.

CHAPTER TWENTY-ONE

The new start – Saturday 2 September 1922

'Tina, you came. And Mr and Mrs Walsh and Rita, how lovely to see you all again.'

'We're very excited for you, Private McLeod. What a splendid endeavour. You should be very proud,' replied Eddie.

'It's just John now, sir. I've been officially discharged from the army.'

The foursome had just inspected the array of work set out in the former front parlour of the McLeod home. Small wooden side tables, writing desks, trolleys and trays were the carpentry work of his partner Michael Sanderson. There was also a selection of John's tapestry and embroidery work: book covers, cushion covers, blotters and framed embroideries for decoration. There was even a magnificent, quilted blanket depicting the seaside. It was clearly Henley Beach, with its distinctive jetty, fanciful kiosk and Tramways Trust cast iron bandstand.

'I had no idea you could make so much. This quilt is a work of art,' admired Clementina.

'Well, it's thanks to my mother, really. Without her sewing help, I probably wouldn't have produced such a wide range. She's out at the workshop, serving tea to other visitors. Won't you come through so you can meet Mike too?'

The old stables at the bottom of the backyard had been spruced up and converted into a modern carpentry workshop with a collection of jigsaws, sanders, lathes and wood turning machines. They were all set at a low height to accommodate Michael who was in a wheelchair, missing two legs from the knees. He was a handsome man, possibly in his early 40s, with dusty blonde hair, freckles and piercing blue eyes. They were the same eyes as the pair on the young gentleman and miss standing beaming behind him.

There were quite a few visitors in the cavernous space, but John directed Tina and her company straight to Mike. He was effusive in his praise for his business partner John, crediting him with having the idea for setting up their own workshop to make a living for themselves. They already had several commissions to keep them busy for a few months and had received more from the locals who'd visited today. Eventually, when a space cleared, John escorted them to the table set up for tea and scones, where his mother, Frances, and his sister, Ruth, and her two eldest daughters were presiding.

'Mother, Ruth, this is my dear friend and tutor, Mrs Clementina Vitale and her companions, Mr and Mrs Walsh and young Rita.'

'No need for introductions, John. Mrs Vitale and Mrs Walsh and I caught up at a social do last weekend. But Mr Walsh, it's a pleasure to meet you, and to see you again, Rita,' said Ruth.

Clementina couldn't help staring at John. He looked so different out of uniform. He was wearing dark blue corduroy trousers, a checked pale blue and beige shirt under a homemade knitted fawn sleeveless vest, topped with a rich brown leather apron. His eyes, which had always seemed a little sad, were bright and eager. As he handed Clementina a plate with a scone, their eyes met.

'You look so happy, John. I'm awfully pleased for you.'

'Thank you, Tina. It's early days yet, but I'm thrilled to see our plans in action. We had all of my father's equipment just sitting here, so Mike's going to be giving me a refresher in some carpentry basics and hopefully extend my skills, so we can produce more together.'

'That's fabulous news. I wish you every success.'

John's mother, Frances, interrupted with a cup of tea.

'Come, sit down at one of the trestle tables, won't you, so you can all enjoy your tea and scones in comfort?'

'It's very admirable of you to have given up your front parlour, Mrs McLeod,' suggested Linda.

'Oh, I was rattling around on my own in this big house. I'm thrilled to have John back, and Mike and Nancy and their two children have moved in as well.'

'And you're doing some sewing for John too. That is going to keep you very busy.'

'Nancy's been an absolute treasure. She's taken over all the household duties, so I have plenty of time on my hands. And it's only basic stitching, not like the fancy things you ladies produce.'

Nancy was duly introduced to their party once she had finished talking to another group. A petite, curly-haired blonde, she gave Frances a fierce hug.

'I can't thank John and Frances enough for taking us all in. We wouldn't have been able to have Mike at home in Norwood. The steps, and our sloping street weren't suitable for the wheelchair. But with this smooth driveway and access through the back of the house, which is lower than the front, Mike can manoeuvre his wheelchair about on his own.'

'Captain Dixon was a real trooper,' added John. 'He organised the building of some ramps up to the house and from the sleepout to the bathroom and kitchen. And it was his idea to have the driveway and floor of the barn concreted, so that Mike could have a smooth run. He even had the Red Cross pay for it all.'

As other visitors arrived, John and Nancy slipped away to tend to them. This gave Clementina the opportunity to watch the McLeods and Sandersons in action. She felt a warm glow fill her. This support was what she was used to amongst the extended family of flax growers and weavers she had lived with in Italy and had been so lucky to find again in this little corner of Australia with Linda and Eddie. Now she saw it between these two families—former strangers coming together in goodwill to support each other. For a few minutes, she was able to forget about her past and see that she could be quite comfortable if she chose to extend her stay here in Australia. It had already been almost a year. Torn by her thoughts of having neglected her duty to her husband, Nicola, she was still agonising over whether she should return to Italy.

As they were leaving, Linda remembered to thank John for the cushion covers and reminded him they had promised him an invitation to see them in their parlour setting.

'Thank you, Mrs Walsh. That would be a most welcome treat.'

* * *

Both John and his mother were invited to dinner for the following Saturday night. Linda and Clementina spent several days discussing the menu. Linda suggested a soup as a starter and a roast as a main, keeping the menu simple for mother and son. But she also encouraged Clementina to think of some flavours which would represent her home.

Clementina thought about making her mother's signature '*pizza docce*,' a sponge cake heavily soaked in coffee and rum and filled with alternate layers of vanilla and chocolate custard. But Eddie cautioned that anyone not used to drinking coffee might find the bitter aftertaste intimidating.

For starters, they settled on a light beef broth, with the addition of the garden's abundant silver beet crop. While silver beet did not have the bitterness of the *cicoria* she would have used in Rapino, it had a similar look and texture. She would add a handful of her *spaghetti alla chitarra* to each serve to give it body. Luckily, they still had just enough of a wedge of sharp, aged *pecorino* cheese from Imma's supplies to grate over the top for a creamy richness.

Clementina went to her bedroom and opened the trunk she'd brought with her from Italy. She pulled out a foot-long rectangular wooden box threaded with sharp metal strings. It had been a wedding gift, made by her grandfather. As she briefly ran her fingers over the contraption, his soft voice belying his stern face, lined by decades of outdoor work at the mercy of the weather, ran through her mind. Normally, memories of her lost relatives made her maudlin, but today, with all the activities she needed to complete, she uttered only a little imploration to her grandfather in heaven for help in her endeavour: '*Aiutami, nonnino*'.

She would roll wide strips of a whole-egg pasta dough over the sharp steel, which would cut the dough to form fine string-shaped *spaghetti*. She'd never used it before, because Antonia and Rosaria had done most of the cooking in her married home. But she'd helped her mother and grandmother often enough to know how to make and shape the dough with her eyes closed.

The main course would be a roast lamb, studded with rosemary and one clove only of the garden's pungent garlic, bathed in red wine and served with carrots and potatoes. It would offer something more familiar to their guests, but with a hit of Italian flavour. Inspired by the spring weather, Clementina remembered that Mother Maddalena had sent her the recipe for *ricotta* cheese she'd asked for. It would make an unctuous filling for a traditional *crostata*, a creamy-centred tart with a strong citrus flavour, which would help with digestion at the end of a copious meal. It was the dessert her grandmother would make at Easter, when fresh sheep's milk and eggs were in abundance. They would look forward to having it after the period of abstinence during the 40 days of Lent.

So first, she had to tackle making the *ricotta*. She started in the sewing room, where she found a large piece of very fine muslin, which she folded over several times and drenched in cold water. She used this to line the bottom of a large sieve, which she set above a tall stockpot to catch the liquid as it drained. Eddie had been out early that morning to the Kirkaldy Dairy and had come home with the required extra flagon of fresh milk and a pint of cream. Clementina poured the milk and the cream into their large copper saucepan and set it on a gentle flame. She added a good pinch of salt, stirring gently but constantly with a wooden spoon. As soon as the mixture came to a simmer, she added a quarter cup of white vinegar, stirring more vigorously for a few seconds until the mixture curdled. Then she immediately removed it from the heat and used a ladle to slowly layer the clotted mixture into her lined sieve, allowing the liquid to drain away. Lifting the sieve, she was very satisfied to see that the whey had collected in the pan, and the *ricotta* had formed into clumps. Moving the sieve over to the sink to drain away the extra liquid, Clementina did a happy little dance.

Next, she scrubbed the kitchen table and poured out a mound of flour, creating a well in the centre. She added salt and four eggs and a little olive oil, which she amalgamated with her fingers, slowly bringing in little scoops of flour from the edges of the well. Once all the flour had been incorporated, it was time to knead the dough. It didn't take long, only a few minutes before the dough was shiny and smooth. Poking a finger into the dough, she was pleased to see the indentation disappear quickly enough. She set it aside under an upturned bowl to rest for an hour.

As she was placing the cleaned silverbeet leaves into her copper pot ready for steaming, a knock at the kitchen door alerted her to Mr Langley, who'd come to deliver the extra block of ice for the icebox. Just in time, as the *ricotta* was now ready to be cooled. Once the silver beet was tender, she drained away the water, pressed the leafy bundle through the sieve and transferred it to her rinsed muslin cloth to wring out more of the water so that it came out quite dry. Then off it went into the icebox too. When cool, she would chop it up finely. She'd made the broth the day before. Using beef bones, carrot, onion, celery and parsley stalks, which she'd allowed to simmer gently for most of the morning. Now that it was cooled, and the bones had released their gelatinous goodness, she could pass it through a fine sieve and leave it in the pot to reheat when it was time to serve.

Back to her pasta dough, she used the rolling pin to stretch it out to the required thickness. Cutting it into wide strips, she laid the dough over her *chitarra* and pushed her rolling pin down hard, up and down its length, so that the metal strings cut the dough into fine, wriggly strands. These she mounded into little clumps, a handful for each diner. She dusted them with a little flour, covered the tray with a tea towel and put it aside. The silver beet and spaghetti would be dropped in to heat up once the broth had come to a slow simmer. They'd only need a minute in the hot broth for her *minestra* to be ready.

Finally, with the *ricotta* suitably cool, she grated orange and lemon rind into the cheese, added sugar, vanilla, almond flour and egg yolks, and beat it furiously until the mixture appeared silky. Then she set it back in the icebox for the flavours to meld together.

Rita and Linda returned from their shopping expedition to the butcher and the grocer with the deboned lamb leg, potatoes and mushrooms for the gravy. Before setting Rita to peel potatoes, Clementina showed her the *ricotta*. She scooped some into a little bowl.

'Go wash your hands, then you can come back and enjoy your morning tea.'

'Yummmm,' was the verdict. 'It tastes like ice-cream!'

Clementina used some red wine mixed with the whey from the ricotta to marinate the lamb. Once roasted, it would come out juicy and tender, and the drippings could be added to the mushroom gravy for extra depth. Linda approved, remembering that her mother used to prepare roasts in this manner. With Eddie's simple tastes, she had fallen out of the habit of preparing fancy meals and was quite excited to sample these enriched marvels. She fervently hoped that the McLeods would appreciate Clementina's efforts and be prepared to try something new.

Clementina had made the short crust pastry first thing in the morning, and now that it had chilled, she was ready to finish the dessert. Linda had borrowed a dozen tartlet cases from the baker, Mr Olsen, who asked only for a sampler and the recipe in return. The two experienced cooks made quick work of rolling, cutting and shaping the cases and then filling the tartlets with the ricotta cream. Over the top, they sprinkled slivered almonds before popping them into Linda's gas-lit oven. There was enough pastry and filling to make two dozen tartlets—plenty for John to take some home to the Sandersons too.

The house smelled divine. Rita couldn't stay out of the kitchen, getting in the way with her thousand questions, so she was dispatched to the front verandah with a jam sandwich, some more of the sweetened *ricotta* and her new paper doll book. Finally, all the components were ready and the kitchen was clean. The deboned leg of lamb was ready to go into the oven an hour before their guests arrived, so Linda implored a limp-looking Clementina to have a bath and a short rest while she and Rita set the dining room table for their guests.

Having started out the day humming and happy, Clementina could now feel her stomach churning, worried that everything in the kitchen should go to plan. She had given little thought to the evening itself, to what would be expected of her in terms of conversation, especially with John's mother. Clementina's English conversational skills had certainly improved, but she found understanding some people's speech quite difficult, in particular that of older people who seemed to mutter between their teeth, sometimes even slurring the ends of their words, rather than enunciating each syllable.

John had understood. He'd spoken to her slowly, using simple words when she had first started at Lady Galway's, but they would be in a different setting tonight. She took several deep breaths before sinking into the scented bath. She was being silly. Linda and Eddie would be with her, so there was no need to worry. Linda had asked if Clementina wanted to invite Caroline Thomson and Captain Dixon, but Clementina had declined. Having to concentrate on too many people speaking still made her quite nervous. Caro and Reggie had been very kind, inviting her, on a couple of occasions, to join them for local events, which Linda and Eddie had encouraged her to attend. She always felt like a fish out of water with them, though, not understanding many of their references and being too embarrassed to keep asking for an explanation unless a comment or a question was addressed directly to her.

Out of the bath and smelling of her favourite violet scent, Clementina arranged her hair simply. She lifted it all away from her face into a loose ponytail, tying a wide black silk ribbon around it and twisting it all into a relaxed knot. She chose a light wool plum skirt and paired it with a matching flared-sleeve top. Black stockings and shoes matched the best. Before stepping back into the kitchen, she slipped out to the front garden and snipped the few remaining violets growing in the shade along the fence. Forming a little posy, with one or two heart-shaped leaves, she tucked this into the side of her bun, just above the ribbon. Linda had finally convinced her to stop wearing black, but she still felt more comfortable in darker, muted colours.

When John and Frances arrived, Clementina greeted them at the door and thanked them for the lovely bunch of pale pink day lilies, which John explained were from his mother's garden. John was at least a foot taller than his mother, who was closer to Linda and Clementina in height.

'We walked over, not expecting it to be quite so cool still,' admitted Frances, who said she would keep her coat on for a little while longer.

'A little nip of sherry before dinner will fix that,' said Eddie, pouring a round for everyone.

'A toast to your success, John,' started Eddie.

'And don't forget the beautiful cushion covers,' piped up Linda. 'Look how perfectly they fit into my décor.'

'Ah, so this is where they ended up,' reflected Frances. 'Now I understand the obsession with getting the clementine trees right,' she said.

CHAPTER TWENTY-TWO

About-turn – Saturday 9 September 1922

Frances' Irish background turned out to be the source of both her and her son's sardonic humour, with the pair of them regaling the others with tall tales, one more fantastic than the other. Clementina was surprised that she had no difficulty understanding them. They were enthusiastic in their sampling and compliments for the dinner. Rita felt very grown up to have her potato mash noticed, and Clementina and Linda lapped up the praise for the rest. Dusted with icing sugar, the tartlets were a huge hit, and Clementina even convinced Frances and John to try a small coffee, the Italian way, with a touch of the smooth almond liqueur she had brought from Italy as a gift for Linda and Eddie when she had first arrived.

While Linda accompanied Rita to her room to put her to bed after a long and eventful day, Clementina and Eddie directed their guests to the parlour. Discussions turned more meaningful without young Rita present.

'How are you both adapting to Australia?' asked Frances. 'I can't believe how well you've picked up English in such a short time, and little

Rita seems to speak like a native.'

'I've been very lucky to have Linda and Eddie's support and encouragement, and I've had help from Sister Marie at the convent, and all the boys at Lady Galway's have been patient and helpful. In the early days, it was difficult to understand, but I wanted to be independent as soon as possible, so making an effort was the only way to get ahead.'

'Well, it looks like you have a lot of pluck. Like my John. There was nothing going to stop him from recovering and starting again, even without a hand.'

On cue, John waved his stumped arm with the shirt cuff neatly folded back.

When Linda returned, she discreetly enquired about the McLeod family origins, to discover that John's father had come from a very staunch Presbyterian family who had cut off communications with his son when he'd married the Catholic Frances.

'We used to live in the city but came out to Henley Beach once our eldest, Ruth, was born, so my husband could set up his own saddlery business, independently of his father. He did well for himself for many years but took ill one winter and never really recovered. The doctor said it was pleurisy, an affliction of the lungs. Luckily, the girls were both married, and John had already left school and found himself a job, so we didn't need to struggle. When John went off to war, I was proud of him, but devastated too, because I imagined that he'd one day take over his father's business. As you saw, I'd kept all his father's equipment in the shed.'

'That was very wise of you, Frances,' confirmed Eddie. 'It's given John here something to aim for, hasn't it son?'

'Well, I hadn't quite thought about it in that way, but I guess it has. Knowing that the equipment was there, I was on the lookout for someone who could put it to use and also train me up as my father had always promised me. He hadn't wanted me to go to work at the flour mill in Port Adelaide, but we'd agreed that it would be good training for me to work for someone else first and understand how hard it was to earn your coin, before I took over the business from him. In the meantime, he would teach me a little at a time, on Saturday and Sunday afternoons.'

'You'll get there. It's clear you've a good head on your shoulders and a determination to succeed,' encouraged Eddie. 'Don't let your accident deter you. You'll work out a way to make use of what you've got, like your friend Mr Sanderson.'

'That's kind of you to say, sir. I'm very touched by your confidence in me.'

'Thank you, Eddie, it pleases me too that someone else can see the potential in my son, regardless of his injury,' added Frances.

Clementina had been listening intently to the exchange, pleased at Eddie's assessment too.

'Well, Mother, it's time for stumpy here to get going. Thank you again, all of you, for a wonderful evening,' said John, as they both stood.

'Just hold on. It won't take me long to get the buggy out, and I'll drive you home,' said Eddie.

'Nonsense,' replied Frances. 'With all the lovely food and wine, I'm warm as toast and full as a barrel. I dare say I'll be able to roll down the street.'

She slipped into her coat, gladly taking the tin of tartlets Linda had packaged up for them.

* * *

The following afternoon, as they were relaxing on the front verandah,

John appeared with the Sanderson family in tow.

'We're heading to the square to hear the Tramways Trust Military Band. Would you like to join us?'

Clementina looked at Linda and Eddie.

'Why don't you take Rita with you?' suggested Linda. 'Eddie and I are happy sitting under our verandah. I'm sure we might even hear the band from here.'

'I'll just fetch our hats and coats, shall I?' said Clementina.

'You'd better take this inside then,' said John, handing over the tin in which Linda had packaged the tartlets last night.

When she reached for it, she found it was quite heavy. Peeking inside, she discovered a small jar of bite-sized red-orange clementine wedges suspended in a thick, pale pink syrup.

'From our garden. My father planted the tree decades ago,' said John. 'It turned out to be the perfect model.'

'Ah, no wonder your embroidery was so lifelike,' replied Clementina, biting her lip, touched by the gift. She looked up and caught them all staring at her, so she quickly rushed inside to fetch their hats and coats.

Clementina could not concentrate on the music. The slow build of the mournful Parsifal March from Wagner stirred up a deep sense of lament in her. John was sitting right beside her, and the Sanderson twins and their mother were to his right. Mike's wheelchair was parked at the end of the row, and Rita was sitting on Clementina's left at the other end of the row. Rita was unsettled too. She began swinging her legs wildly and turning around constantly to see if she could spot any friends. Clementina hoisted Rita onto her lap, but Rita kept squirming, protesting at Clementina's tight grip. The woman sitting in front of them turned around at the disturbance. It was Mrs Price, one of Linda's older clients from the local area, a busybody and a gossip par excellence. She frowned at Clementina, but the frown turned to a conspiratorial smile when she spotted John sitting next to her. Clementina was mortified by the unwanted attention and the thought of becoming a subject of Mrs Price's usually salacious rumours. She blushed furiously, the heat crawling up her neck. Her heart started pounding, and a sense of panic invaded her. She gripped Rita tighter, shushing her, but Rita wrung herself from Clementina's grip and squeezed past John to sit on young Greta Sanderson's lap instead.

John had winked at her, probably trying to comfort her about Rita's fussing, but it was just then that Mrs Price had turned around. Clementina's embarrassment deepened, suddenly acutely aware of her physical closeness to John. She'd been this close to John many times before, but the throbbing rhythm of the drums, keeping pace now with her elevated heartbeat, created an intimacy that was making her nervous. Her hands were gloved but sweaty palms made her itchy. She rubbed her hands vigorously across the sleeves of her coat to find relief for their prickly heat. She knew she was being foolish. Apart from the odd smile he threw her way when their eyes met ever so briefly, his focussed expression revealed little. She wondered what he was thinking, what he hoped from her? She was happy to be his friend, but was he expecting more? And what was this strange turbulence she was feeling? Linda's words came back to mind. Was she being honest with herself, imagining him being just a friend? The unwanted attention from Mrs Price, her unsettled thoughts about John, not appeased by the sombre music which made her feel like crying, sent her mind reeling to images of Nicola—images she'd never conjured before.

He was in his uniform, lying in a ditch, his face bloody, eyes staring at her, arms imploring her to come to him. When the trumpets exploded and the cymbal crashed, she imagined bombs going off, and Nicola being lifted in the air, his body split in two but his eyes open, still staring at her with his mouth moving, crying her name. Involuntarily, she let out a shriek. She shut her eyes tight and shook her head, wishing away the terrifying image that had formed. Her senses became heightened. She could smell rotting flesh and hear anguished cries all around her as the violins reached a crescendo. She jolted when John placed his hand on her arm and leaned in to whisper, 'Tina, is everything alright? Are you unwell?'

Clementina's eyes flew open, but she stared blankly at John's lips, still lost in her nightmare. As the movement ended and the crowd started clapping, bile rose in her throat and her head began pounding. She leaned over to grab Rita's hand and murmured something about having to go. Perplexed, John stood, but she motioned for him to stay where he was and scurried away, practically lifting Rita off the pavement in her hurry to get across the road and back home. Rita started moaning. She was frightened.

'What's happened? What's wrong?'

But Clementina had no words. She just shook her head and hurried the young girl along, gripping her hand ever more tightly.

Back home, Linda and Eddie were still on the verandah. Lowering their newspapers, they were startled to see two terrified faces breach the gate.

'What's happened?' asked a confused Linda.

'Out …' was all Clementina managed to say as she clutched her mouth shut and rushed off to the outhouse. She vomited the contents of her lunch, again and again, until there was nothing left.

Linda arrived with a towel and a glass of water, turning Clementina around to feel her forehead. The younger woman was shaking, and her forehead was clammy. Taking charge, Linda steered her into the house and to her bedroom. She helped Clementina to remove her soiled outer garments and shoes and then helped her slip under the covers.

'Shhh, there, there. Rest now,' she said, leaving a towel and a bucket by the side of the bed and tiptoeing out of the room with the smelly clothes.

When she went back to find Rita, the little one was curled in Eddie's arms, still whimpering.

'It's alright, my darling. Everything's going to be fine. I've put Tina to bed. She's not feeling very well. She seems to have a tummy ache.'

'She scared me. She couldn't speak. She didn't explain. What's going on?'

'I'm not sure exactly. We all ate the same thing, and the rest of us aren't sick. We'll let her rest and hope she recovers quickly. How about we go inside to clean up your face and find you some milk and biscuits? It's time for your afternoon tea, isn't it?'

'Is there any *ricotta* left?' Rita brightened at the thought of a sweet treat.

'Maybe we'll give the *ricotta* a miss, just in case it's gone off. But you can have some of Tina's aniseed *pizzelle*.'

'Yippee!'

With Rita calmed, Linda hunched her shoulders trying to communicate to Eddie that she had no idea what was going on. Feeling completely out of his depth, Eddie returned to his newspaper, pretending to read while Linda and Rita were in the kitchen. When they returned, Eddie suggested he and Rita go out the back to the stable and give Charlie a good rub down, leaving Linda to go check on Clementina.

Clementina was fast asleep, crunched into a cocoon under the blankets. Linda could see she was no longer shivering. Her colour had returned to normal, and her forehead had lost that clammy feeling. Deciding it was better to let her sleep, she tiptoed back out of the room without waking her.

Linda stepped out onto the front verandah to tidy the newspaper and the plates and cups left on the table when John and the Sandersons arrived at the gate.

'Is Tina here?' They all seemed startled and confused.

'Oh yes. She has an upset stomach, so I've sent her to bed. I'm not sure what's brought it on, but hopefully some chamomile tea will see her better in a few days. Thanks for stopping but go on home. Don't concern yourselves.'

Linda smiled brightly, trying to placate them, but she was just as confused. Clementina slept on, all through the night. Linda asked Eddie to bring the camper bed that was normally kept in the sleepout into their bedroom so that Rita could stay with them and not disturb Clementina. In the morning, Eddie had just left to accompany Rita to school and call in at the convent to let Sister Marie know Clementina was unwell when Clementina dragged herself into the kitchen in her dressing gown. Her face was still grey and her eyes puffy, but she mumbled about having to get ready. Linda gently guided her to a chair, put the kettle on for some chamomile tea and just sat beside her holding her hand, without speaking until the kettle whistled.

When Mrs Booth arrived, Linda's eyes told the woman everything, so without her usual cheery salutations, she went straight out to the laundry. Linda got Clementina to take a few sips of the tea and offered her a plain piece of bread, which Clementina numbly chewed, but had difficulty swallowing.

'*Cara*,' whispered Linda, 'can you tell me what's going on? Where you're hurting?'

Fat, silent tears rolled down Clementina's face, but slowly, between sobs, Clementina recounted her terrifying experience. At a loss for how to placate or counsel her, Linda resorted to admonishment.

'Come now, Clementina. You're being irrational. It's just your imagination. Nicola's long gone and a long way from here. You have a new life now.'

'That's it, you see. I can't have a new life. I can't leave him in that condition.' She stared at Linda without really seeing her. She had understood something. Nicola was calling to her from beyond the grave, begging her not to forget him. It was time for her to return to Italy. She stood abruptly.

'I need to write to Mother Maddalena. I need to get to the post office today.'

Rushing from the kitchen, she closed herself in her room and set to writing her letter.

Linda was never so glad to see Eddie return unexpectedly.

'I sensed something might be wrong. Is there something I can do to help?'

'Go fetch the doctor,' she implored. 'She's gone mad.'

Eddie returned within the hour, with Doctor Muirhead following in his own buggy.

Clementina was dressed and ready to head out to the post office, but the doctor convinced her to hear him out. They sat in the parlour for more than an hour, with Linda and Eddie wringing their hands at the kitchen table, watching the wall clock tick the minutes away.

When Clementina and the doctor emerged, they came into the kitchen and sat at the table. Clementina had streaks down her cheeks where tears had fallen and was still clutching the envelope she had addressed to Mother Maddalena. Gently, the doctor tried to explain.

'It seems some very violent feelings have set off Mrs Vitale's imagination, and she's had a terrible shock, believing a nightmare she experienced to be real life. I'm going to leave a draft with you for Mrs Vitale to take, stirred into some warm milk if she can tolerate it, or into some warm water if she prefers. Then, I recommend she go back to bed for some rest. I'll pass by tomorrow morning again, and hopefully a quiet sleep will have helped. She has a letter she wants to send, but I've suggested she give it to you, Mrs Walsh, for safe keeping, until she's feeling more like herself. Then she can decide if she still wants to send it.'

Eddie and Linda both had eyes the size of saucers, perplexed and worried for their dear Clementina.

'Thank you, Doctor. I'll see you out,' said Eddie.

Clementina looked at Linda and in a quiet voice, finally tried to explain herself.

'The doctor's right about the nightmare. I want to go back to bed, but I don't want the draft. I need to think clearly. He's right about the letter too. I won't send it today. I want to think things over. I need to make sense of what's happened inside my head.'

Looking up, taking Linda's hands and giving them a reassuring squeeze, she muttered forlornly, 'I'm sorry to have frightened you. I promise I'll explain once I've sorted out my own thoughts.'

Linda could only nod and watch the younger woman shuffle back to her room.

Later that night, after a teary Rita had been convinced to go to sleep on the little camper bed again, Clementina emerged. In the parlour, with the door closed, she spoke in a quiet, measured voice, trying her best to explain herself to her dear friends.

'This is something I've been thinking about since the day of the dedication of the Soldier's Memorial. I saw how proud John was to be recognised for his service and of the memorial for his lost friend, and I couldn't help but wonder what happened to my Nicola. It was only that day that I realised I don't even know where he died, where his body was laid to rest, or even if he was still in one piece and able to be buried. I wrote to Father Ernesto that afternoon and posted the letter the next day, but I haven't had a response from him yet. I feel like it's my duty to go back to Italy to make sure Nicola's sacrifice has been honoured and remembered, and his body laid to rest. Until I do that, I don't think I can be at peace.'

'But do you intend to come back?' asked a frightened Linda.

'I don't know,' muttered Clementina, casting her eyes down, unable to meet the searching glare of her friends.

Eddie had been silently listening, not making any comment. But after a few minutes of mutual confusion, he asked both Linda and Clementina to hear him out.

'Is it possible, Clementina, that this sudden resurfacing of memories of Nicola is just guilt at your own happiness? This week, you've been joyfully discussing recipes and remembering your childhood favourites. Could it be that those memories triggered thoughts of Nicola too? And then when we had such a good time with John and Frances, is it possible that you felt guilty about having so much fun? After all, when you arrived here, you were determined not to change, not to let yourself forget you were a widow. Is it possible that you've developed feelings for John, and the guilt is making you look for excuses to deny these feelings?'

Linda looked across at her husband of 30 years, a little taken aback by the profound nature of what had just come out of his mouth. And proud too of what she knew was a very accurate reading of the situation. She didn't want to interrupt Clementina's thinking process, so she sat still, throwing Eddie a small, grateful smile and just watched Clementina, sure her mind was ticking furiously because the younger woman's face could not hide the depth of her emotions.

'Yes, Eddie. You may be right, but I still need to find out what's happened to Nicola,' she mumbled.

'I understand that completely, but shouldn't you wait for an answer to your letter? It's only been around 6 weeks since you've written. You know very well that an answer to a letter from Europe can take 3 to 4 months. Could you perhaps write home to your family first, and see what they say?'

'I guess I should,' Clementina sighed, accepting Eddie's wisdom.

'Thank you, Eddie, Linda. I feel a little calmer. And you're right about waiting. A few more months won't make any difference, and I don't want to abandon Rita without preparing her. And I certainly don't want to miss her First Communion. Mother Maddalena in Chieti would never forgive me.'

'And perhaps you need to speak with John, to let him know that you're not ready to pursue a relationship, so that he doesn't hold out false hope,' added Eddie as gently as he could.

'I'm not sure that's necessary, but I'll think about it.'

The next morning, Annie arrived with a sweet get-well note from Sister Marie at the Henley Beach Convent scrawled behind a French postcard depicting a young girl sitting at a sewing machine and with the words *Vive Sainte Anne* written across the corner.

'Saint Anne is the patron saint of seamstresses,' Linda enlightened both Clementina and Annie.

Sister Marie asked Annie to pass on the card to Clementina when Annie had dropped off her little sisters at school that morning. A few hours later, an army truck showed up with a delivery of a bunch of flowers and a handmade get-well card, signed by the boys in the Sewing Studio. Eddie had contacted Matron Heritage to let her know Clementina wouldn't be coming in the previous afternoon. The kind gestures made Clementina feel even more guilty and brought more tears to her eyes. Complicating matters further was the vision of Frances McLeod making her way through the gates. Clementina fled to the back of the house and hid in her room, leaving Linda to deal with the concerned visitor.

What had she unleashed? Yesterday, she'd been resolute in her decision that she should return to Italy. Today, she was panicking about how she was going to leave her life here. What was she going to say to the confused and frightened Rita, who'd tiptoed around her this morning, unsure and terrified by Clementina's sudden change in demeanour? And how could she leave her Rita? Maybe she should take Rita with her? But she had no right to do so, and what would be the purpose? She was just thinking selfishly.

And what about Linda? How could she abandon her and the business? Linda was relying on her to keep it going. Hadn't she given her this magnificent opportunity to take the business beyond anything a single person could ever have hoped to achieve? Was she going to throw it all back in her face? The guilt and uncertainty plagued her. Doctor Muirhead had admonished her for not taking the draft, and now she had a headache and was feeling nauseous again. Oh, why? Why was this happening to her? Preferable to this stomach-churning anxiety were the 4 years of numbness which had accompanied her from the time news of Nicola's death had been received until her arrival here in Henley Beach. At least in the numbness, she hadn't had to think. Thinking was too exhausting!

Clementina went out to the back garden and picked up a trowel, a garden fork and her old basket. She slipped into her wooden gardening clogs after checking for unwanted creepy crawlies. Pulling on her gardening gloves, she dug at the weeds in her vegetable patch, each forkful of turned earth calming her nerves and giving her mind some respite.

After a while, she sauntered over to the rabbit hutch with some of the lettuce leaves and parsley she'd pulled, taking the time to hold the two rabbits in her arms and feel their warmth and heartbeats close to her own heart. With the rabbits still in her arms, she sat on the bench outside the laundry where she could hear Mrs Booth humming at her washing tasks. After returning the rabbits to their hutch and changing her shoes, she peeked into the laundry.

'I have some lettuce and silverbeet here, Mrs Booth, if you care to take some home.'

'Don't mind if I do, Miss Tina. The silver beet is good for strength, and my little Millie has been looking quite pale these last few weeks.'

'Oh. She's not sick, is she?'

'Just growing too fast with this good sea air, I expect.'

'I'll bundle it up in some newspaper and leave it on the kitchen sink, Mrs Booth.'

'You're very kind Miss Tina. And I'll take this opportunity to say thank you for taking my Annie under your wing. She's so excited by what you've been teaching her. She can't stop talking about all your fabulous ideas.'

'You should be very proud of her, Mrs Booth. She's a quick learner and she's working hard. She's very conscientious and never idle. You've brought her up well.'

'Thank you, Miss. That brings the mother in me much joy. I hope you have the good fortune of raising a daughter one day too.'

Clementina forced a smile before she dashed out to deposit her load into the kitchen. She stood clutching the sink, heartbroken by her thoughts again. Antonia's warning scrawled at the bottom of one of Rosaria's letters came back to her. Was Eddie right? Was she running away from any potential happiness and the opportunity for a new relationship and the chance to have her own child? She was 24 years old. If she returned to Italy to sort out Nicola's needs, it would be at least 2 years before she returned here, if she were even able to return. And then, if she wasn't working here, what would they all live on? If she stayed in Italy, she would probably have to set herself up in a bigger town somewhere, and where would the money for that come from? Oh no. Why was life so complicated?

CHAPTER TWENTY-THREE

Special Delivery – Monday 18 September 1922

Clementina made the effort to return to her usual routine as much as possible. It was Monday, and as she was accompanying Rita to school, she forced herself to focus on the little one, whose excited chatter and concerns centred around her upcoming First Holy Communion in late October.

'I know exactly what I would like for my dress. I saw a photograph in one of your tailoring magazines, and Zia Linda said she loved it and thought it would suit me. She said we could go shopping for fabric when she was next free.'

'Well, you must show me too this evening, but I think your Zia Linda would very much like to make this special dress for you herself.'

'Yes, I know. She told me. But she said we should ask you to do some special embroidery on the veil, like you do for your brides.'

'I would be honoured, my darling.'

'Thank you, Tina. Are you feeling better now?'

'Yes, *cara*. I'm sorry if I frightened you. But you don't need to worry about me.'

'I prayed very hard for you, like Sister Mary-Paul tells us to. She says our prayers are sure to be answered if we pray for our loved ones before we pray for ourselves.'

'I'm very proud of you Rita and so pleased to hear you prayed for me. I'm sure it helped.'

'Tina, Sister Mary-Paul was explaining about the prayers we needed to say before our Communion Day so that our communion will be extra special. She says we must pray for the souls of our dear departed so that they can get to heaven quicker.'

'And you do that, don't you, *cara*. Do you still pray every night for your family, like I taught you?'

'Of course. You told me to pray for them in Heaven. But Sister Mary-Paul says they are in a place called Purgatory and they won't be called to Heaven unless their loved ones pray for them. Only, I'm worried, you see, that I'm the only one praying for so many of them, and I don't know how long it's going to take for them to get to Heaven?'

Clementina stopped and bent down to be at Rita's eye level, giving her a quick hug before looking deeply into her eyes.

'You're not alone in your prayers, my darling. I pray for your family, as does Zia Linda and Uncle Eddie. And you still have the whole convent in Chieti praying for them, remember that.'

'Really? Oh, that makes me much happier. I was feeling very heavy-hearted. I thought they might get stuck in Purgatory if it was only me praying.'

'I'm not sure about the rules, but your brother and sisters and your parents and grandparents were all good people, I'm sure that their journey through Purgatory will be very speedy, and they may have already moved into Heaven. Don't you think?'

'That's what I thought, but when I asked Sister Mary-Paul, she said only God knew the plans for each person's soul.'

'Oh dear. Seven years old is much too young for such worries.'

Tina was holding Rita's hand and brought it to her lips to kiss it as they continued walking.

'Let me ask Sister Marie today. She's much older than Sister Mary-Paul. I'm sure she'll be able to sort us out, and I'll let you know what she says tonight. How does that sound?'

'Oh yes, please. I'd really like to know for sure.'

'Don't worry, my darling. I'll be sure to have an answer for you tonight.'

After a final hug and kiss, the two parted, with little Rita skipping off to her classroom and her zealous Sister Mary-Paul. Clementina headed to the convent kitchen for her usual Monday English lesson while she assisted Sister Marie with the week's bread production.

Sixty-nine-year-old Sister Marie immediately set out to allay Clementina's fears.

'Oh, you know, these young Irish girls, they're very big on following the rules. We European girls, we're more philosophical. We are happy to understand the intent of the ruling. We hope only to prepare young people to develop a charitable mindset and to think about the welfare of other people before thinking of themselves. Daily devotion to prayer is also to encourage them to value spiritual comfort above material comforts. As long as they're praying earnestly and developing habits of kindness towards others, surely that's all we can ask of our young ones. You tell your Rita that Sister Marie will make sure that she asks God to send a sign to let us know her family is in Heaven.'

'A sign?'

'Yes, my dear. There's always a sign. And through your prayers, you'll find a sign in answer to the question that's recently been troubling your heart too.'

Clementina nodded, acknowledging within herself, that she hadn't done much praying these last few weeks. She'd allowed herself to succumb to anxiety and had not found the peace she needed to help her decide on a path forward. Tonight, she would attempt to pray for guidance, and maybe even a sign. She desperately needed one, though she was sceptical of Sister Marie's blissful belief in a direct message from God.

Returning from Lady Galway's that afternoon, Clementina let herself in through the parlour entrance. The house was very quiet. Even Mrs Booth had gone. Linda had probably been to collect Rita and they must have stopped at the shops. Eddie, she guessed, was caught up with last minute affairs for the new convent which was due for handover in mid-November. She went to the room she still shared with Rita and changed into her house dress and voluminous apron with enough pockets to keep her basic sewing tools at hand. Her bedside table still displayed the cards which were delivered to her last week. There was the big get-well card from the boys in the Sewing Studio and the smaller one from Matron Heritage, and the card with pink pansies from Reggie Dixon and Caro Thomson, with a gentle note scribbled on the back from Emmeline Thomson. There was also Sister Marie's Saint Anne postcard and a small card from Frances and John McLeod with one of John's miniature embroideries glued to the front with a pretty painted cardboard frame. It was a cross-stich of a violet bush with its heart-shaped leaves and a single violet. The words inside simply said 'Wishing you a speedy return to good health' with both their names signed, probably by Frances, she suspected.

Clementina scooped them all up to put them into her bedside drawer, making certain to put Sister Marie's card into the back of the Latin prayer book that Mother Maddalena had given her at the convent before she'd left for Australia. With the prayer book was a little velvet pouch in which she'd placed her rosary beads. She hadn't looked at these more than once or twice since getting off the ship. Leaving the pouch behind, she popped the beads into one of her apron pockets. It would be a good reminder to turn to prayer instead of panic the next time her anxieties besieged her. At the back of the drawer, kept safe in one of her embroidered linen towels, were the photos of her parents and Nicola in their thick cardboard frames. Opening the smaller one of Nicola in his uniform, she traced her finger over his face and body. He looked so proud here. He was young and vigorous—nothing like the image she had recently conjured of him, bloodied and lifeless. Quickly folding the photo back into its linen cocoon, and returning it to the depths of her drawer, Clementina placed a hand on her prayer book. Could she ask for a sign, as Sister Marie had suggested?

A noise from the kitchen alerted her to the fact that Rita and Linda were home. An excited Rita came crashing through the bedroom door.

'Tina, Tina, we found some shoes! They're so beautiful. Let me get changed then I'll come to the sewing room.'

Chuckling, Clementina headed to the kitchen and seeing Linda's beaming face too, relaxed herself.

'So, you've found what you need.'

'Yes, I picked Rita up early and we went by train to Port Adelaide, to Crawford's on Commercial Road. I was glad to see they still specialised in children's wear, but I was taken aback by the number of ready-to-wear items they were carrying, at very reasonable prices too. I suspect that for those mothers who don't sew well, it's a blessing to be able to purchase off the rack, given the way children grow.'

'You didn't buy a ready-made dress, did you?'

'Oh, of course not! How could you think that? No, Miss Gill had already organised a few bolts of fabric for Rita to choose from, so we stopped in at her shop first, then went to Port Adelaide for shoes and gloves to match.'

'Did you remember netting for veils? Rita asked me if I'd embroider her veil?'

'Yes. I picked up a bolt of plain netting. Annie told me last week that her sister will be wearing the Communion dress she had worn, which was cut down from her mother's wedding dress, but that the veil was a little worse for wear. She asked me for advice on how best to patch it. But I thought you could teach her how to make one from scratch. I think she'd be so proud to make her sister a new one. And she and Rita are the same colouring, so I've bought netting in an ivory tone.'

'That sounds perfect. But can I help you with dinner first?'

'No need. I stopped in at Mr Poole's, the butcher, for some of his sugar-cured beef silverside which everyone has been talking about, and I prepared the green beans and carrots from the garden this morning. I just need to heat everything up and make a white sauce. You get Rita started on her homework. I promised Sister Mary-Paul that she wouldn't neglect her reading and her spelling practice.'

Rita never needed reminders about doing her homework. She was already in the sewing room, swinging her legs furiously on the chair with her new shoes on and reciting her spelling aloud. Clementina smiled at her and went to the sideboard where she spied the fabric bolts wrapped in brown paper. Next to them was a stack of mail, and rifling through, she saw one envelope was addressed to her. Clementina gasped when she saw Father Ernesto's name and address on it. She picked it up and found it to be unexpectedly heavy, as if there were more than just the usual one sheet of fine paper in it. She didn't want to open it now, so she put it into her front apron pocket. She'd promised to have a chat with Rita about her existential crisis, so once she'd tested her on her spelling and listened to her reading, they'd look at the fabric and then have a little discussion about Sister Marie's advice. Clementina was dismayed by the thought that Rita felt burdened by her responsibility for getting her family out of Purgatory and wanted to reassure the little one as soon as possible.

Finally, after dinner, Clementina sent the others into the parlour while she tackled the dishes and tidied the kitchen. With the kettle on, ready to fill the teapot, she sat down and opened Father Ernesto's letter. There was a 4-page spread from a national newspaper. She looked at it, puzzled at first, then realised there were tables on the pages, listing names of the deceased soldiers, unit by unit, who'd been buried in one of the memorials to the fallen. This memorial had been constructed in a place called Monte Calvario, outside the city of Gorizia in the Friuli region of northern Italy, right where some of the bloodiest fighting had taken place. There was an article describing the monument and a drawing of the tall, impressively carved sandstone spire which had been erected at the top of the hill. Looking at the tables, Clementina saw that Father Ernesto had circled Nicola's name. And then elsewhere, the name of Rita's father had been circled. A tight lump formed in her throat. Nicola had not been forgotten. Her fears had been unfounded. The remains of the fallen had been removed and taken to an ossuary nearby, which was in the process of completion. He'd be re-interred where he fell, with the men alongside whom he'd valiantly fought. One of these men had been Rita's father. It was quite extraordinary considering that the article claimed that an estimated 650,000 Italian men had died and a further 947,000 were wounded from 1915 to 1918. Was this what Sister Marie meant as a sign—could it suggest that she and Rita were cosmically linked?

Also in the letter was a form for the local *Cassa di Risparmio* bank in Rapino which she was to complete. Father Ernesto had sent instructions regarding her entitlement to a war widow's pension. He explained that the sum was meagre, but that Rosaria and Antonia were already benefitting, and that if Clementina filled and returned the form, which needed to be countersigned by the Italian consular authority where she lived, she too could receive the modest sum allocated to her. Then, if she did not need it sent to Australia, she could nominate Rosaria or Antonia to be the ones to access her account on her behalf, and there was a form for that purpose too.

When Linda came in to check on her, she found Clementina with her face flooded in tears, but with a wide, beaming smile. She couldn't speak. She could only hand over the contents of the letter. Linda didn't need to read all the details—a cursory glance told her Clementina had found her answers. She called out to Eddie. He'd been wise to tell them to wait for the priest's reply.

Clementina reached into her pocket and clutched her rosary, silently saying a quick prayer of gratitude for Father Ernesto. He was probably in his late 70s now and for nearly 50 years had been solicitous of his little mountain flock, even when one of them was so far away. She'd send a letter first thing tomorrow, thanking him profusely and letting him know she'd received all the documents, which would follow as soon as she could complete all the regulatory requirements.

While at the post office, she sent a lettergram to Mr Patterson, the Italian vice consul, to request an appointment for the following week. When she heard from Mr Patterson, she'd let her friend Imma know she was coming into the city. She needed a heart-to-heart with her friend. Linda was wonderful, but Clementina needed a fresh, younger woman's perspective.

Before getting into bed, Clementina took Father Ernesto's letter and bundled it up with Nicola's photo in her linen towel, giving the bundle a kiss as she tucked it back into her drawer. She pulled out the photo of her parents and grandparents.

'I'm sorry, *mamma*. I haven't been able to find Francesco.'

She'd let the family in Rapino and Father Ernesto know of her efforts and lack of results. She'd even attended the Italian Red Cross benefit ball with Imma and her family, and despite being introduced to many new people, no-one had heard of a Francesco Vitale.

'It's up to you in heaven, *mamma*. I've done all I can do on my own.'

★ ★ ★

On a Saturday afternoon a fortnight later, the sewing room treated two little girls to a Castlemaine Couture consultation, complete with jam fancies and pink lemonade. They spent time looking at dresses and veils in magazines, with Linda and Tina offering advice about the relative merits or pitfalls of each one. When each girl had chosen her preferred style, Annie was instructed on how to take and record all the necessary measurements. Then, Eddie accompanied them back to the Booth home on Marlborough Street, where the girls could play with younger sister Millie for the rest of the afternoon.

As they were farewelling their final clients, a bridal party for a wedding in Grange the following February, a clean-shaven gentleman in a dark suit and straw bowler hovered at their gate. Linda smiled, thinking he might be related to the ladies and had been waiting to accompany them home. But he let the group pass and kept looking at the house, trying to peer into the sewing room window.

When the coast was clear of other people, he raised his hat.

'Excuse me, Ma'am, am I at the premises of Castlemaine Couture?'

Intrigued by the gentleman in the sharp suit and polite demeanour,

Linda replied in the affirmative.

'I'm looking for a Miss Clementina Vitale.'

Linda noted immediately that he pronounced her name correctly in the Italian manner though his English was impeccable.

'May I ask what your enquiry relates to, sir?'

'I believe she may be my sister, Ma'am,' he replied, his eyes searching behind her.

'Just wait there a moment, won't you, sir,' gulped Linda as she rushed off to find Clementina, who was returning the dirty plates and glasses to the kitchen.

'Tina, could you come back to the sewing room, please?'

Clementina followed her to the internal door of the sewing room, where Linda had stopped, and pointed to the man at the gate that they could see through the window.

'He says he's your brother.'

CHAPTER TWENTY-FOUR

A welcome sign – Saturday 7 October 1922

Clementina stepped out to the verandah, with Linda hovering behind her.

'Francesco?'

The gentleman swivelled at Clementina's voice and stood back, hesitating. Her curated, elegant appearance, nothing like what he was expecting.

'Is it really you, Clementina?' he stammered, quickly coming up the steps. 'The last time I saw you, you were only 10 years old, and there was talk of sending you to the nunnery in Guardiagrele. You don't look like a nun now … But you do look like … *mamma*,' he uttered in disbelief, shaking his head. He slowly approached and then reached out for her, to envelope her in a fierce hug.

'Francesco, I can't believe my eyes. I'd given up on ever finding you! How on earth did you find me?' Clementina furiously wiped away the tears clouding her vision.

'I saw your name mentioned in a newspaper article. I wasn't sure, but I promised myself that the next time I was in Adelaide, I'd make some enquiries.'

'I've been looking for you for more than a year! I even had announcements put in all the newspapers across the country asking for your whereabouts.'

The two of them were still standing outside, holding outstretched hands, just staring at each other.

'Tina, *cara*, why don't you bring Francesco inside?'

Installed in the parlour, perched together on the settee, hands still clutched, the two of them couldn't take their eyes off each other, needing to examine every square inch of the face in front of them.

'You look like *papà*, but fairer. You have *mamma*'s colouring and *mamma*'s grey eyes.'

'And you look just like *mamma*, but with *papà*'s brown eyes, his wavy hair and olive complexion. I can't believe you're here. What *are* you doing here? How on earth did you get here?'

Slowly, Clementina told her sorry tale, stopping to give Francesco time to take it all in and digest the tragedies that had befallen their family.

'You sent that one postcard and then you never wrote again?'

Choked by emotion, Francesco needed to take some time to compose himself before he could explain.

'I was sent to Libya, in North Africa, for my military service. It was a brutal experience,' he said, shaking his head, his eyes glazing over.

'When I finished my 3 years, there was talk of war between Italy and the Ottomans, and I knew I'd be called up to fight. We'd been returned to barracks in Naples, and my sergeant had already tried to convince me to re-enrol in the Army proper. My friend, Andrea, he was a local *Napolitano*, and he heard about a ship going to America. You see, my military pay had been miserly, and I thought that if I could get to America, I could make some real money before returning home.

So, we snuck onboard, and once we'd left port, we convinced the captain to take us on as labourers. The only problem was that the ship was coming to Australia. I was fine the first week, while we were sailing in the Mediterranean, but 60 days in the open ocean was my undoing. I'd never been so sick in my life. I nearly died. Only the fear that they'd feed my body to the fishes if I didn't make it, kept me alive.

The captain dumped me here in Port Adelaide, at a small hospital, the first one willing to take me. Andrea had jumped ship in Perth. I never saw him again. I was very weak, but the doctor was kind, and his wife made me broths until my stomach settled, and I could eat again and regain my strength. They'd been given my military discharge papers, and using some of his Latin, the doctor guessed my name was Frank Henry, and that's how he registered me in the hospital records.

The doctor helped me find accommodation with a family he knew who had two young boys just starting school. So, I learned to read and speak a little English through them. I found work on the docks and after a few months, I recovered my mind and my strength. The only problem was that work on the docks was haphazard. There were too many of us day labourers, and the Italians were treated like vermin, so I kept away from them, not revealing my identity.

A few months later, through the family I was boarding with, I found out about a quarry near the Barossa Valley that was looking for fit young men. They helped me find accommodation with a cousin in the region. The quarry work was steady, and the pay was good. That's when I sent the postcard. I didn't know what to say. I'd hoped that after I'd worked a few months, I could send some money home with a proper letter, but the longer I was away, the more I imagined *papà* would be angry with me. I knew I'd never get on a ship again, so I thought it would be better if everybody forgot me,' he concluded.

'We never forgot you. Even in her delirium when she had the fever, *mamma* would call your name. She made me promise to find you and bring you home.'

The news of his mother's reaction broke his composure, and Francesco covered his face, weeping noisily in his distress. Linda had been sitting in the armchair, knitting under the window, not wanting to leave Clementina alone with a stranger. She glanced up, catching Clementina's turmoil, with a sad, compassionate grimace.

'When I arrived here, Linda helped me approach the vice consul, who contacted all the other consulates around the country, and when that resulted in nothing, we put advertisements in all the newspapers. Then someone local came forward and said you'd been repatriated to Italy to fight in the war.'

Francesco shook his head.

'It wasn't me. Francesco Vitale is a fairly common name. There were three of us in my unit during my military service.'

'Really, I never thought of that. We were the only Vitale family in Rapino, and *papà* had been the only son.'

'No, no. I heard about the Italians being carted off, but I was lucky. You see, I wasn't registered with the Italian Consulate. I didn't know that I was supposed to do that, and the doctor at the hospital, he just registered my name as Frank Henry and that's the name I used.

I was already at the quarry in Nuriootpa when war broke out and so many German men were carted off to internment camps that the quarry was desperate for workers. So, I got extra shifts and eventually I was made a shift foreman. If the police or military authorities came calling, my boss vouched for me, telling everyone my accent was Dutch—a cousin on his mother's side. If questioned, I told them I'd been robbed and lost my papers when I arrived.'

'Is that where you are now?'

At the end of the war, I bought a house and some land near Nuriootpa, and then I got married to a local girl, Barbara, and we have a son, Frank Junior.'

Clementina perked up at that news.

'Does that mean I'm an aunt in Australia too?'

'Of course it does. I hope you'll be able to meet Barbara and Frankie soon.'

'Francesco, that's just wonderful news.'

Clementina flung her arms around her brother's neck, both of them taking comfort in this renewed physical closeness. After several minutes, Clementina whispered: 'I know if *mamma* and *papà* were still alive, they'd be so happy for you.'

'I hope so. I know I've done the wrong thing, but I'm so glad you're here.'

'But please, Francesco, tell me how you found me.'

'Just after Easter, I came down to Adelaide on quarry business, and I was reading the newspaper on the train. I intended to buy Barbara something nice—a hat or a new coat, and a toy for Frankie—so I was looking at the fashion advertisements. The same page had an article about you creating a feather dress for a debutante ball. It said you were a very accomplished embroiderer. I thought nothing of it at first, except that there was a woman with the same name as my sister. Then when I got home and told Barbara, she said I should have pursued it, just in case it wasn't a coincidence. I really came here today to please Barbara. I didn't know what to expect. I certainly didn't imagine that it could actually be my little sister in the flesh.'

The sun was setting, and a noise from the backyard suggested that Eddie had come home with Rita.

'Well,' said Linda, 'what should we call you? Do you prefer Francesco or Frank?'

'Oh, I think Frank. I'm sorry, but I've forgotten most of my Italian. Before military service, I only completed two years of compulsory schooling—*papà* needed me to look after the sheep. They tried to teach us some Italian during training, but since most of us came from the south, we all spoke our dialects amongst ourselves, so I didn't learn much there either. I really improved myself only when I came here. When I moved to the Barossa, there was no Italian spoken around me at all, so, surrounded by English, that's what I spoke too.'

'But Titina,' he said, reverting to her childhood nickname, 'how did *you* learn to speak English so well, and in such a short time?'

'I had a lot of help. Linda and Eddie Walsh have been my towers of strength.'

On cue, Eddie, who'd just been apprised of the situation by Linda, walked in with Rita, and introductions were made.

'You'll stay for dinner, won't you, Frank?'

'That's very kind of you, Mrs Walsh.'

'Please, call us Linda and Eddie.'

'Were you planning to return to the city tonight?' asked Eddie.

'I took the precaution of booking a room at the Del Monte Guesthouse. I thought that even if the search for Clementina proved futile, I might enjoy some sea air for an afternoon. Quarries are very dusty places and hard on the lungs.'

'Well, let's have dinner, then we can walk you back to Del Monte's.'

Clementina, Linda and Rita excused themselves while Eddie poured a couple of glasses of whisky. Rita was dispatched to set the table in the dining room with the good crockery and cutlery while Linda and Clementina scoured the scullery for something they could rustle up.

Usually, when they had late clients, they would have a simple soup and sandwiches for dinner. With some cabbage and leek from the garden, some bacon and potatoes, they pulled together a hearty thick soup followed by their bottled peaches and an almond crumble with the leftover ginger biscuits adding some oomph. The women worked quickly in tandem to pull off the preparation at lightning speed, but Linda did ask the important question: 'Are you sure that he's your brother and not an imposter who knows something about your family?'

'He has my father's and my grandfather's face, my mother's mannerisms and her calm, polite way of speaking.'

Clementina went off to her room and came back with the photo of her parents taken on their wedding day. Even though it was faded, Frank's face was all his father's, and his piercing gaze matched his mother's.

After dinner, Eddie and Clementina accompanied Frank back to the Del Monte Guesthouse which had been built high on the sand dunes with a wraparound balcony facing the sea. They stopped in the guest lounge to talk some more. Frank wanted to know about Clementina's wedding. Of course, he had known their neighbour Nicola Della Valle, his older brother Lorenzo, and younger brother Domenico very well. He was equally saddened to hear of the demise of their town and the devastation brought on by war and the influenza epidemic.

'Do you ever plan to go back to Italy, Clementina?'

'A few weeks ago, I thought I would need to go back. But news came that Nicola's body has been properly interred in a specially built ossuary, and a war memorial has been put in place to commemorate the place where he fell. Father Ernesto has submitted a request to the military authorities so that I can claim a war widow's pension, which will help Antonia and Rosaria with Lorenzo's children, so I don't think I need to go back. I miss my home, but I left only sad memories there. I'm happy here, especially now that I know I have done my duty as *mamma* would have wanted.'

Eddie's face lit up and he winked at Clementina. 'I can't believe your good fortune at finding each other again on the other side of the world. After those first advertisements drew a blank, I didn't think this would ever happen.'

Francesco smiled, but he was troubled. 'I earn a good wage, but I have to support my wife and son, and possibly other children who will come along, so I won't be able to send regular remittances like you do, but if I sent you a money transfer, could you send it to Father Ernesto? I'd like it to go towards some masses for the family. It would go a long way to putting my mind at ease. I was young and selfish. I didn't understand what it meant to be a father until a few years ago. Now I can imagine how devastated I would be if my son cut me off with no explanation.'

Frank hung his head in shame and ran a finger under his collar, trying to ease the feeling of being choked and the sudden heat which had suffused his body at the thought of how callously he had acted.

'Certainly, I can do that,' replied Clementina, reaching out to stroke his arm to comfort him as best she could. 'And I'm sure Father Ernesto would put any donation to good use in the community.'

Frank needed to return to Port Adelaide early the next morning so he could catch the quarry train back to Angaston, but he left his address with Clementina, promising to be in touch by letter again and to arrange a time for Clementina to meet his wife and son.

Clementina was thrilled when, by the end of the week, she had received the money transfer Frank had promised, and a sweet letter from her new sister-in-law Barbara. There was also a photograph of the three of them taken at the christening of their baby son. She was looking forward to meeting all of them, especially her 3-year-old nephew.

CHAPTER TWENTY-FIVE

Moving forward – Thursday 12 October 1922

'Mrs Vitale, I'm delighted to hear that your brother has been found. How wonderful to have this mystery finally solved.'

Clementina was sitting in Mr Patterson's office in Currie Street and had just recounted her brother's tale.

'The next time you communicate with him, you must tell him I'd like to see him so that we can make an official application for a name change and to have him registered properly, if he is still an Italian citizen. I can assist with an application for naturalisation if he desires. And for you too, Mrs Vitale, when the time comes. You need to have been living here for 5 years before we can apply.'

At the conclusion of her business affairs with Mr Patterson, Clementina made her way down a busy side lane to Hindley Street. She called in on a few of the drapers and other retailers she usually frequented, including Caroline Delaney's Hat Shop. There, she made an appointment for her current bridal party to come in for selections and fittings the following week, giving Caroline swatches of fabric they would use in their dresses. The two businesses had developed a close association. Linda and Clementina advised their clients to book in with Miss Delaney, if they hadn't already sourced their own hats, and Caroline recommended the trip to Castlemaine Couture in Henley Beach for the best work in the west.

'I think it might be time Castlemaine Couture moved into premises in the city, don't you think? I have so many customers who would come to you but are daunted by the distance. Even if you offered consultations only once or twice a week, you'd see tremendous growth.'

Clementina smiled, grateful for the older lady's enthusiasm.

'The only problem is that we are already at capacity, in terms of what we can produce. How would we fit in all the extra work that a new shop might bring in? It's really not feasible.'

'You could expand—hire others to work for you.'

'But then, their output wouldn't be our work. That's what makes us special. Our work is actually made by us. We fit and cut exactly to our client's requirements, and we treat each client as if they are royalty. That's why they come to us,' explained Clementina. 'Besides, Linda is happy with the way things stand, and so am I. Anyway, why don't you think about coming to the seaside? There's no other milliner in the area. You could be very popular.'

'Oh, at my age, I'm not sure I could start a new business. But retiring by the seaside sounds very enticing. I might just have to come out and have a look around.'

'Why don't you come to lunch one day?'

'That sounds like a wonderful idea. I'll let you know.'

By noon, Clementina was knocking on her friend Imma's door. She was proud to give Imma the ribboned package she was carrying with the two hat pins she'd purchased from Caroline's, one for her friend and one for her daughter Teresina. Teresina was working with her father and brother at their shop at the Central Market today, so that Imma could be free to spend time with her friend.

Imma was just as astonished as Mr Patterson to hear of the resurfacing of Francesco Vitale, and terribly heartbroken to hear of her friend's anguish in relation to her husband's fate on the battlefield.

'*Cara*, you've been so busy trying to re-establish yourself, learn English, care for Rita, support Linda and Eddie and still do charitable work with whoever asks for your assistance, that you haven't given yourself much time to think. It's only natural that at some point, thoughts of home and of Nicola would resurface,' Imma suggested.

'But that vision I had was so real. It truly terrified me, Imma.'

'That vision was your worst fears played out in your mind. You must have thought about what happened to him when he died, but then you had the shock of dealing with his death and the end of your marriage and then your parents' deaths and those of Antonia's family so soon after your own tragedy. You must have buried those thoughts. Now that you're feeling more settled, they've resurfaced. It's only natural.'

'Do you really think that's all there is to it?'

'How else can you explain it?'

'I wondered … if it was a sign from God … or a message from the afterworld …'

Clementina kept her chin down, afraid to look into Imma's eyes.

'The afterworld … Clementina, *Santo Cielo*! Where are your thoughts taking you now? No, *cara*, I'm inclined to side with Eddie. I think he's spot on. Now that you are finally moving on with your life, as I've been encouraging you to do for a while I'd like to remind you, well … you simply panicked, and your mind threw up this excuse, so you didn't have to handle the emotions you feel for this John fellow.'

Lifting Clementina's chin, Imma continued, more calmly, mindful of not spooking her friend. 'Of course, Nicola was your first and only love, so when your heart starts to feel this way again, it's only natural that it returns to Nicola in the first instance. Don't you think? But it's time to set aside those memories and open your heart and your mind to create new experiences of love. I'm sure Nicola would want that for you, and his mother has confirmed that she wants that for you too. You have everybody's permission to move on, except your own!'

Clementina was listening and nodding, but she was still feeling raw and uncertain.

'You can't expect that things will be the same between you and John as they were with you and Nicola. To start with, you're not a naïve romantic 16-year-old anymore! You've had to grow up quickly. And you're independent now. You've been used to making all your own decisions, and hard ones at that! You don't want to lose that independence, but that doesn't mean you can't open yourself up to love again.'

'The thing is, I haven't seen or even had a word from John since that Sunday, so maybe this attraction I'm feeling is all in my own mind. He might not even be interested.'

'Well, he sent you that card, didn't he?'

'I'm sure that was his mother's doing,' she sighed.

'I don't believe that. His mother wouldn't have known about your fondness for violets.'

'It's probably just a coincidence.'

'Still, it's up to you now to make a move. You need to go to him to let him know that you're still interested.'

'Oh, I couldn't do that!'

'Of course you can. You don't need to say it in words, you just need to show your face, to show that you're not afraid of him. Remember, Clementina, the man has a missing hand. Don't you think that maybe he's feeling rejected? He might have come to the conclusion that you're not interested in anything more from him because of his injury. Many men like him would feel that way—like they wouldn't be good enough.'

'Oh, no, I'd never feel that way about John. He's so gentle and kind and determined to do well. He's very clever and has worked so hard to become independent again.'

'Well, he needs to know that you think that way.'

'But I've already told him that … at dinner and before.'

'But then you ruined it all by running away. My dear, if you want to make sure he understands your interest, you're going to have to be the one to reopen lines of communication between you, to give him a chance to understand your feelings. Don't forget, men need direct information—in general, they're not so good at guessing women's thoughts,' added the world-weary Imma, folding her arms and sitting back, pleased with her summary of the situation.

'But how am I supposed to do that?' muttered a confused Clementina.

'Well, you've a perfect excuse to go see him!'

'I do?'

'Rita's Communion of course. You're going to need a special gift made for the little one, aren't you? What about a little desk and a cover for her prayer book?'

'Imma … Oh, my goodness … You're a genius.' Clementina marvelled at her friend's ability to pinpoint the correct way forward. 'I knew I had to talk to you and that you'd have a solution to my dilemma.' Throwing her arms around her friend, their unrestrained laughter reverberated in the small kitchen, putting an end to Clementina's restlessness.

After lunch and some more light-hearted gossip from Imma, the older woman walked her dear young friend to the electric tram stop on West Terrace. She'd filled her basket with vegetable seedlings for the new season, some paper bags of dried lentils and chickpeas, some spicy sausages, well wrapped in several layers of cloth and newspapers to mitigate the strong smell, a small wheel of dried, salty pecorino cheese, which she'd made herself, and two glass bottles with rubber stoppers full of precious olive oil.

'I look forward to coming to celebrate little Rita's Communion and meet your famous brother, and hopefully this John of yours. Don't disappoint me, *cara*,' she concluded as she planted firm kisses on both sides of her friend's face and waved her off.

★ ★ ★

The next day, Clementina decided to 'grab the bull by the horns,' as her friend Imma was very fond of saying. With Linda in tow, she walked down to the end of Main Street for the McLeod house on East Terrace. She hoped it would be suitable to turn up without an appointment. Knocking on the parlour door yielded no results, so the women boldly set off down the wide path on the left side of the house to the workshop at the end of the garden.

Fortuitously, the double doors were wide open, and Mike Sanderson looked up as they approached, switching off the noisy lathe. John had his back to them and only looked up when Mike called him, indicating that they had visitors.

Turning around to see who had come, John lit up with obvious pleasure at the arrival of the two women.

'Ladies, you are definitely a sight for sore eyes. What brings you here on this day, made all the more glorious by your presence.'

Linda beamed at both gentlemen, making a polite reply. She subtly squeezed Clementina's arm, still entwined with hers, to encourage her to speak.

Comforted by John's warm welcome, Clementina lost her nervousness and launched into their reason for coming. Very soon, they'd agreed on a writing slope with a pen rest and an ink well at the top and room below the hinged lid to store papers.

'We could put a decorative motif and her name on the side. What do you think?'

'Yes. Her real name is Margherita, which of course stands for the marguerite daisy, so if you could incorporate that, I'm sure she'd be delighted.'

'And I'd like to order a jewellery box to match, maybe with some of your lovely embroidery to decorate the lid. Something substantial to sit on her dressing table and in which she can store all her treasures. She loves collecting seashells and pebbles from the beach.

'We would be honoured, ladies,' said Mike. 'But when is the big day?'

'On the last Sunday in November, the 26th. Does that give you enough time?' asked Clementina biting her lip and staring up into John's warm brown eyes who were focussed entirely on her own matching pair.

'Of course. We'll make it a priority,' confirmed Mike, smirking at his friend's sudden muteness.

John glanced at Linda who was happily chatting to Michael Sanderson. He reached for Clementina's hand and pulled her away to his own work bench.

'I have a question I wish to ask you,' he said, swallowing nervously. 'My mother has reminded me many times that the annual parish dance is coming up at the end of January, and she would like me to attend. May I ask you to come join my family and I … as my dance partner that is?'

Clementina's worried face broke out into a wide smile.

'I'd be honoured, John,' she replied. 'But I must warn you, I've never learned to do your sort of dances.'

'Well, we can remedy that. Mrs Franklin gives dance lessons on Tuesday and Thursday nights at the Institute on Seaview Road. May I come collect you at 7, for a 7.30 start, next Tuesday?'

'Oh, that's a wonderful idea. I look forward to it,' she giggled.

CHAPTER TWENTY-SIX

Special events – Thursday 16 November 1922

John and Clementina had attended six of Mrs Franklin's dance classes. So far, she'd learned to do the regular waltz, which allowed for a fairly slow turn around the dance floor, and the Allies' waltz, for which the music was much quicker. The fast music meant that John had to step in much closer to her and hold her much tighter, which made her head spin for reasons other than the faster tempo. They chose to sit out when the class launched into a tango. That dance made her underarms prickle with a sudden rush of heat. They didn't do the foxtrot either, which looked too complicated, but they didn't mind jumping back in for the hilarious turkey trot that didn't require much skill and finished the night with high energy.

The best part of the dance classes was when Clementina and John made the leisurely walk to and from the Institute. They stopped for refreshments after the class and then wandered back home again, chatting all the way. This week, Clementina found the right moment and the courage to explain herself and her actions to John. He was attentive, listened to her without interrupting, and said he could understand her reaction. He praised her loyalty to her husband and his memory.

'Since the Soldier's Memorial opened, I feel I've discharged my duty to my friend, Bert. He'll be permanently remembered now, especially since his parents have died and his siblings don't live in the area anymore. I felt I had the responsibility to make sure his name was still amongst us. I know his older sister has had a bench named in his honour at her local church. She lives in the country, and she wanted a place she could easily visit to remember him, especially since his remains are still overseas. Maybe you could take her example and do something for your husband and your lost family here.'

'I never thought of that. It's a lovely idea, and especially for Rita too. I felt so sad when she told me how burdened she felt by the thought that she is the only one who remembers and prays for them.'

'Why don't you talk to Father Kenny? He's a good sort. Even if he can't do anything himself, he might have other ideas of how a private memorial could be established.'

★ ★ ★

The following Saturday, Caro and Reggie had their engagement party at the Convalescent Home, hosted by Matron Heritage who organised a supper dance in the dining room. Some of the men had cobbled together a band and played what they could. A phonograph provided music for the rest of the time. All the couples' local friends, the nurses, and the resident returned soldiers were invited, along with Clementina, John, Mike and Nancy. A family lunch was being held the following day at the home of Captain and Mrs Thomson, so this evening was really for the younger set. Only Captain Dixon's parents had arrived from Brisbane for the engagement. They were staying with the Thomsons for the week. More of his family planned to come for the wedding. Clementina travelled to the party with John and the Sandersons. Arrangements had been made to pick them up in a special army truck to accommodate Mike's wheelchair. Clementina and John were able to show off their burgeoning waltz skills for a few numbers but spent most of the evening mingling and chatting with a whole range of people. Clementina was delighted to catch up with Nurse Harrison, who introduced her to the other nurses.

'Tina is the brilliant lady who designed this dress for my sister's wedding.'

'Ooh, you are clever, Tina. The fabric and the colours are muted, but still eye catching, and we're all very jealous of the asymmetrical cape thing you designed. It's so whimsical,' said Noreen.

'That's the sort of thing I need for my blue dress. Would you consider making me just the cape?' Jeannie tucked away Tina's business card with glee.

Caro wore a simple ivory silk straight shift Clementina had decorated with a triple row of increasingly larger pearls at the high front neckline and all the way to the much lower back. She paired it with a deep black, lustrous fur stole. Caro was tall and willowy and had bobbed her fair hair for the occasion, wearing it sleekly combed down and pomaded to frame her face. She was a replica of the modern miss from the *Vogue* magazines and drew many admiring glances from both sexes, and most of all from the besotted Reggie Dixon, whose pride was bursting from every angle of his trim, muscular body and whimsically waxed moustache.

Supper, organised by the Thomsons, consisted of an assortment of savoury and sweet foods all laid out on white linen-covered tables lined up against the back wall of the dining room. Clementina tried many new things: fresh oysters with a squeeze of lemon, devilled eggs, and slices of cold ox tongue in aspic served on thin buttered toast. All were easy to eat without cutlery, though she'd had to remove her gloves to avoid greasy spots. Then there were a number of sweet dishes she'd never tried. A colourful sponge trifle was made with tinned peaches and raspberry jelly. The lamingtons were in honour of Captain Dixon's Queensland origins, as were the copious amounts of fresh mango, which had arrived with his parents the day before, but which were too sour for Clementina's palate. The nurses had made a dried fruit cake served with a very strong brandy sauce, which the couple ceremoniously cut with Reggie's sword at the end of the champagne toasts raised in their honour.

The servicemen had even organised some games. Charades using song titles was popular. They also played pin the tail on the kangaroo, which Clementina happily joined in, and even a hilarious musical chairs, where Nancy Sanderson took out first prize sitting in Mike's lap—a spot no-one else dared to claim.

Clementina was dropped off home, exhausted and exhilarated. She had felt very comfortable, for the first time—not worried about her ability to fit in or to participate in conversation. She felt accepted, just like everybody else, regardless of their circumstances or social standing. In Italy, neither she nor her parents would ever have dared to socialise with anyone outside of their peasant origins. Even when she was young and the flax and linen trade had been booming, her entertainment was strictly tied to religious festivals and family events. She had seen the *grandi signori* with their exquisitely tailored modern outfits and shiny leather shoes bought at city cobblers, but everyone she knew wore the village dress and homemade shoes. Despite some minor instances of snobbery she'd experienced, life was more egalitarian here. In the shops, even though they were frequented by all classes, everyone mostly took their turn, being served on the basis of their arrival at the premises rather than on their financial status. Once, at the post office, when Mr Reynolds had tried to serve the stationmaster ahead of her, Mr Flaherty had insisted that she be served first. Mr Reynolds had apologised to her, giving the excuse that he assumed Mr Flaherty might be in a hurry, but the gentleman had gently explained, 'I'm here on personal business, and I'll wait my turn like everybody else.'

★ ★ ★

The following morning, after the church service, Clementina approached Father Kenny with John's idea.

'Let me think about it. It sounds like a wonderful gesture. I'll need to obtain permission from my superiors, but it is something that has been done before, so I don't see why we couldn't come to a suitable arrangement.'

Sunday afternoon was set aside for finalising Rita's Communion dress. Linda had already sewn the dress, according to Rita's exacting instructions. They had chosen a light cotton damask in ivory that was cut as a simple shift with a plain, round neckline. Pin tucking was used at the front to add interest and structure. The dress reached to just below her knees and at the base were six layers of thin, tight ruffles. The sleeves were elbow length so that she could wear the elbow-length white silk evening gloves, already purchased. Tiny pale ivory silk ribbon bows were sewn onto the bottom central gather of the sleeves, which also ended in a single frill. A few more petite silk ribbon bows were sewn at the bases of the pin tucks at alternating heights. The veil was to sit on her forehead, and through some smocking, form a crown effect, cinched at the sides with more ribbon and a large fabric bow on either side. The veil would then flow in a double layer over her shoulders, ending at her hips. Clementina had scalloped the edges and sewn a thin hat elastic at the base of her head to create a substantial cap which could simply be secured by a bobby pin on either side. She embroidered a run of marguerite daisies with tiny yellow pearl centres along the edge of the veil. The dress would be paired with fine white stockings and the white Mary Jane leather shoes with a single buckle on the side and a small, elevated heel. To surprise her, Linda had also sewn a small fabric drawstring pouch to carry on her arm, using the leftover dress fabric.

At the end of the fitting, Linda returned to the sewing room with a plush deep green velvet box. She drew Rita onto her lap.

'My darling, in here is the jewellery set my parents bought me when I was a girl. In my day, we had our Communion and Confirmation ceremony together, when we were 12 years old. My parents saved money for 2 years so that they could afford to buy this gold jewellery, so you can understand how precious it is?'

Rita nodded solemnly. 'Can I see it?'

Linda opened the box and set it in front of Rita. Clementina came to sit with them to look at the special treasure.

Rita didn't say a word, but Clementina gasped. 'Oh my, how exquisite.'

Set into a display compartment was a rope-like gold chain with a penny-sized medallion featuring a veiled Madonna with a prominent heart surrounded by flames. The bracelet had tiny hearts set at intervals and there were a pair of slim hoop earrings, each with a tiny heart charm attached.

'Can I try them on?' asked Rita, almost breathless.

They all went to the cheval mirror, Clementina ceremoniously holding the box while Linda picked up first the chain and secured that around Rita's neck. Then she attached the bracelet around Rita's slim wrist. With the earrings, she held them up to Rita's ears to show her the effect they would create. While Rita had probably had her earlobes pierced as a baby, the holes had long closed over.

Rita fingered each of the pieces, relishing in their ability to make her shine.

'Zia Linda, they're so beautiful. I feel like a queen.'

'It would be my great honour if you wore the necklace and bracelet on your Communion day. And then when you're older, maybe for your Confirmation, we could organise to have your ears pierced, so you can wear the earrings too. What do you think?'

'I think I'm the luckiest girl in the world,' she said as she hugged Linda ferociously. Detaching herself, she added. 'But you'll hold on to them, won't you? They're too beautiful. I'd be too tempted to play with them all the time, and I might break them.'

Linda nodded and gave Rita a warm smile, discreetly wiping away the tears forming at the corners of her eyes. Clementina hugged her too and helped return the jewellery to the box. Further words were unnecessary.

* * *

On her Communion Sunday, the house was woken by a very enthusiastic young girl at 4 o'clock in the morning. Her little eyes were shadowed, and the strips of muslin that Linda had woven into her hair the night before had almost all fallen out. Rita confessed she had been too excited and nervous to sleep and had tossed and turned most of the night. She'd also eaten very little the night before, and Linda and Clementina were worried for her stamina. It was traditional for adults to fast before receiving communion at mass, but Rita had always been given a glass of warm milk. Today though, she refused it, as she said she had promised Sister Mary-Paul that she would observe the fast for her First Communion and forever after, each time she planned to take communion.

She tried to be very pious and serious but jumped into Linda's arms and then Eddie's with unrestrained glee when she was presented with a crystal container with scented talc and a powder puff, and a matching small vial of eau de cologne.

'It's like yours, Tina, but it smells of roses! I feel so grown up!'

She turned solemn and pensive again when she unwrapped Clementina's special offering—a slim brass plaque engraved with the names of her grandparents, parents and siblings and the month and year they passed away. When Clementina explained that next week, Father Kenny had been given permission to allow her to choose one of the benches in the church on which to attach the plaque, she was overcome with emotion and climbed into Clementina's lap, wrapping her arms tightly around her neck.

'Tina, do you think this is a sign that my family are in heaven now.'

'Undoubtedly, my darling. And today, you can carry your family with you in your little pouch.'

A little tear spilled down Rita's face. Wiping them away, Clementina quickly changed the subject. She wanted Rita to look back on this special day with joy rather than the sadness that had marked her young life.

The church was crowded with locals who had turned up in force, and many visitors too. The families of the communicants had all been allocated a bench near the front and the group of 12 candidates took up the two front rows on either side of the aisle. When they arrived, Sister Mary-Paul was all aflutter, sorting seating arrangements. Once Father Kenny indicated he was ready, the little ones were ushered down the side aisle and gathered at the back of the church to walk in solemnly with their hands clasped reverently in prayer held at chest level. They walked in behind Father Kenny, waving his lit incense burner, who was preceded by three altar boys. The first two carried the two candles in their polished silver stands and the third one carried the large brass crucifix.

The little ones were directed to stand at the altar rail, where Sister Mary Dolores, the principal of the school, distributed their blessed rosary beads and little white leather-covered prayer books with their names inscribed on the frontispiece. Father Kenny then welcomed them and impressed upon the whole congregation the importance of this day. By the end of the service, with a choir of schoolchildren leading the singing, even Eddie had to wipe a tear from the corner of his eye. Linda and Clementina had not bothered to try to retain the tears of pride which flowed, both of them dabbing at their eyes with handkerchiefs from the minute Rita and her little friends had processed down the central aisle.

After the service, the communicants and the whole congregation were shepherded into the church hall, where short tables had been festively decorated to fit the little legs of the communicants and taller tables, set out buffet style against one wall, accommodated the adults. The children were served glasses of cold milk and little plates of plain butter and strawberry jam sandwiches, a small piece of chocolate cake and an apple. They chattered amongst themselves while the adults mingled with tea and scones provided by the Ladies Committee of the parish. In this way, even the children of the families who could not afford an extended celebration could mark this special day. In the alcove of the hall, a photographer had set up a canvas backdrop and a bench with an enormous basket of silk flowers adorned with a gilded card with 1922 written on it. All the families were encouraged to have their children photographed, so that they could be displayed in the church for a few weeks. The opportunity was made available for any families who could afford to purchase their own photo, to pick up a little calling card for the studio. Clementina asked Eddie to order an extra copy so that she could send it to Mother Maddalena in Chieti.

Francesco and his wife and son were with them. They'd arrived on Friday morning and booked themselves into the Del Monte Guesthouse until Tuesday, so Clementina had an extended opportunity to meet the new additions to her family. Imma and her family and their hat-maker friend, Caroline Delaney, were due to arrive for lunch by tram. The 7.30 am church service was too early for them to get to Henley Beach from the city on time. Eddie had booked the private dining room of the Del Monte Hotel for lunch. It had a splendid reputation for elegant, yet hearty meals and good wine, and was further away from the noise of the activities around the Henley Jetty. Linda had invited the Captain and Mrs Thomson as well as her first local friends Mr and Mrs Ferrier, the drapers, and Miss Gill who worked for them. Eddie had invited some of his colleagues from the school board, Dr and Mrs Muirhead and the accountant Mr Metcalfe and his wife. Father Kenny had promised to drop in at home in the evening, because he'd had many other invites for the day, but Sister Marie had been delighted to accept an invitation. Clementina had hoped to invite John, but his niece Lucille Jones, Ruth's youngest daughter was also a communicant, so his sister was hosting her own family lunch at home, but he promised to stop by as soon as he could and definitely spend the evening with them. He didn't want to miss out on meeting the famous Imma and getting to know Clementina's brother better.

CHAPTER TWENTY-SEVEN

Closing out the year – Monday 4 December 1922

A week after Rita's Communion, a letter arrived from Caroline Delaney. She informed them she was coming down to Henley Beach the following week for a few days and had booked a room at the Ramsgate, so that she could be close by. She also wanted to make an appointment with Mr Gray, the land agent, who had advertised some properties for sale in the area. She asked if Eddie would be free to accompany her to the appointment and eventual inspections, because she felt she would be treated more seriously and fairly if he were there. The little shop in Hindley Street had been purchased by her father. She had inherited it upon his death and taken over the hat-making business, where she had worked since she was 13 years old. Eddie, proud to have been selected for the task, immediately organised a lettergram to both parties, suggesting times he would be available to make inspections.

Cosily ensconced in the sewing room with her friends, Caroline, who had never married, explained that she had been totally charmed by the little seaside town the previous Sunday. She marvelled at how much it had grown in the 5 or 6 years since her last visit. That had been during the war years, when everything had seemed rather dour and shabby.

'I turned 60 last month and I didn't bother to celebrate because I have no siblings and my parents and other relatives are either long gone or no longer live in Adelaide. I found there was really no-one I wished to invite, except perhaps you two darling ladies.'

'You have no cousins or close acquaintances?'

'I do have cousins, but we've never been close, because they are either 10 years older than me or considerably younger. Apart from when they need a hat, I rarely see them. As for acquaintances, Hindley Street has changed so much that the people I once knew well as a young woman, and with whom I socialised, have all moved away too. I don't even recognise most of the people at my church anymore.'

'But your business is still doing well, isn't it?'

'Once upon a time, people came to a milliner to be personally fitted for all their hats, but these days, it's mostly only for special occasion wear. The new department stores and large drapers are stocking so many pre-made items at prices I can't compete with. I don't blame people for choosing the more sensible option, but I have seen a steady decline in business, which has suited my declining energy levels well, I might add.'

Linda nodded vigorously.

'Yes, I believe the same thing is happening to our business. Thankfully, with Clementina's talents, we have been able to pivot almost exclusively to special occasion wear ourselves. I've seen less and less of my regular customers for their everyday frocks. Especially now that sewing machines too are also an affordable option. Any woman with a modicum of intelligence can run up the modern trend for simple shifts. All they need is to buy the paper patterns so widely distributed through the newspapers and women's magazines, and they can make a dress to fit, without any training in tailoring.'

Clementina had not stopped to consider the shift in their customers, but she nodded too when, on reflection, she realised that their current clientele were mostly after event attire.

'So, what are you saying, Caroline? Are you going to give up your business?' asked Clementina.

'I'm not quite ready to give everything up. But most of my equipment would easily fit into one room, so I thought if I found a two-bedroom cottage, I could use one room for a workroom and maybe set up a parlour to receive clients. Then I thought, since so many of my customers are coming from Castlemaine Couture anyway, why don't I move closer to you ladies, that way I'll have your friendship and company, as well as easy access to your customers.'

'Oh my goodness,' gushed Linda, standing suddenly. 'Caroline! Mrs Fenwick, just a few doors down and across the street from here was telling me that she was considering selling up and moving in with her daughter whose husband is being transferred to Melbourne with his job!'

'Has she listed it with an agent yet?'

'I don't know, but I'm sure she'd be happy to hear that there's someone reliable interested. I could send Eddie around for you to make enquiries?'

'Capital idea! I knew I could rely on you and Eddie to help me,' beamed Caroline, reaching out for Linda's hands. 'A cottage all on one floor, would be ideal. I've noticed that my knees aren't what they used to be, and my narrow, two-storey place is causing problems, anyway.'

Within a month, a price had been agreed upon for Mrs Fenwick's house and a buyer found for Caroline's shop and upstairs apartment in Hindley Street. Eddie promised to organise some reliable carters to help Caroline pack all her equipment, transport it out of the city and install it in the bedroom at the back of the Henley Beach house, which received the best light. Most of the furniture she had in her little shop fit perfectly in her front room. The dining room next door was big enough to accommodate her compact table and six chairs, as well as a settee and a couple of comfy armchairs. All that was left was to have her dear friends come help her celebrate with a cosy housewarming dinner.

* * *

There were many other celebrations too for them all to enjoy. In early December, Eddie very proudly handed over the keys of the newly built convent to the Congregation of Mercy Sisters. The blessing and official opening ceremony, which attracted an enormous crowd, was led by the Archbishop, who praised the quality of the build and its timely completion. Eddie was particularly proud of his work record: none of his men had been injured, and the architects extolled their excellent workmanship.

The building had been designed in Spanish Mission Style and built of brick and cement concrete. Spanning two stories and facing the Gulf St Vincent, it was also an important landmark when viewed from the sea. The roof was covered in red Mediterranean-style clay tiles, and the building, composed of a central entrance and two wings on either side, featured a deep verandah on the ground floor and an equally sizeable balcony on the top floor. The windows were all shuttered to keep out the bad weather in winter or to allow cross-ventilation in the heat. On the ground floor of the left wing, the schoolroom could hold over 100 children and opened up to the courtyard at the back of the building, affording the children protection from the wild winter winds. There was also a kitchen and laundry situated here. On the other wing, immediately off the entrance, there was a sacristy for the priest to store his vestments and prepare himself to say mass in the well-appointed chapel and gallery, fitted with a beautiful stained-glass window. Upstairs, a community room and refectory, two parlours and music rooms, and 16 small single bedrooms had been built. The entire building had been fitted with the latest devices and was electrically lit.

The Archbishop thanked Mother Cecelia, whose relatives in Buenos Aires had been the generous benefactors. This resulted in the building incurring no debt for the sisters or the diocese. He explained that the Henley Beach convent would allow the hard-working sisters in Angas Street and at Parkside the opportunity to come in shifts for respite, especially to restore their physical and mental health with beneficial sea breezes and the opportunity for quiet contemplation during the school holidays.

After the successful conclusion of this project, Eddie, who was now almost 60, decided that he would prefer to take on smaller building projects in the future. He only wanted to deal with individual clients, rather than committees with large numbers of interested parties. Thanks to the building boom in the area, there'd be no shortage of work.

* * *

With Christmas approaching and the already busy summer wedding season in full swing, Linda, Clementina and Annie were working non-stop. Rita was now on holiday and eager to be of help. Though her skills were still too rudimentary to do much in the sewing room, she was invaluable for running errands, especially with Eddie's supervision.

At the convent, Sister Marie decided that her baking days were beyond her now. She suggested that Mr Olsen's bakery should be commissioned for delivery, so the bread-baking and English lessons came to a natural halt. The workshops at Lady Galway's also closed for the duration of summer, freeing Clementina to get more done in the business. It also meant that she could spend more precious time with John, who had taken to dropping in after dinner most evenings to chat with Clementina as she completed her work. His mother, Frances, had invited all four of them and Caroline Delaney to Christmas dinner. They would clear away the equipment in the stables and set up trestle tables for all the McLeod family and guests, with everybody contributing one or more dishes, so no-one had to work too hard in preparation.

Clementina was feeling nervous about John's expectations and decided that she should talk to him frankly.

'John, I need you to explain to me what to expect on Christmas Day, and especially what your family will expect from me. For example, do I need to organise gifts for everyone?'

'What did you do last year?'

'It was only the four of us. We went to early mass and then Linda and I worked together to cook a nice meal. We exchanged small gifts. I made Rita a new dress, a new lace veil for Linda to wear to church and bought some wine for Eddie. What about you?'

'Well, as young adults, my sisters and I were usually given a silver coin, and a small sugary treat on Christmas mornings. So, since my nieces are young, we've continued in the same tradition, giving them some money in a card and their own box of sweets or chocolates, but only after Christmas lunch. It's their parents' job to provide them with toys, books or clothes, depending on their age and circumstances, and that usually happens at their own home in the morning. We adults just provide the items for the meal. I've always made sure to give my mother extra money in advance so she can shop for what she needs. But, since Rita has thoroughly captivated my mother, I'm sure she will treat her as an extra granddaughter and have a little envelope and sweet treat set aside for her too, like she's organised for Mike's twins.'

'But should Linda and I also provide something for your nieces and the Sandersons?

'Well, even Ruth's older girls at 14 and 16 still love pretty things. What about fashioning a bow they can put in their hair? I'm sure they'd be very proud to say they have an original Castlemaine Couture item.'

'John, that's wonderful, because that's exactly what I was thinking. And what about us? Will we be exchanging gifts?' she asked more hesitantly, not sure if she should have been so forward.

'Well, I've already had plenty of time to organise my gift for you, which I've made myself, so if you had the time … how about some of those delectable tarts of yours?'

'Oh, that's too easy. Anyway, I was going to bring a plate of special chocolate ones for the Christmas table. But I know exactly what I'm going to make you too,' she teased.

'Any hints?'

'Of course not!'

'Can I ask you another question then?'

Clementina stopped what she was doing to look up at John when she detected a more serious tone to his voice.

'What is it, John? Please be frank. That's one thing I appreciate about your company—you're always honest and open with your feelings.'

'Well,' John swallowed and paused until he had her full attention. 'I think you know how much I appreciate you and your company, and I wouldn't want to lose you, but … well … I'm not ready to move into a more serious relationship,' he finally blurted. His eyes were focussed on hers and his unusually anguished look startled her, but she nodded in encouragement, her face serious too, given the importance of where this discussion would lead them.

'You see, I feel I haven't had enough time to establish myself yet, and … I wouldn't be able to support … a wife. Not just yet. Do you understand what I'm saying?'

'John,' she gasped. She reached out for him, her hand trembling. Searching his eyes and looking into them without shying away, she answered him.

'John, you mean the world to me, but I'm not ready either. I'm not interested in anyone else, but I'm not ready to move on yet. It's hard to explain, but I've found so much fulfillment in this work and this business, and I don't want to let it go, ever. Can you accept that? Whatever develops between us, I would expect to keep working. How do you feel about that? Would you be able to allow that?'

'I've been wondering if you felt that way about this work. I can see how important it is to you, and I'm so proud of you, and your creativity and hard work. I would never want to stand in your way.'

Clementina stood and pulled him to her. 'I miss the closeness we had during our dancing lessons,' she smirked cheekily.

'We can pretend the music is still playing just for us,' he murmured as he held her close and slowly waltzed her around the sewing room table. He gave her a brief, tentative kiss and then returned her to her chair.

They were both blushing furiously, but soon the embarrassment of their first kiss turned into broad smiles. The comfortable silence between them as they looked into each other's eyes, unabashedly, was precious to them both, especially after having cleared the air of any uncertainties.

When she finally sank into bed that night, Clementina turned to open the top drawer of her nightstand and withdrew the little package enveloped in tissue paper she had secreted away in there. Opening it, she smiled with great satisfaction at the bottle green silk damask tie she had created with the popular Windsor knot. She had stitched it down to hold it in place and threaded a broad elastic through the back so that John could put it under his collar without needing someone to help him tie it.

CHAPTER TWENTY-EIGHT

Bad news likes company – Friday 5 January 1923

Linda and Clementina were expecting Emmeline Thomson and her daughter Caroline for their final fittings. The wedding was scheduled for the following weekend. But it was Reggie Dixon who showed up at their door instead. Clementina was about to make a quip when she noticed Reggie's clenched jaw and grey face.

'What is it, Reggie? Do come in, sit down. Do you need some water? Has something happened?'

Linda quickly poured out a tea and added several teaspoons of sugar when she saw Reggie's wild eyes and inability to focus. Gulping down a mouthful of the hot beverage, Reggie swallowed with difficulty, his eyes downcast and his head shaking from side to side as if he were debating with himself. The women stared at each other, dumbfounded and increasingly alarmed by this development. Young Annie had stopped her activity at the sewing machine and sat stiff-backed in her chair. Reggie cleared his throat and looked up.

'Ehmm … the thing is, we've just had news. Something terrible's happened. It's Albie Thomson …' He hung his head again.

'Something's happened to Albie …?' prompted Linda.

'We've just had news that he died yesterday,' he finally blurted.

'He died?' repeated Linda and Clementina, echoing each other. 'How?'

'We're not sure. I came to tell you that the family is travelling to Melbourne on the overnight train. The wedding will need to be postponed.'

'Of course, Reggie. Thank you for coming to let us know. Are you going with them?'

'Yes, I'm off to secure tickets for the train now.' He stood up abruptly and put his hat back on. 'I must be off.'

'Take care, Reggie. Our thoughts and prayers will be with you all,' sighed Linda as she showed him to the door. 'Do let us know if there is anything we can do to be of assistance, and please pass on my condolences,' finished Linda.

Clementina had dropped herself into her wicker chair by the window and watched as Reggie turned his motor around and headed off towards Henley Beach Road and presumably on to the Adelaide Railway Station to complete his task.

'My goodness,' was all that Linda could say as she came to stand and stare out the window too. 'Another enormous blow for my dear Emmeline. I wonder what could have happened to such a young man?'

'Do you think it could have been the alcohol?' suggested Clementina, thinking back to the last time she'd seen him, completely in his cups at an important and public event. She knew that she and his family had not been the only ones shocked at his behaviour that night.

'Who knows? Since the return of the men from the war, there's been so much change in what is considered acceptable behaviour.'

Both women slowly resumed their tasks, eventually returning the

Thomson outfits carefully to the wardrobe where they were being stored.

'Poor Caro and Reggie. They've been so happy these last few months.'

When John arrived that evening, Clementina relayed the shocking news. They were all sitting on the front verandah, trying to catch the sea breeze. John turned bright red and dipped his head when he heard the news.

'Do you know something, John?' whispered Clementina.

'Later,' he whispered back. 'When Rita's in bed.'

At that cue, Clementina called Rita and asked her to go inside to wash up and put on her nightie. Once she was out of earshot, John was about to speak, then hesitated.

'This might not be suitable information for ladies either,' he directed this to Eddie, looking for approval from the older man.

'Best just be open and honest, son. We're all adults.'

On a sigh, John began. 'The rumour among the men at the convalescent home was that he was admitted to a VD clinic.'

'VD?' questioned Clementina.

'Venereal disease.'

'Oh!' uttered Clementina and Linda in unison, not expecting this sort of information at all. The newspapers regularly mentioned the concerns of the Armed Forces in treating this disease in returned troops, but it was still a shock.

'But I don't understand? Do you die from that?' asked Clementina.

'In some men, the disease is dormant for a long time, then when it resurfaces, it can be very painful. That may have been why he was drinking so much. And in some cases, the disease attacks internal organs and can lead to heart or liver failure.'

'My goodness. I had no idea it could be so fatal,' replied Linda.

'But you've heard this as a rumour. How do you know it's true?'

questioned Eddie.

'I don't know if he died from complications of VD. But I do know he did contract the disease. He told me himself.'

Linda and Clementina looked over at each other, jaws dropped open.

'We shared a table one night at Lady Galway's, and he was drinking a lot. He was bragging, telling us about his port-side adventures and said he'd been lucky because the sores had disappeared after a month at sea. He thought he'd been cured. But the Army doctors used to lecture us infantry men endlessly about the dangers of secondary infections developing long after the first minor symptoms had disappeared. We were told about the risks of passing on the disease to female companions once we returned home, even when there appeared to be no more symptoms.'

Rita came back out, ready for bed, so Clementina accompanied her and stayed with her for a while, going through the motions of reading her a story and saying her prayers with her, but all the while thinking about Albie Thomson. She wondered if the family knew about his possible VD and had kept it a secret, or if, as John suggested, Albie himself had been blissfully ignorant of the danger he was in. In any case, she herself had dodged a bullet. Thankfully, nothing had ever developed between them. He was much too brash and self-important, and they had absolutely nothing in common. In her brief encounters with him, she could see that he enjoyed a good time, and he was certainly amusing in company, but she sensed a dark side to his affected humour. Still, he had been a very glamorous and handsome man, and both his mother and his younger sister doted on him. They would be devastated, no matter how he had died.

When Rita finally dropped off to sleep, John had gone home, and Eddie had taken himself to bed too. Linda was in the kitchen and was putting away the teacups.

'John left. He said he had a delivery to make tomorrow, so wouldn't be around until tomorrow evening.'

Clementina nodded and was about to say goodnight but instead pulled out one of the kitchen chairs and sat down. Linda did the same.

'Can you believe it?' whispered Clementina. 'What a cruel way to die.' She brought her hands to her mouth and shook her head, still in disbelief.

'I'm distraught for Emmeline. Just when the family fortunes looked like they were turning around. That's four sons she's lost. I don't know how she's going to cope.' Linda sighed sorrowfully. 'All we can do is pray, I guess. I wonder if Father Kenny's been told. Do you think I should let him know?'

'We don't know for sure what the circumstances are. I'd be wary of spreading rumours. I hope John doesn't tell anybody else.'

'Eddie did ask him not to tell anyone else for the moment, even the lads at the convalescent home.'

'Probably a wise move. Thank goodness for our dear Eddie. He's such a treasure, Linda.'

'I know, I'm very lucky. But what about you, *cara*? I see you and John have become great friends and are very comfortable with each other now. Is there a chance anything else will develop beyond friendship?'

Clementina looked up into Linda's hopeful eyes and rewarded her with a soft smile and a nod.

'Something's happening, but we've both admitted that neither of us is ready for anything formal at this stage, so we're happy just getting to know each other better.'

'That's very sensible. Take your time, but for what it's worth, I think you've found a good one too.'

Linda pushed away from the table to stand up and tuck in her chair, and when she stepped over to Clementina, she bent over from behind the chair to give her a hug and plant a kiss on the top of her head. Clementina stood, returning the hug with a kiss on her friend's cheek, then she too made her way to the bedroom, wondering why a sudden sense of dread had come upon her.

★ ★ ★

Two days later, young Billy Preston from the Post Office turned up with a telegram. Thinking it might be from Reggie or Caroline, Clementina opened it eagerly but quickly dropped it like it had been a lit match about to scorch her fingers.

'What is it, *cara*?' Linda stopped what she was doing and picked up the telegram off the floor.

'Oh no. I'm so sorry, Tina.' She immediately gathered the shocked Clementina into her arms and shepherded her towards her chair. 'Annie, be a dear and pour some tea for Tina, and make it very sweet.'

The telegram had come from Italy, from Giovanni, letting them know that Antonia, Clementina's mother-in-law, had passed away in her sleep a week before and the funeral had been well-attended. He advised that a letter from Rosaria was following.

Clementina went to her room and threw herself on the bed, allowing her sobs and her tears to flow without shame. She cried for her wonderful Antonia who'd welcomed her, cherished her and looked out for her. Antonia had been her rock when her world had crumbled around her. Even though she too had lost a son, her focus had been on making sure Clementina survived the shock of becoming such a young widow.

Then, when more died, she'd been the one to rally everyone to the necessary tasks of burying the dead with dignity and rebuilding their lives. Antonia was probably only in her early 60s, yet the hard, physical labour she had endured most of her life had inflicted many more years on her tired body. Clementina was also plagued by anguish for her sister-in-law Rosaria, now left unaided with two young children. Although Rosaria was a few years older, they'd been childhood friends and neighbours. Then their closeness had been further cemented when they both lost their husbands. Rosaria had been the first to encourage Clementina to go to Australia, to grab at any opportunity to change her destiny—a constant battle against the elements, against hunger, against misery.

When she'd finally spent her tears, she went out to the bathroom to wash her face. She would go directly to the Post Office and wire some more money to Rosaria. She would need it now, to have Antonia's name engraved on a headstone alongside her husband's. On the way, she stopped at the newsagent and bought a sympathy card. She chose one with lilies growing by a babbling stream. That's where Antonia had spent most of her life, at the river's edge, on her knees, washing other people's clothes. She scribbled only a few words in Italian, to let Rosaria know of her heartbreak at the news and her desire to support her in any way she could. She sent another note to Father Kenny to have a mass dedicated to Antonia's soul, for her eternal repose—she certainly deserved her moment of blissful rest. The only other thing to do now was to wait for Rosaria's letter. As she began walking home, her thoughts were a jumble.

How impotent she felt and what a curse it was to be so far away. Really, she wanted to be there, to be holding Rosaria. They should have been together through this painful time. Instead, here she was, walking the street of this foreign town, where nobody knew her private business and nobody could guess at her anguish. If she'd been in Rapino, there would be signs pasted on the wall of the *Commune* with black borders and Antonia's name and funeral details, letting the whole village know, inviting them to remember Antonia's life and pray for her departed soul. Before the funeral and well after it, visitor after visitor would come to the house to console her and check on her welfare. When she walked to the well, she'd be stopped and hugged and people would recount stories of their encounters with Antonia over the years. The pain wouldn't go away, but it would diminish through this shared remembering.

Turning the corner onto Main Street, she saw Caroline Delaney coming out of her house and heading towards her. Reaching her, Caroline tucked Clementina's arm into hers.

'My dear Tina, I was looking out for your return. I've heard the news of your mother-in-law's passing. How devastating for you to be so far away from the important people of your childhood. It's the curse of the immigrant. I remember my grandparents suffering every time they heard of someone's passing in Sheffield, even if it wasn't a relative. My grandmother once said it was like someone taking an eraser to the picture book of her childhood, removing one figure at a time, until the only thing left was a blur of faint lines, too indistinct to mean anything.'

Clementina nodded and hugged her friend. 'Yes,' she choked. 'Thank you. I needed that reminder. I need to remember that I may have lost a significant person from my past, but I have new people here, significant to my future.'

At the following Sunday's mass, Clementina had pulled her lace veil well over the sides of her face, to give herself a private space in which to contemplate. So, she'd been surprised by the number of local acquaintances who had offered her their condolences and their support. Over the next few weeks, when she stopped at the local shops, everyone had a kind word for her. She was astounded each time. She wasn't in Rapino, but maybe she wasn't a foreigner here after all. All this attention and genuine sympathy made her realise how much she'd become integrated and embraced by this tight-knit community. It did much to lift her out of the doldrums she'd fallen into because Antonia's death vividly brought back to mind all the awful deaths she'd endured in a few short years.

Clementina was not alone in her experience of grief. Caroline Thomson eventually called in, several weeks after they'd heard about Albie's death.

'Caroline, how lovely to see you again. Do come in. May I serve you a cup of tea?'

'I'm sorry to drop in on you unannounced, Mrs Walsh, but I'm only back in Adelaide for a few days. Mother's still in Melbourne and I need to get back to her. I just came to check in on Freddie and accompany my father back.'

She was talking quietly but rapidly, as if she were in danger of running out of breath if she stopped.

'Here, my dear, come sit and have some tea. Take your time, and tell me about your mother,' encouraged Linda.

Linda had directed her to the settee at the far end of the room and sat next to her, speaking in hushed tones. Annie was at her machine, whirring away, and Clementina stayed at the sewing table, not wishing to overwhelm the young woman, who was looking very gaunt and fragile.

'Mother's in hospital. She had a nervous collapse when she heard about the circumstances of Albie's death. We had no idea that he'd come back from the war with a nasty disease which attacked his liver. His drinking didn't help.'

'I'm so sorry to hear that my darling girl. Is there anything I can do to help?'

'Would you keep an eye on Father? He's been so distraught at mother's undoing. He can't cope seeing her senseless and uncommunicative, so Reggie and I have brought him back here. Freddie will still live with him, and his sister Maude, who was widowed last year and is living alone, has offered to come stay with him for however long it takes. But he'll need a friend, and I hoped I could impose on you and Mr Walsh to let some of his acquaintances know that we'd love for them to drop in to restore his spirits.'

'Of course, we will do whatever we can, my dear. And we'll let you know how he's faring. Is there somewhere I can write to you?'

'Reggie's been wonderful. He's organised a little flat in a boarding house near the hospital. I need to be there. I don't want mother left amongst strangers, otherwise I fear we may never get her back.'

'But you'll be alone Caroline, dear. Are there no other relatives you could call on?'

'I'll have Reggie. Look …' Caroline held up her left hand to show them the slim gold band on her wedding finger. 'We decided to get married at the Registry Office in Melbourne before bringing father back to Adelaide, and Reggie has applied for a transfer with the Army to a Red Cross facility in Melbourne which has come through. We're taking the train back on Friday, so he has time to clear his desk here and transfer any important information to the next chap.'

'That's lovely news for you, Caroline. The next few months are going to be very hard, but I'm glad to hear Reggie will be with you.'

'I came to ask about our dresses. Could you hold on to them for me? It's my greatest wish that I could be married properly at our church with mother in attendance. I'm hoping that the prospect of a proper wedding, even if it won't be how we planned, will bring mother back to her senses.'

Caroline had started weeping, and Clementina quickly joined the pair to proffer her a handkerchief.

'I'm so sorry, Caro, for the heartbreaking circumstances you find yourself in. Your mother had asked for silk roses to be made to trim her hat for the wedding. I have them here. Could I wrap them up as a little posy for you to take to her. They might help?'

'That would be lovely,' she stammered. 'She'd been so assiduous about managing her own rose garden in preparation for the wedding. She said she wanted to flood the church with their perfume.'

Clementina went over to her notions drawer to find a ribbon and a scrap of lace she could use to arrange the fabric rose posy. They had a tiny bottle of rose oil they used to scent their ironing water, so she dabbed just one small drop on one of the green ribbons that she twisted and folded over to look like leaves, before handing the posy to Caroline.

When Eddie returned from visiting Captain Thomson, he relayed more sad news.

'It looks like he's aged at least 20 years, and he's so frail. I suggested a stroll to the jetty, but he said he wouldn't manage. A month ago, he did that every day. He was always so strong. His sister says he's not eating. I went straight over to alert Doctor Muirhead. He's going to need much more than moral support.'

CHAPTER TWENTY-NINE

At last, a letter – Wednesday 21 March 1923

A week before Easter, Clementina finally received the letter from Rosaria she'd been apprehensively waiting for. The news was grim. More and more people, Rosaria explained, especially those whose economic circumstances allowed them to hire someone outside of the home to do their laundry, had been leaving the small mountain towns for more advantageous prospects in the bigger cities; an exodus which had a drastic flow-on effect for Rosaria's and Antonia's laundry service.

Last summer, her brother had organised for her to take up laundry work at a hotel in Pescara. It was only going to be for a month, so she'd left the children behind with Antonia and had gone to the hotel for the live-in position. The pay was good—much better than she or Antonia had ever earned for similar work, and she was pleased to have found a buffer. Between Clementina's remittances and access to her war widow's pension, and Antonia's allowance for having lost her youngest son in battle, they were managing, despite the downturn in their business.

Then, in early September, she'd been offered a permanent position at the hotel laundry. Antonia advised her to take the job, saying that she'd keep the children and make sure they were fed and stayed at school. Giovanni, from next door, had promised that he'd bring the children one Sunday a month when she was entitled to a day off. It wasn't an ideal solution, but it worked. Until Antonia died. After the funeral, Sabia and Giovanni, had taken the children in, so Rosaria could return to Pescara. But her children were suffering.

Father Ernesto had suggested that the children be boarded at an orphanage in Pescara, so she could see them more often, but the thought of separating them, and maybe never being able to get them back, terrified her. And then, at the end of March, Antonia's cousin Filomena died too. Giovanni had been hanging on while his mother was alive. He and his son Tonino spent their days wandering across the region to find whatever odd jobs they could. Their flax fields, once the mainstay of their community, remained empty because there weren't enough labourers to prepare the soil and plant the seeds, let alone do all the work needed to harvest and prepare the crop for linen production. In any case, for the last two years, they'd been forced to sell their linens for below production costs. The pride of their little fraternity, on the outskirts of their village, had disappeared overnight.

Now Giovanni too was talking about leaving. He couldn't see another way out of the misery his family was enduring, getting skinnier and skinnier, the clothes hanging off protruding shoulder bones. His daughters, Teresina and Antonietta, one 14 and the other 15, didn't even have a decent dowry. He often expressed the great shame he felt at not even being able to provide them with the basics. How could they ever get married, except to another miserable *affamato*, with nothing to his name and no prospects for the future? He'd told Rosaria that the only hope he had was to beg his cousin in America to sponsor him. He'd asked Father Ernesto to write to Philadelphia, but he didn't even know if the address he had was still relevant. Anyway, Sabia was terrified of going to people they'd never met. Her mother and her sisters all still lived in the village. She kept crying at the prospect of being buried alone, away from all she knew and held dear.

For Easter, Clementina and the Walsh's had been invited to Nuriootpa to celebrate with her brother Frank and Barbara's family. They took the train to Gawler and Frank came to pick them up in his motor truck. Eddie and Rita were thrilled with their seat in the tiny cab up front with Frank, but Linda and Clementina, riding on a bench seat on the open back of the wagon, protected from the wind only by a canvas tarpaulin, were mightily relieved when they were deposited at Barbara's door.

Rita immediately begged to be allowed to wander in the open fields, and went rushing off with Linda, Eddie and Frankie Junior for company. Clementina had offered to help in the kitchen, but instead found herself sitting in the sunshine under a grape vine whose leaves were turning the red gold of autumn, enjoying a coffee with Frank and pouring her heart out to him about the new developments in Rapino.

'Clementina, if they want to migrate, why don't we offer to sponsor them. I'd have plenty of work for Giovanni and Tonino, and I'm sure Giovanni's pay alone would allow them to rent a decent place in the area. Sabia and Rosaria and the older girls would probably find domestic work or fruit picking in the area, and there are plenty of good schools for Rosaria's younger ones.'

'Really, but how would we go about that?' Clementina wondered aloud.

'I think we'd need to get on to your Mr Paterson, the vice consul, as soon as possible. I'm sure he'd know the ins and outs.'

They continued to discuss the possibilities of the plan over lunch, with Eddie and Linda encouraging them, telling them that the process to sponsor Rita and Clementina had been straightforward and had only taken a few months for approval.

Lifted by this unexpected possibility of being reunited with her last link to her Italian family, Clementina returned to Adelaide feeling much more optimistic, much to John's delight. He had been concerned for her sadness over the last few months.

Within days, Frank had made inquiries with Mr Patterson to discover that while immigration was not as simple as they hoped, there was a demand for agricultural and domestic workers, especially in country areas. Frank, as the sponsor, was able to provide a glowing reference from his boss at the quarry and accompany it with a written offer of employment for both Giovanni and the 16-year-old Tonino. Barbara had used her family's long connection in the region to secure an affidavit from their local Member of Parliament, outlining the employment needs of the district, including work in fruit and vegetable picking, packing and canning and domestic work.

When Clementina put all this information in a letter, she thought carefully about how she would word this opportunity. She wanted to be absolutely honest and also encourage them to make the leap. She'd written to them last year about finding her brother Francesco and about how well he was doing for himself. They knew what she had been up to through her regular correspondence over the last 2 years. She hoped fervently that they would consider coming to join her. That they could all be a family again!

'I hope I'm not too late and they haven't already accepted an offer to move to Philadelphia.'

While waiting for a response, both from the Immigration Department and her family, Clementina tried to remain optimistic and positive. A reply from Rosaria came first. She was scared but infinitely grateful. Her brother had urged her not to pass up this opportunity, regardless of what Giovanni and Sabia decided. And anyway, they hadn't heard anything from the cousin in Philadelphia. Rosaria's only concern was that if she came on her own, she wouldn't want to be so far away from Clementina. Despite Frank's generous offer, she hardly knew him; it had been 16 years since she'd last spoken to him to wish him well before he left to do his military service.

This thought had been plaguing Clementina too. When she relayed the content of Rosaria's letter to Eddie that night, he told her not to worry, that he'd see what he could come up with in the next few days. Clementina had great faith in Eddie's powers of persuasion. He was well known in the area and highly respected. Clementina knew that if there was an alternative solution, Eddie would find it.

She'd found it hard to focus on anything else these last few months. And the worst thing had happened. She was working on some embroidery for a bride's dress and had cut her finger with the tip of her embroidery scissors—blood drops stained the dress right at the front hem. Linda reassured her it could barely be seen, and she could cover it with new embroidery thread, but Clementina felt it was an omen, and one of bad luck, too. She didn't wish '*una disgrazia*' upon her bride, but neither did she wish bad luck to fall on herself or her nearest. The incident disturbed her more than it should have, preventing her from sleeping properly, and for days, she couldn't shake off the heavy sense of dread that had enveloped her. She knew she was letting her imagination terrorise her again. Her years at the convent had instilled in her an understanding that these long-held superstitions only had power over you if you gave into their insidiousness and let them erode your confidence. She reminded herself that now was not the time to succumb to pagan beliefs.

Eddie had thought long and hard about Clementina's request, sifting through all the people he knew who might be able to provide a solution. The problem was simple: If Rosaria came to Henley Beach, she would need employment and accommodation for herself and two children—her son Rocco, age 5 and her daughter Antonietta, age 7. He and Linda had only bought a small house when they first moved to Henley Beach, because it was only the two of them and their priority had been to set Linda up with a shopfront, so that her clients could come to her. But there was no reason they needed to stay there. When he'd made enquiries with the agent Mr Gray for Caroline Delaney, he'd become aware of the large number of vacant lots going up for sale, filling in the space between Henley and Grange and further south between Henley and Glenelg as more people fled the unsanitary conditions in the city for the salubrious sea air. He quite liked the idea of building himself a bespoke house before he retired, but he knew Linda would be reluctant to lose the close contacts she had in their central little pocket.

The next easy alternative would be to convert the sleepout into insulated bedrooms. If he were honest, he hadn't used it as a sleepout in several decades and it had simply become a storage room for the excess bolts of fabric Linda and Clementina acquired when they were working on large bridal parties. He could still accommodate that need at one end of the sleepout by building a bespoke storage system and extend the other side to create extra bedrooms. Another bathroom and toilet wouldn't go astray if they were adding all these extra bodies to the house. Clementina would lose some of her garden, and Charlie's stable would probably have to be reduced in size. Anyway, Charlie was getting old too. Eddie wasn't sure how long he'd still be able to pull the buggy and dray. He chuckled at his next thought: If they didn't need a buggy and dray anymore, there'd be plenty of room to extend, and dear old Charlie could be retired. Eddie could then get himself that swish motor car he'd been eyeing off at Mr Millner's Motor Garage over on Henley Beach Road.

As for a job, Clementina had explained that Rosaria had been the third daughter in her family, so her mother had only taught her very rudimentary weaving and embroidery skills. She had been doing laundry since she was 12 years old, first working for a rich family in a more substantial home in the village. Then, when she married, she assisted Antonia. Eddie assumed that, since she would already be frightened about coming to Australia, it would be best to see if she could continue the same line of work. They had their Mrs Booth coming in twice a week to do their laundry, maybe Rosaria could pick up work with three families? However, Eddie remembered that most families did their washing on Mondays and ironing on Tuesdays, so the likelihood of a family wanting her on a Wednesday and Thursday was slim, let alone on a Friday and Saturday. No, he would need to find a commercial venture that accumulated substantial laundry most days of the week.

Opening his trusty notebook and unscrewing his pencil from the attached holder, he began making himself a list. There were a few small private hospitals in the area. There was Lady Galway's, of course, but he also added the larger guesthouses and hotels. Tomorrow, he would start with one across the road from them—the Ramsgate. The proprietress, Mrs Sophia Nicholls, was very community-minded, and she knew what it meant to lose a husband and become a solo mother. The community had rallied around her when her daring son, a member of the Australian Flying Corps had been made a POW in Germany and she'd opened her doors to the community to celebrate his release, relatively unharmed, in 1919.

'Eddie Walsh, you've brought music to my ears. I've had Mrs Jensen doing my laundry for over 20 years, and didn't she say to me just last month that she wanted to retire at the end of the year at the latest? This

Rosie girl you're talking about sounds ideal.'

'You understand she won't have English language skills at first, but we'll help her with that.'

'The sheets don't care what language you talk to them! She'll be working in the scullery, and my maids will bring all the laundry down to her. All she'll have to do is get on with the job. In summer, I usually have two young girls who come in to help Mrs Jensen. That could continue, so she won't be overwhelmed. We're a busy place and getting busier every year.'

'Mrs Nicholls, Linda and Clementina will be delighted to hear of your generosity, and if you were after a new frock, I'm sure we can come to some arrangement.'

'Wouldn't you know it, but my son Alfred has gotten himself engaged, so I'll take you up on that offer. Now, you let me know what paperwork or letters need writing and I'll get on to it straightaway.'

She stood up to accompany Eddie to the office door and back into the central reception area.

'I'm going to tell Mrs Jensen right now. She'll be so relieved. She keeps ranting about those grandchildren of hers and not wanting to miss out on being with them while they are still young.'

Item number one was crossed off the list. Eddie gave his suspenders a satisfying snap as he returned his notebook to his inner jacket pocket. Next stop, Pengelley's woodyard over on Military Road, to discuss the amount of lumber he'd need to convert the sleepout, and maybe a stop in at the Grange Hotel front bar, where his building trade mates gathered. It wouldn't hurt to have a word with Mr Bennett, the architect, and Mr Kinnear from the council about the permissions and drafting he'd need.

* * *

When approvals came through, it transpired that Giovanni and Tonino had accepted work in a large agricultural holding in the south of the region, where they had contracted to remain for a year. Sabia and her daughters had elected to stay in the village, but arranged to move in with Sabia's elder sister, who was still working a loom, but had shifted to using wool instead of flax, because her in-laws still owned and managed a substantial flock. The rudimentary carpets and blankets they were making were a significant departure from Sabia's fine linen work, but her skills were adaptable, and her output would come in very handy. Her daughters too now also had an opportunity to learn this new craft and participate in the family's recovery. Rosaria, however, with her circumstances still dire, had Father Ernesto use his connections to organise tickets for her on the first available ship.

The houses on via Giardino would be abandoned. Some of the furniture could be sold off, but no-one was interested in the houses or the fields, where wildflowers and tall grasses were quickly returning them to the state they were in before centuries of cultivation and specialised management by the flax families and their forbearers.

With a secure offer of employment and accommodation, Rosaria and her children's fares had been subsidised by the Australian government. Frank was prepared to make up the shortfall. Linda was a little daunted by the impending changes but took it all in her stride, especially since Eddie was energised by the modifications to their home.

When they finally arrived, 9-year-old Rita took on her role as older sister seriously, and replicated what Imma's daughter, Teresina, had done for her when they were on the ship. She set up a schoolroom in the parlour, using games and a portable blackboard that John had made up for her to teach the younger ones practical, rudimentary English.

Rosaria was relieved to be able to get straight to work but was tired at the end of the day and not overly interested in studying English. She relied heavily on Clementina to translate for her. However, about 3 months after their arrival, she was dismayed when she realised that her children could now ostracise her from their discussions, which were increasingly conducted in English. Linda calmly stepped in, waiting till Rosaria finished her laundry work in the early afternoon, so she could take her to the local shops. Slowly, she introduced her to the names of goods they regularly bought and had her practice simple interactions with the shopkeepers and regular customers, like she'd done for Clementina. Once this fear of stepping out of her defined domestic space eased, Rosaria herself became more confident, asking Rita for help with reading the easy primers her children brought home from school.

When Rosaria sent her first letter home to Sabia, in time so it would arrive for Christmas, she was able to include a photograph of all the Walsh household gathered around her daughter Antonietta, dressed as a little bride in Rita's handed down dress and veil, on the day of her First Holy Communion. She described her employer's generosity in insisting that the family and a few friends come to the hotel dining room for lunch, which was offered on the house for Mrs Nicholls' most valuable and efficient employee ever.

CHAPTER THIRTY

John and Tina – Sunday 4 May 1924

Little Rocco followed his Uncle Eddie to the purposely built garage and stood back as the heavy, wooden double doors were prised apart and pinned down.

'Hop in, little man,' encouraged Eddie as he opened the front door to his five-seater motor. Rocco put his foot on the riser and, with Eddie giving him a boost, pushed himself up and clambered across the seat. Eddie used a chamois tucked into the side of the door to wipe off the sandy footprints left behind on the Moroccan brown leather seats before sliding in himself, behind the wheel of his new cream Dodge with a black hard top. Releasing the handbrake, he allowed the car to roll backwards to the end of the driveway before re-engaging the brake. That's as far as they were going for the moment. Rocco watched Eddie in his new black tails and black silk top hat stroll up to the garage doors to release their pins and shut them again. When Eddie bent to adjust his tie in the side mirror, Rocco pretended to do the same to his bow tie, eliciting a laugh from the older man.

'It's going to be a long day, young Rocco. I hope you're ready?'

'I'm ready, Uncle Eddie.'

Six-year-old Rocco was the ring bearer. They had been to the church a few days before and practised all their roles. He knew he had to wait for the invitation from the priest to come forward and present the little pillow Annie had made, onto which the rings were tied with gold ribbons. *Mamma*, his sister Netta and cousin Rita had made him rehearse at home so many times because it was a special day for Zia Tina, and he wasn't to do anything to upset her. He repeated this directive to his Uncle Eddie.

'Don't fret, lad. Stick with me. I've got you.'

The neighbours had started gathering in the street. They were waiting for the bride and her retinue to come out of the house to make their way to the church. When Linda, in her mauve silk dress and fox fur stole, her hat at a fetching angle, opened the front door and Rita came out in her lilac taffeta dress, the gathering crowd started clapping. The noise intensified as Clementina finally emerged, a picture of radiance in her cloud-white dress of many layers of chiffon and lace. She was wearing her veil low on her brow with a circlet of silk flowers to keep it in place, and her lace train was wound around her arm to protect it. She blushed to see so many people in the street clapping, whistling and cheering her on.

Today, standing at the cheval mirror in the sewing room before leaving for the church, Linda reminded Clementina of the evolution of her colour choices. They chuckled over her heavy black skirt and her enormous wool shawl. The unexpectedly warmer weather had encouraged her into lighter wear, but still mostly black. After nearly a year, when she'd felt more comfortable in the business and her surroundings, she'd transitioned to no-nonsense navy blues and greys as her staples. Then, when her fondness for John burgeoned, she'd delved into rich plums, purples and greens. She'd naturally switched to dusky pinks and ochres when John's love had eased her last fears. Today, all in white, she had thrown off the shackles of the past and the sadness she thought might never leave. She was ready to turn a new page and write the future with John by her side.

Eddie opened the back door and offered his hand to facilitate her entry into the car. Then he went around to the other side to settle his wife in the front seat with Rocco, and young Rita next to Clementina. A couple of young men from his building company had agreed to spend the day at the house to keep it safe while the whole family was away, and Eddie waved to them, sitting on the front verandah with the beers and the ploughman's lunch they'd been left. He slipped behind the polished oak dash and wheel, ready to drive his family to the church.

In the car, Margherita fidgeted with Clementina's silk flower bouquet. She caressed the white silk roses, peonies and orange blossoms. But she especially loved the trails of marguerite daisies with their bright yellow centres, included to represent her. Nestled deep in the bouquet's heart were tiny silk violets with their heart-shaped leaves, Clementina's favourite flowers. Before they'd left Italy, Clementina had promised never to abandon her, and even though she loved Linda and Eddie with a fierceness she couldn't explain, Clementina was the only link that Rita had left to her first family, one that she felt duty-bound to remember and honour. She was ecstatic for Tina and John, but relieved too when she'd learned that they had decided to keep living at the Walsh house. Rita had been easily persuaded to give up her room and move in with her new cousin Netta, so that Tina could still be close to the business. Uncle Eddie had added on a little alcove to the bedroom, so that Tina and John could have a cosy, private place to sit and chat at the end of the day. Maybe, someday soon, Rita hoped, it would fit a cradle too. In that event, Linda said that she could call herself 'Aunty Rita' and wouldn't that make her the envy of all her friends?

At the church door, Rocco's mother handed him his special pillow and guided him to the front of the church where he was to stand with Uncle John and the best man, Uncle Mike. Rosaria glanced at the alcove beyond where her daughter Netta was standing with a handful of other girls, all dressed in white, singing the service replies with Sister Mary-Paul at the organ. After a year in Australia, she was beginning to feel free from the dread that her hardship had instilled in her. She had married Domenico Della Valle wearing her traditional village dress, but unlike her sister-in-law, she hadn't had the luxury of being able to marry for love. Her father had arranged her marriage, and like all grateful and faithful daughters, she'd accepted the match with Domenico. He had seemed calm and kind and came from a good family. As the first son, he would inherit his father's property, and therefore he had good economic prospects. He was quite handsome in his own way, making her the envy of many of the village girls. Affection had come later, after getting to know each other and certainly after the birth of their first child, as they faced new responsibilities together. But the love she witnessed between Tina and John or between Linda and Eddie, no, she had never known that, not even with her own parents. With an arduous job that left her physically exhausted most days, and with two young children still to raise, she wasn't in a hurry to find a new partner, but she did wonder what that love might feel like.

Frances was sitting with her daughters and their families, watching John's face as he waited for Clementina to enter the church. He was all smiles, sure of himself and sure of their love. She couldn't have wished for a better partner for her devoted son. He'd been her rock when her husband had died. She worried that she'd relied too heavily on him, making him miss his chance for young love. Then, when he returned from the war, maimed in body, mind and heart, she'd felt so guilty at how she'd stood in the way of his happiness. Today, she felt relieved and blessed.

She had her three wonderful children, their three incredible partners and her gorgeous grandchildren. She hoped there would be at least one more while she still had the physical capacity to run after a toddler. Still, she couldn't complain. She'd had the added blessing of having Mike and Nancy's delightful twins, Kit and Greta, at her dinner table every night for almost 2 years and Rita, Rocco and Netta kept her amused, when she was occasionally asked to watch them after school, when the other women were busy with their work.

Annie was sitting with her parents and sisters in the pew behind the Walsh family. She'd made Rita and Rosaria's dresses and had even succeeded in making a suit for little Rocco, as well as the new peach chiffon dress she was wearing today. Caroline had been giving her lessons, so she'd also made her own hat. She'd fashioned it in a matching peach chiffon with a large fabric rose attached to one side. She loved sewing, but hat-making was much more satisfying on a creative level. The offer Caroline had made her, to teach her the ins and outs, so that she might take over the business in a couple of years, had her buzzing. Her parents had been very impressed, encouraging her to take up the opportunity, with a view to eventually being able to incorporate her younger sisters into a family business. But for today, feeling grown up and elegant in her new outfit, she was eagerly looking over at one of the young men sitting in the pew opposite hers. He'd given her a shy smile as her family had walked in. She crossed her gloved fingers, hoping he would be at the reception and that he might ask her to dance.

In the foyer, Eddie slipped on his white silk gloves and positioned Rita in front of him. She was looking regal in her silver, pearl and diamante crown and she carried a basket of pale pink rose petals to scatter before her. Eddie gave her a quick wink for reassurance. Clementina was standing ram-rod straight while Linda fussed with her train, fanning it out in a wide arc behind her. She planted a quick kiss on both Clementina and Rita's cheeks, tapped Eddie on the arm and whispered, 'Wait till you hear the music.' Then she slipped down the side aisle to her seat in the front pew.

* * *

Clementina had thought long and hard about this second wedding. From the moment she met John, she'd had a great admiration for him and had appreciated his kindness and his attention, not only for her welfare but also for the welfare of all the people in his circle. Their friendship and mutual respect had come first and built slowly. A physical attraction had only developed when she had become more secure in herself and ready to move on from her difficult past. Still, she questioned the idea of another marriage. For many months, she couldn't shake the guilt she suffered, believing that a second wedding would be breaking the vow she'd taken to treasure her first husband and forsake all others except him. She'd made a promise before God to give herself physically to Nicola for evermore, at a time when she didn't fully understand what that meant. Despite her affection for John, it took her a long time to fathom the thought of laying with anyone else. Could she possibly allow herself to meld physically into another being, to be consumed, so that you became one with that person, your heart beating in unison, the other's essence pulsating through your body until you were transformed into one entity, one soul, one thought, one energy?

John had sensed her reticence, because it matched his own. He'd foregone the idea of love and partnership before the war, feeling he had a duty to his mother and his deceased father to be the head of the household and ensure his mother's financial security. Then, after the war, after the horrors he'd seen, of humanity's depravity, of power disguised as nationalism, after his injury that made him less whole, less of a man, he'd closed himself off to the possibility of ever finding someone who would understand him. He thought no-one would appreciate his gentle nature and accept, let alone love, a cripple. Initially, he admired Tina for her talent and inner strength. Yet, when he'd come to understand her and truly believe he could allow her to see the real him, with all his vulnerabilities, that's when he saw what other people appreciated about her—her natural elegance, her diminutive, trim figure, and her large brown eyes, clear skin and chiselled features. By that stage, he was in love, and secure in her love too. Only then was he able to rejoice in her physical beauty. Today, as she walked down the aisle, with the light pouring in from the front doors and the tall windows on both sides, casting beams which criss-crossed over the polished floorboards of the central aisle, she glowed like an angel. He felt uplifted by the glory of their love. To share his life with her, to commit to her for eternity, body and soul, would be the privilege of his life.

When she passed the alcove from where the schoolgirls' choir was singing the Ave Maria, she lifted her head, her nerves dissipating at the soothingly familiar aria. At the altar, John turned to watch her arrive. His face tried to contain his emotions, and he swallowed hard to avoid shedding a tear. When he lifted her veil, Clementina looked confidently into John's ardent eyes and into her future.

THE END

Acknowledgements

This book was imagined and written on the unceded land of the Kaurna people. I acknowledge the Traditional Owners of Country throughout Australia and their continuing connection to their country. I pay my respects to Elders past and present, custodians of their own story traditions.

When my father passed away in 2020, I became very conscious of the fact that I had now become the repository of family history and had a duty to pass it on. Unfortunately, most of what I knew was quite sketchy, so by the end of that year, when I decided to retire, I began researching our family. This led to the discovery of the once vibrant flax-growing and linen-weaving cottage industry in my father's tiny town in Abruzzo, an industry which sustained many families and villages across Italy. This industry, like many other cottage industries, succumbed to industrial progress and led to phenomenal internal migration and mass migration to other European countries, the Americas and eventually Australia and New Zealand. So my first thanks are to my paternal ancestors, whose voices felt very present during my writing journey.

The inspiration to write the character of an embroiderer came from the stories of the many women I encountered during my research for the Italian Gloryboxes of Love exhibitions held in Adelaide from 2023 to 2025. I was privileged to see a mountain of treasures, mostly handmade, which fed my thirst for all things embroidery. The stories and history of Italian Gloryboxes can be viewed at www.italiangloryboxesoflove.com. Many thanks to HistoryTrust SA for financial support to launch this website.

Many thanks also to Tina Morganella who edited the completed manuscript and helped me to improve my writing. I had wonderfully supportive Beta Readers who gave me early feedback on content: thanks to Diana, Rita and Loretta who shared their Abruzzese culture with me, to Concetta, whose reflections helped refine Clementina's inner thoughts. To Marie of the Henley Beach Historical Society, for her insightful feedback and encouragement and to Jen and the members of the Novelist's Circle for the many pointed questions and suggestions about structure and voice. To Robyn and Robyn, my final readers, thanks for giving me the courage to press send.

Finally, my gratitude to The City of Charles Sturt, for the grant which helped with all facets of publication and to Rochelle Sideris of Ngutungka Henley Beach Library whose encouragement and enthusiasm for all my projects has been unending and uplifting.

Author's note

A **Shimmering Thread (2026)** is based on research into my paternal family, in particular the life of my great-grandmother Laura Cinosi, who was a weaver, from a flax-growing family in Rapino (Provincia di Chieti), Abruzzo, Italy. It is also a tribute to the many Italian migrant women all over the world, who from the 1860s to the 1970s, made their way in new lands, using their sewing and embroidery skills to support their families. The choice of the setting in Henley Beach was based on research into the activities of the Adelaide Red Cross Society and their efforts to rehabilitate injured men after their return from World War One, and also the influence of the first global conflict on societal change.

For further communication and for information about books and appearances, please email: lauradimartino.author@mail.com

I am a proud, independently published author of two previous books. Please see overleaf for details of both titles.

Cremona House: an Italian Migration journey 1900-1950 (published in 2024)

This historical fiction novel is based on the experiences of six Italian families living in Adelaide in the 1920s and 30s. Told through the eyes of Carlo Bodoni, an enterprising ice-cream maker who started with a factory in Port Adelaide and in 1922, built a factory in the city on South Terrace. In 1928, he purchased the mansion next door to the factory and re-named it Cremona House. This house became the scene of many glittering events, hosting glamorous international visitors. However, by 1941, Carlo's social activities with the Adelaide Fascist Party marked him as an Enemy Alien, and along with 5,000 other Italian men from across Australia, he was interned at Loveday Internment Camp, outside Barmera (SA) for six-years at the end of which his factory and his business was destroyed and he had to find a new way forward. To do this, he sold the house and factory to Pultney Grammar School, which used the factory as its primary campus for many years. The house was restored and remains in the grounds of the school. Photos and information about the house and the background to the book can be found on my website: https://linktr.ee/lauradimartino.

Working it out (published in 2024)

This contemporary romance novel follows the lives of two sets of sisters who are cousins. They are in their early 20s and at a point of transition in their lives where they need to make decisions about their futures, in particular their careers. In this snapshot of a year in their lives, they discover more about themselves and their ultimate desires. Like many young people, they experience the highs and lows of workplace and personal relationships, but with each other's support, they eventually work it out.

Independent authors rely on genuine reviews posted on websites like *Goodreads.com* to promote their book. Please consider leaving a review if you have read any of these books, it makes an enormous difference to the algorithms!

With many thanks

Laura x

Clementina's Abruzzese Kitchen Treats

In 1983, 20-year-old Laura spent the month of December, snow-bound in the little village of Rapino with very little to do, as everyone her age was away at school or working. Her cousin, *Maria Cellucci*, was a trained pastry chef who ran a little *Pasticceria* (pastry shop) on *Via Giardino,* which was very popular for its local specialities.

Laura's love for baking and for the history of traditional recipes was born here, following Maria's gentle but firm instructions and listening to her many wonderful stories about village life.

Laura returned to Australia with her favourite recipes hastily scribbled into a little notebook. Mostly the ingredients were listed in Italian and the method written in English, based only on Laura's observations in the kitchen. Over the decades, they've been re-written and adapted to a domestic kitchen and Australian ingredients and shared many times over in written form or on platters!

Clementina made them in the pages of this book to keep her homesickness at bay.

Buon appetito x

Pizzelle — aniseed wafer biscuits

To make these traditional 'little cakes' a Pizzelle iron *(il ferro da pizzelle)* is a must. The plates, often made of cast-iron, create ultra-thin, crisp wafers. The dough is traditionally flavoured with crushed fennel/aniseed or lemon rind. Modern versions with cocoa batter and slathered in fig jam or hazelnut paste are also very popular. Electric pizzelle irons are readily found online and make the task so much easier.

INGREDIENTS (FOR 18-20 PIZZELLE)

6 large eggs
12 tbsp caster sugar (2 per egg)
6 tbsp light olive oil
6 tbsp sunflower oil
2 tsp anise extract or 1 tsp of ground star anise
3½ cups plain flour

METHOD

- Whisk together eggs and sugar until the mixture is pale and fluffy, and the sugar has dissolved. Add oils and anise extract and whisk to combine. In a separate large bowl, sift the flour. Slowly incorporate wet ingredients until you have a smooth paste (should be the consistency of cake batter). Set aside for at least a half hour for flavours to develop and the flour to properly rehydrate.
- Heat the pizzelle iron and brush with a little oil. Drop one heaped tablespoon at a time onto one side of the pizzelle iron. Close the iron and cook for 40-60 seconds or until steam stops escaping from the sides. Carefully lift the wafer biscuit from the iron with the tines of a fork and set aside on a tray lined with absorbent paper. Continue to cook the remaining batter.
- To serve: dust liberally with icing sugar or use a favourite spread to sandwich two pizelle together.
- Store in an airtight container.

Note regarding flavourings: Instead of the strongly flavoured anise, use a liqueur of your choice, vanilla extract or the grated rind of 1 lemon or orange. For chocolate ones, add 2 tablespoons dark cocoa to the flour mixture and enhance with a pinch of salt and vanilla extract.

Biscotti alle Mandorle — whole almond biscuits

The Italian word for 'biscuit' *(biscotti)* means twice*(bis)*-cooked *(cotti)* and this recipe is a perfect embodiment of the method used by ancient bakers when they returned their enriched bread dough to the dying embers of their oven to crisp up. These almond biscuits are cooked all over Italy, using the nuts or dried fruits typical of each region. They are sometimes called '*cantucci*' or '*parigini*'. Being free from fat, these biscotti are hard and designed to store well. They are traditionally eaten dunked in wine or coffee to avoid teeth shattering! In Rapino, the traditional wine served with these biscotti is *Cerasuolo d'Abruzzo* – a type of rosé. They are breakfast favourites.

INGREDIENTS

2 eggs, at room temperature
¾ cup caster sugar
1 tsp vanilla extract
1 tsp zest of lemon, grated
2¼ cups (340g) plain flour
1 tsp baking powder
1 cup whole raw almonds, with skin left on

METHOD

- Preheat the oven to 180°C. Cover a baking tray with baking paper.
- Beat two large eggs and the sugar until pale and frothy. Gently stir in the vanilla and lemon extract with a spatula.
- In a separate bowl, sift the flour and baking powder. With a spatula, gently incorporate the wet ingredients into the flour mixture. Stir in the almonds.
- On a floured board, shape the dough into one or two log shapes approximately 5cm wide. If necessary, incorporate a little extra flour to make the dough easier to handle. Place the logs onto a parchment-lined baking sheet. Press down with floured hands to flatten the logs. You want them to be around 2cm thick all over to ensure even cooking.
- Bake the dough logs for 20-25 minutes at 180°C until they are lightly golden. The centre will be slightly soft. Remove from the oven and set aside to cool for at least 10 minutes.
- Transfer the cooked and cooled log to a cutting board. Slice the logs on the diagonal, pressing a sharp knife straight down into the dough.
- Place the biscuits back on the baking tray, cut side up. Bake the biscotti a second time, for 5 minutes on each side, until golden brown and crisp.

Note: Slicing at a greater angle will give you longer biscotti, and less of an angle will produce smaller ones (called *biscottini* or *cantuccini*).

Taralli di San Rocco — lemon-glazed shortbread rings

In the blazing heat of the summer, around the 18th of August, the feast of San Rocco, patron saint of the harvest, is celebrated in Rapino with a procession of women carrying copper water conches filled with flowers and grain stalks and hung with lemon-glazed shortbread rings which they leave as an offering at the saint's altar in gratitude for a bountiful harvest. They traditionally carry the conch on their heads, a method once used to transport water to individual homes from the town fountains.

INGREDIENTS

2 eggs
130 g sugar
Grated rind of 1 lemon
50 g of light olive oil
60 g milk
370-400 g plain flour
1 tsp baking powder

For the glaze

150 g icing sugar
1-2 egg whites
a few drops of lemon juice
coloured sprinkles

METHOD

- Pre-heat oven to 180°C. Line two large baking trays with baking paper.
- In a large bowl, using a fork, beat the eggs with the sugar and lemon rind. Pour in the olive oil in a thin stream and then the milk, continuing to work the mixture with the fork until well incorporated.
- Sift 370g of the flour and baking powder, then add a heaped tablespoon at a time to the egg mixture. You should obtain a smooth batter that is firm enough to shape with your hands. Add more flour if necessary.
- Pinch off a heaped tablespoon of the batter into your floured hands, shape into a ball and then poke your finger into the centre, rolling it around your finger to form a doughnut-style shape.
- Place on your lined baking trays and bake for 20 minutes or until lightly golden. The bottoms should be firm to the touch. Transfer them to a wire rack to cool completely.
- To make the glaze: put the icing sugar into the bowl of an electric mixer. Add the egg white, a little at a time, to create a thick paste. Add a few drops of lemon juice to create a more fluid consistency. If necessary, add a little extra egg-white to obtain the consistency of a pancake batter.
- Dip the top of the cooled rings into the glaze and set them back on the wire racks to dry. Once nearly dry, they can be decorated with coloured sprinkles.
- Store in an air-tight container for a few days.

Pupi cù l'ova — Easter shortbread figures

These biscuits have ancient pagan origins, representing spring-time fertility. The dough is shaped into a doll (complete with breasts and a boiled egg for the tummy) and horses (complete with flying manes and galloping feet with a boiled egg shaped into a saddle). Girls were given the doll and the horses, probably representing vigour, were destined for boys. They are great fun to make with children. Around Easter, Facebook and You Tube groups abound with incredibly beautiful and/or frighteningly ugly Pupi competition entries. They can be decorated before cooking as suggested below, or baked first then decorated with coloured icing, much like classic British gingerbread men.

INGREDIENTS

400g plain flour
100g almond meal
1 tsp baking powder
Pinch salt
150g sugar
125g lard or butter
2 eggs
1 tsp vanilla extract
grated rind of half a lemon
2 tbs milk

For decoration

4 hard-boiled eggs
coffee beans or chocolate drops for eyes
egg wash for a shiny finish
coloured sprinkles

METHOD

- Preheat oven to 150°C fan-force. Line a large baking tray with baking paper.
- In a large mixing bowl and using a fork, combine the plain flour, almond meal, baking powder and salt. Add remaining ingredients and mix well. Using floured hands, knead the dough until soft and pliable.
- On the lined baking tray, begin building the shapes you desire – perhaps make yourself a paper template to form the bases. Add small strips of dough for features, e.g. hair, lips, earrings, necklaces, aprons, manes, tails, saddles, reins, etc. Use coffee beans or chocolate drops for eyes. Insert the boiled egg in the centre, covering it with strips of dough (traditionally in a cross shape) to secure the egg to the pastry base.
- Whisk an egg yolk with a tablespoon of water. Brush all over the dough and cover with coloured sprinkles.
- Bake for 30-40 minutes, depending on the size. The bottoms should be firm and easy to lift off the baking tray.
- Store in an air-tight container for 2-3 days.

Crostatine alla Ricotta e Mandorle — ricotta and almond tartlets

These are popular spring-time or Easter desserts. If buying ricotta in tubs - make sure to strain it well. Line a fine sieve with a clean *Chux* cloth and allow to sit over a bowl in the fridge until ready. Don't throw out the whey - it's a great tenderiser, especially for pork or lamb roasts.

INGREDIENTS

For the tart shells

350g plain flour
15g baking powder
120g softened butter or lard
120g sugar
2 whole eggs+ 1 yolk
Grated rind of 2 lemons

For the filling

2 eggs
500g fresh ricotta, well-strained
130g caster sugar
80g finely ground almonds
Grated rind of 2 lemons
15ml of lemon juice

For decoration

100g slivered almonds
50g icing sugar

METHOD

- In a large mixing bowl, rub the softened butter or lard with the flour and baking powder. Mix in sugar and eggs and the grated rind of the lemons with your fingers. Knead well until all the ingredients have been well incorporated. When you are able to poke a finger into the dough and it springs back, the dough is ready. Wrap the bowl in cling film and place in the refrigerator for 30 minutes.
- In the meantime, add the filling ingredients to a bowl and beat with a hand whisk to obtain a smooth cream. Store in a covered container in the fridge.
- Preheat your oven to 180°C. Brush or spray your tins with oil or butter.
- Turn dough out onto a floured board. This quantity of dough should make the top, bottom and sides of 1 × 20cm cake tin or 6 muffin-tin size smaller tartlets. Use a rolling pin to roll out the dough and cut out bottoms, sides and tops as required for your tin shape.
- Fill the base with the ricotta and almond cream. Top with the remaining dough, pinching the sides together. Sprinkle the top with the slivered almonds.
- Bake for 25-35 minutes, depending on size. The base should be firm and the tops lightly golden. Remove to a wire rack to cool. When ready to serve, dust liberally with sifted icing sugar.

Pasticci di Rapino — Christmas sweet pies with chocolate and almonds

These little tarts are symbolic of Christmas throughout Abruzzo and as each town seems to have its own variation, there are hundreds of 'authentic' recipes from the region. This is the *Rapinese* version. They are flavoured with the locally produced **mosto cotto* – a syrupy confection made by boiling down 'must' (grape juice). In Australia, I have usually substituted it with plum jam, or more recently, date syrup. These are meant to be dainty little mouthfuls, and as they are extremely sweet, I usually bake them in a mini-muffin tin.

INGREDIENTS

For the filling

300g white sugar
500ml water
Rind of ½ lemon, in strips
1 cinnamon stick, approximately 5cm
300g dark cooking chocolate, grated
300g whole toasted almonds, coarsely ground
7 egg yolks
1 tbs mosto cotto*

For the pastry

250g unsalted butter or lard
400g sugar
6 egg yolks+2 whole eggs
1 kg plain flour
2g baking powder

METHOD

Filling

- In a heavy-based saucepan, boil water and sugar, lemon rind and cinnamon until sugar is dissolved to form a sugar syrup. Remove rind and cinnamon. Add chocolate and almonds. Stir well and set aside to cool. When cold, beat in egg yolks and add a tablespoon of the *mosto cotto*. Mixture should have a firm, jam-like consistency.

Pastry

- Combine all ingredients, kneading well to form a smooth dough. Set aside to rest for a minimum of 30 minutes. On a lightly floured board, roll out the dough to ¼ cm thickness. Butter and flour the pastry cases. Line each with the dough. Fill ¾ of the case with filling.
- Roll and thin out the remaining pastry dough (should be slightly thinner than the cases). Cut out rounds. Top each pastry case with a piece of dough, making sure the sides are joined to the bottom cases by brushing the edges with a little of the leftover egg white.
- Bake in a pre-heated medium oven (180°C) for 10-15 minutes until pastry is golden.
- Allow to cool completely, removing them from their pastry shells as soon as cool enough to handle and transfer to a wire rack. To serve, dust liberally with icing sugar.

Pizza Dogge (or Pizza Dolce) — celebration 4-layer sponge cake

This is a rich, indulgent recipe used only for very special occasions. Made with 100 eggs, this cake was once a favourite for weddings. As a child, I hated the liqueur-soaked sponge layers and would use a spoon to scoop out only the fillings, but the adults in my circle flew into raptures over it! It's expensive and time-consuming to make, but if you can master the sponge cake, it's actually quite a straightforward recipe. You can always substitute the liqueurs for whatever you have on hand — I often just use Sherry or Marsala with a vanilla sugar syrup. The important thing is to make sure the sponge layers are well-moistened. This will make them quite delicate to handle, so you'll need to build the cake directly onto your chosen serving platter (one that will fit overnight in your fridge, as this cake needs to mature before serving).

INGREDIENTS

For the sponge cake

5 fresh extra-large eggs, room temperature
150 g caster sugar
100 g plain flour
100 g cornflour
Pinch salt
1tspn vanilla extract

For the wetting agent

1 cup water
1 cup caster sugar
1 cup Alchermes Liqueur
1 cup Rum
¼ cup Anisette Liqueur *(Sambuca or Ouzo work well too)*

For the almond spread

250 g icing sugar
250 g almonds, peeled
1 tsp vanilla extract
Juice of 1 lemon
¼ cup Amaretto liqueur or 1 tbsp almond extract

For the vanilla + chocolate custards

400 grams caster sugar
100 grams plain flour
4 eggs
1 L full-cream milk
Rind of half a lemon (cut into 1 long strip)
1 Cinnamon stick
1 Vanilla bean
100g dark cooking chocolate, grated

For the mocha icing

1 kg butter, preferably organic
200 g icing sugar
2 cups freshly brewed espresso coffee
½ cup toasted crushed hazelnuts

METHOD

Sponge cake

- Preheat your oven to 150°C. Line 2 × 20cm × 5cm round cake pans with baking paper or grease tins well.
- Use an electric mixer to beat 5 extra-large eggs with 150g caster sugar until very pale and foamy and the sugar has dissolved. Mixture should be at least three times the volume of the original. Gently fold in the vanilla extract.
- Sift the flours and salt and fold through the egg mixture using a whisk.
- Pour the sponge cake mix into the 2 pans and place these in the oven for 1 hour or until the centre bounces back when pressed, or a skewer inserted into the middle comes out clean. Remove and allow to cool on a wire rack.

Wetting agent

- In a microwave-safe 1L jug, add 1 cup of water and 1 cup white sugar. Cook for 3 to 4 minutes, stirring after each minute until the sugar has dissolved. Once cool, add the liqueurs and rum.

Custard filling

- In a heavy-bottom saucepan, place 400g sugar and add 100g of plain flour. Mix using a whisk to get rid of any lumps. Slowly add 1 litre of fresh milk and 8 egg yolks, whisking all the while. Add a slice of lemon rind, then the cinnamon stick and vanilla bean. Mix gently, then put your saucepan on the stove on medium heat and stir continuously using a wooden spoon. It should take between 5-10 minutes to become thick and creamy. Remove the lemon peel, cinnamon stick and vanilla bean.
- Remove half of the custard from the saucepan and transfer it into a bowl to cool and set. Place a plastic film directly onto the surface of the custard to stop it from forming a skin.
- To the remaining custard in the saucepan, add 100g of grated dark cooking chocolate and mix well off the heat. Continue to mix until the chocolate is well-incorporated and the mixture takes on a milk chocolaty appearance. Transfer to a bowl and also cover with plastic film as above.

Almond cream

- Combine all the ingredients in a food processor and mix until smooth. Set aside.

Mocha icing

- Using an electric mixer, combine one kilo of room-temperature butter with 200g icing sugar, mixing until the sugar has dissolved. Add 2 espresso-sized cups of freshly brewed espresso coffee (around 4 mouthfuls!) and continue to mix until the icing thickens. Keep refrigerated in a sealed container until needed.

HOW TO ASSEMBLE

- Once the sponge cakes have cooked and cooled, use a large, flat knife to cut them in half, forming 4 even layers.
- Starting with the bottom layer, place it securely onto the centre of your serving platter. Generously wet this layer of the cake with approximately ¼ cup of the wetting agent. This will help to keep the Pizza Dolce moist. Spread a generous amount of the thick almond mix on top of this layer, making sure to evenly cover all of the base, leaving a 1 cm gap from the edges of the cake.
- Then, place the next layer of sponge on top of the almond cream layer and wet it with ¼ cup of the wetting agent. Add a generous amount of chocolate custard to the centre of this layer, and then spread it thickly and evenly, again leaving a 1 cm gap from the edges of the cake.
- Add the third layer of sponge cake to the top of the chocolate custard and use ¼ cup of wetting agent to moisten it. Then spread the vanilla custard on top. Make sure each layer is evenly distributed to avoid a lop-sided cake.
- Add the final layer of sponge on top of the vanilla custard. Use a long strip of baking paper to wrap the cake so as to keep all the fillings tightly packed. Add the remaining wetting agent to the top layer of the sponge. Cover the top with loosely fitting plastic film, then place in the fridge for the flavours to infuse, preferably overnight.
- The next day, remove the baking paper and the plastic wrap and cover the whole with the mocha icing. The icing can be piped on in fancy patterns or just spread over the top and sides with an off-set spatula. Use the crushed hazelnuts to decorate the top of the cake.
- Serve in thin slices.

www.ingramcontent.com/pod-product-compliance
Lightning Source LLC
LaVergne TN
LVHW091119080826
845145LV00008B/1979

* 9 7 8 0 9 7 5 6 2 1 4 4 8 *